Kerry Taylor is originally from Sydney, and her life so far has been as unpredictable as it has been varied. After a career teaching in suburban schools, she took a holiday to Central Australia that changed the direction of her life. Kerry became a nurse, researcher and academic focused on Indigenous health, and she is published widely in the field. After almost thirty years in the Northern Territory, another change of direction has seen her enjoying new passions of rowing on the Murray River and walking and photographing the coastlines of the Fleurieu Peninsula, South Australia. *Mr Smith to You* is her first novel.

MR SMITH TO YOU

KERRY TAYLOR

First published by Affirm Press in 2023
Boon Wurrung Country
28 Thistlethwaite Street,
South Melbourne, VIC 3205
affirmpress.com.au

10 9 8 7 6 5 4 3 2 1

A catalogue record for this book is available from the National Library of Australia

ISBN: 9781922863379 (paperback)

Cover design by Alissa Dinallo
Cover photograph by Lukas Gojda/Shutterstock
Typeset in Garamond Premier Pro by J&M Typesetting
Proudly printed in Australia by McPherson's Printing Group

Mum. I was listening, more than you knew.

Abbreviations Used in This Book

BNO	bowels not open
BP	blood pressure
crackles	lung sounds made on inhalation due to congestion
CWA	Country Women's Association
DoB	date of birth
High Fowler's	position in which a patient is placed upright to encourage respirations
hrly	hourly
Hudson's	Hudson Mask, used for the delivery of oxygen
Hx	history of
in situ	in place
LLL	left lower lobe
NFR	not for resuscitation
nocte	at night
O_2	oxygen
obs	observations
o/night	overnight
P	pulse
PAC	pressure area care
pt	patient
resp/R	respirations
sats	saturation
specialling	one-on-one nursing care
TB	tuberculosis
temp/T	temperature
U/O	urine output

Prologue

There was no reason to set the alarm these days. It was habit – muscle memory – that made Bill Smith reach for the small leather-bound travel clock on the nightstand. Set for 4am, and wound five times, its face was always turned away from the bed even though the luminous paint on its hands and numbers had dulled considerably.

The horses were long gone, but Bill continued to get up pre-dawn, while the misty blanket still covered the valley and the birds of night and day changed shift. He kept a trainer's watch in his vest pocket, pulling it out each night to check that it was also working before securing it back where it belonged. Both Bill and his timekeeping companions were still ticking, but tonight he felt a little like he was winding down.

There was no one to tend to him the way he tended to the things he cared about. And now there was little to care about. What's the point? he thought? No more horses; no dog to listen to his musings and opinions about the world, without argument. Tonight, Bill Smith sighed deeply, with the weight of all his seventy-six years.

He bent down to take off his shoes, knocking his head on the corner of the nightstand and sending the clock tumbling to the floor. Bill followed.

Wedged between the bed and the window, he was unable to move.

'Bugger,' Bill said as he considered his predicament. 'Wouldn't that rot your socks.'

And then the world went dark.

Part 1

Far North Queensland, 1978

The horses were long gone ...

1

Bill Smith's life felt like one long fight. He had been in this position before. He hadn't let them win then, and he wasn't going to let them win now. His liver-spotted hands gripped the top of his pants and, body contorting and legs flailing, Bill struggled to fight off his assailant.

'Bugger off. Bugger off, the lot of you.'

Nurse Maureen Bannon looked around, wondering who 'the lot of you' were, given that she was alone. She stepped back from the patient's bedside as if to signal her surrender, her hands held out open-palmed in a battlefield show of peaceable intent.

'Come on. Be a good boy now, Billy. We need to get you changed before Doctor can see you.'

Her voice was singsong, infantilising. A voice some would use when talking to the elderly. Like nails on a blackboard, and with much the same effect on Bill Smith.

'Who are you calling "Billy"? It's *Mr* Smith to you, you cheeky little twerp.'

The forced smile dropped from Maureen's face.

‘That’s right, Missy,’ he continued. ‘That might work on some, but not on this one.’ He swatted away her cajoling, leaving her in no doubt that this fellow was not like the docile, compliant characters she might usually encounter.

‘Going to be like that, is it?’ Hands on hips, Maureen addressed her patient with a solemnity that her age rendered comical. ‘Alright, *Mr* Smith,’ she said, with emphasis on every syllable. ‘But we will get you out of those clothes one way or the other. They smell to high heaven. Doctor won’t be examining you like that, let me tell you.’

‘Just piss off now, before I— you should show some respect for your elders,’ said Bill Smith. The same Bill Smith who had always prided himself on his appearance, had never left the house anything but clean and smartly turned out. When Nurse left the room, he pulled his shirtfront to his nose and sniffed. The mix of sweat and old vomit elicited a begrudging agreement, but he wasn’t about to tell her that.

Bill surveyed his surroundings. He was in hospital – Leichhardt Memorial, he assumed, the small rural hospital at the far edge of the Atherton Tablelands. He could smell the rich, black soil that permeated the air so completely that it cut through his disinfected surroundings. But there was no escaping the hint of old man’s bowels that also wafted past now and then. Bill felt his mouth fill with saliva and swallowed hard. Through the louvred windows, he could hear a choir of cane toads enjoying the end of an afternoon downpour. At least he wasn’t down in Cairns Base. He could walk home from here.

He scanned the room, noting the other occupants, who seemed unperturbed by the ruckus. The gentleman to his right made Bill ponder whether they hadn’t already departed this world – mouth agape, yellow-purplish skin that looked like it would tear if touched. He certainly wasn’t someone who would be up for the physical battle Bill had just engaged in.

The old bloke in the far corner was asleep, but cradled a transistor radio to his ear, its failing battery making it sound like a rundown gramophone record as the music heralding the four o'clock ABC News bulletin played forlornly.

The news warned of an unseasonal tropical cyclone building off Cairns. Bill thought about his sheds and hoped this one would not cross the Gillies Range like some cyclones managed to do. He didn't miss living down on the coast, where he had been through his fair share of destructive cyclones. Still, he thought, the timbers holding the stables together had seen better days. One more big blow could bring them down, even if the rainforested mountains might take some of the puff out of the wind. He didn't have the horses to go in them these days, but those sheds held something almost as valuable to him: memories – rich, sensory memories.

Directly across from him was a gentleman who, save for the few wispy strands of white hair above the blue hospital blanket, resembled a bag of bones in the bed. Considering the company, Bill began to wonder about his own condition, having been placed in what he thought could be God's waiting room. He tried to recall the events that had brought him here.

As he shifted position, his body provided some painful reminders. A fall, was it? But how long ago? It wasn't from a racehorse – he knew that much. Those days were behind him. No, this was from doing something meant to be far less risky than riding. He had leant down to take off his shoes, and tumbled forward between the bed and the window – and that's where he'd stayed. He thought he remembered at least two sunrises through partly opened curtains before experiencing uncharacteristic relief at hearing his closest neighbour, Ivy Jenkins, yoo-hooing from his yard. He was missing time. How much, he didn't know. A wave of nausea sent sweat running down his face.

Bill had managed to avoid hospitals – and neighbours – for most of his life, despite having lived through far worse than a fall in his bedroom. He'd even set the odd broken bone or two himself. Not the most elegant of jobs, he'd have to admit, but no need for wasting the doctor's time. He didn't belong here, in a hospital. He didn't need people fussing and pulling at him, this way and that. He would be quite fine back home, thanks all the same. Bill pulled the sheets up as high as they would go, as if by hiding behind them he could make himself disappear.

But there was no disappearing, and no relaxing. He tossed and turned in his hospital bed, unable to settle. The large ceiling fans did nothing but move hot air around the ward, flecks of peeling paint hanging on tenaciously beneath their whirring blades. The fan above him wobbled in its orbit, while the living dead around him snored so loudly as to make sleep impossible. Every now and then there would be a long silence, when Bill wondered whether one poor bloke hadn't breathed his last. But just as he considered whether to call for that cheeky miss to come and check his roommate, there would be another sucking sound and the chorus would start again. No, Bill certainly didn't belong here. What business did those bloody ambos have, bundling him out of his own home?

A fragment of memory. Yes, that's right – two burly blokes with Queensland Ambulance insignia. Ivy must have contacted them. He recalled being taken out on a stretcher, when all a man needed was a hand up off the floor and maybe a cuppa and some toast before they left. Home was where he should be, not whisked away to be tormented by some young upstart pawing at his trousers.

~

Bill loved his miner's cottage in the hills behind Leichhardt. It had been his reward after a life of hard slog, spent moving around with no real place to call home, until a final winning purse and an aged pension had meant he could retire to the little house he'd bought for a song. Bill thought it a bargain. All he wanted now was to be able to see out his days there in peace. Keep to himself. Mind his own business, and hope others would mind theirs.

There was much to love about the timber and tin building nestled on the banks of Pannikin Creek, just above the '57 flood line. Bill called it a home. Some of his neighbours called it a shack, and a ramshackle one at that in later years, but he didn't see it that way. There was a wild-growing veggie patch that pretty much looked after itself, having emerged without any effort from scraps thrown from the verandah. If you stood still too long in that volcanic landscape, Bill was certain, something would grow over you. Tomatoes self-seeded there, as did watermelons, corn and pumpkins, and when he made a small effort there would be spinach and a few other offerings too. There was a mature mango tree, hunched over by the weight of the flying foxes that congregated in it each night. Bill didn't mind sharing the fruit with them when it was available, but he was less fond of the noise they made, especially during mating season.

Most loved of all, however, were the stables and the little blacksmith shed down the back. For the first few years of his retirement, Bill still had two mares to look after, so he'd earned a few quid for their feed by making leatherwork, horseshoes or cattle brands for anyone who'd asked. There were no horses left now, but Bill could still smell their memoried presence every time he went there, and he went there often.

The closed-in verandah needed restumping, but it was where he watched the world go by without having to interact with anyone unless it suited him. A few local trainers would pass by on their way to the creek, when it was high enough to exercise their thoroughbreds in the strong current. Although he was no longer active in the racing industry, there were some who would still seek Bill's advice when it came to their animals' welfare. He would study each horse's gait as they came and went and, if asked, would call out his assessment and suggestions from a distance, never inviting anyone in. Not that anyone tried to come in these days – most accepted Bill's hermit-like ways. Apart from Ivy Jenkins, who was always angling to get a look inside her neighbour's house – without success, until now, it seemed. The thought of people poking around his home prompted Bill to sit up straight in his hospital bed.

'I've got to get out of here,' he said to no one in particular. 'This is bloody ridiculous.'

Bill pushed back the sheets and felt along the bedrails with arthritic hands, trying to work out how to put the sides down. He rattled them in frustration when he found himself unable to press hard enough on the lever. Hands that had once commanded a thousand pounds of racing thoroughbred now could not muster enough strength to push a lever on a hospital bed. For Bill, that realisation was worse than any pain.

He sank back, exhausted, wishing for the sleep that had eluded him while he'd lain on his bedroom floor. How long ago had that been? Before or after he'd collected the eggs? The eggs his neighbour left on his front steps were part of their weekly routine. An exchange without words. Bill would put half a dozen tomatoes or whatever else was in season on his front steps, and Mrs Jenkins in turn would leave him produce from her Isa Browns. But he'd never made it outside to collect them that day.

Bill rubbed his hip, reliving the pain and panic of trying to get up from his bedroom floor and finding himself unable to move. As had been the case back then, he now finally had to accept that he would not be going anywhere soon. He took advantage of the young nurse's absence to close his eyes. The radio playing in the background was reviewing the weekend races, which turned his mind to the time when he'd ridden for one of the top trainers in the north – old Charlie McInnes, the man who'd given Bill his first job as an apprentice jockey, in Cairns in the early 1920s.

'Make sure you hold him back until the final turn. Give him too much, he'll want to get in front and exhaust himself. Bastard of a horse – can't stand staring at other horses' arses, so don't let him go too early.'

'I'll hold him. No problem, Boss.'

'You flaming well better, Son, or we'll be staring at your arse as it goes out the gate.'

~

Cradled in crisp, white hospital sheets, Bill's hands reached out in front of his body, as if on reins, his arms employing old, familiar muscles. The clunky rhythm of the ceiling fans sounded like galloping in the distance. The cane toads in full voice outside the window echoed the high excitement of a crowd on race day. Bill was smiling at the memory – until he was startled from his recollections by Nurse Bannon trying to adjust his pillows.

'Oh, it's you,' he said. 'Good, you can take these bloody rails down and show me the way out.'

'That won't be happening, Bill— *Mr* Smith,' she said. 'You're in no state to go anywhere, I'm afraid. Now, those clothes.' She moved towards him once again, but the look on his face gave her pause.

'Over my dead body, Missy.'

She took a step back. Defeat or strategic withdrawal, Bill wasn't sure, but he was pleased that he seemed to have won this round.

'That can always be arranged,' Maureen said under her breath, as she retreated to check on the gentleman with the radio.

'I heard that, Missy!'

Mr Smith might have won this battle, but he sensed the war was far from over.

2

Maureen Bannon sat down at the nurses' station. The shift was still young, but she dropped onto the chair as if it was the end of a long and difficult day.

'Anyone want to swap patients?'

No one answered. All her colleagues were suddenly very busy writing up their patient notes. Things had been frantic all day – the casualty department had been overwhelmed since early morning by a multiple-vehicle accident on the Gillies Highway, and the wards had been asked to triage the less-serious cases directly to help with the bottleneck. With no one making eye contact, Maureen reluctantly took out the scraps of paper that formed her first notes for this latest admission and began to write them up.

Getting a patient history from Mr Smith had been as challenging as getting him changed was proving to be. Bill Smith didn't have an existing record at Leichhardt Memorial, so she'd had to ask him all the basics. 'It was like pulling bloody teeth,' said Maureen to her workmates. 'Next of kin? None. Marital status? No answer. Past medical history? None. How does someone get to be his age without ever having seen a doctor?'

But she was talking to herself. No one was interested in her mysterious patient. Maureen had found early in her nursing career that sometimes, if she feigned incompetence or vulnerability, one of the Year Three girls would feel obliged to offer help. But not today. They weren't buying. She continued transcribing her notes.

Nursing notes: 2/5/78 16:40. Name: Bill Smith, 76 yrs, male, DoB 7/2/1902. Next of kin: Nil known. Religion: Unknown. Direct admiss. Monitor on ward. Uncooperative, noncompliant with efforts to assess. Hx query fall at home, found by neighbour × 3 days, dehydration, confusion, risk pneumonia. Fluids not commenced. Awaiting review by Dr.

When she'd finished, Maureen scanned the team once more, spinning herself around on the new swivel chair recently donated by the Country Women's Association. She swung left, reaching out her hand to colleagues, Shirley and Jen.

'Swap with me?'

The pair exchanged glances and, in perfect coordination, shook their heads no. It had been a long shot, Maureen knew – especially since she'd called them a pair of stuck-up cows only two days before.

She swung the other way, towards Franny and Petra, both of whom remained absorbed in their notes. Maureen was about to implore her best friend for help when she noticed that Franny was scribbling furiously on her own patient's file, head down, avoiding any attempt at communication except for the unambiguous middle finger that was pointing straight up. Petra was her last hope.

'Petra, mate, you've got a way with the grumpy old buggers. I'm hopeless with geries – they don't like me. I swear Matron just puts me there to break me. That old person smell – ugh,' she said, holding her nose in mock disgust.

'You'll be old one day, you know, Maurs,' said Petra.

'With my teeth in a jar – put me down before that happens!' Maureen responded, following up with an imitation of a gummy, toothless mouth, opening and closing wordlessly.

Scattered giggles rippled through the room. Maureen swung around and around on her chair, like a preschooler on a merry-go-round, until something in her peripheral vision brought the game to an end.

'Is that so, Nurse Bannon?' said a voice from behind her. The room felt like the oxygen was being sucked from it, and all life waited for permission to breathe again. Matron Kelly was old-school. Not a hair out of place, starched veil crisp enough to cut a sandwich. The kind of matron that kept tissues in her office for baby nurses who inevitably left in tears. 'Pan room then, Nurse,' said Matron. 'Perhaps the aromas in there will be more to your liking.'

Without meeting Matron's unyielding stare, Maureen sprang up and marched off down the corridor, leaving the chair spinning slowly in her wake.

~

'You know who you've got in there, don't you?' said Franny.

Maureen jumped at the unexpected presence.

'Gawd, don't do that! Don't come up behind me like that – I thought it was old Kelly,' she said, relaxing her shoulders. 'Yes, I know who I've got – it's *Mr* Pain-in-the-Bum. Why do I always get the difficult ones?'

'It's Bill "Girly" Smith, Maurs – the jockey. Your granddad probably knew him. *Girly*,' she said again, as if that explained everything.

'Girly?' Maureen repeated, without recognition.

'Not sure how he got the name. Some people used to think he was a little bit ... *flighty*,' said Fran, flapping her wrist and giving a knowing wink.

'Flighty? You mean ... a *poof*?' said Maureen, scanning the corridor before allowing the word to fall out.

'You don't say that these days, Maurs – you say "gay".'

Maureen looked at Franny, standing there with her wrist still bent at a right angle, and wondered why that gesture was acceptable but not her own expression. She shook it off. Her friend had always seemed more worldly than her about most matters. Fran had lived in the city for a bit, while Maureen's only trip out of North Queensland had been on a cruise to Fiji with her family when she was thirteen – and she'd spent most of it in her cabin with terrible seasickness.

'I don't know if he actually was,' continued Franny, unfolding her hand. 'Doesn't matter, anyway. I just remember hearing about this funny fella, Girly Smith, who never got changed at the track. Always came and went from meets with his colours under his clothes.'

Maureen pulled Franny into the pan room and closed the door. 'That is queer. Strange queer, not gay queer,' she said, as she contemplated why someone would do that. 'Anyway, I don't care. He's still a grumpy old bugger, and I need him changed before Doctor comes.'

Fran Patterson sat up on a bench and watched Maureen fish a bedpan from the trough of boiling water, holding it out at a distance with the large metal tongs, even though it had just been sterilised.

'You'd be grumpy too if you were in his shoes,' she said. 'Some young girl trying to take his gear off. He wouldn't get changed in front of other jockeys – he won't appreciate you trying to get him undressed.'

'That may be so, but what am I supposed to do? Can't you give me a hand?'

'Have you seen my load? A fractured hip and a gall bladder, for starters,' said Franny. 'Try telling him who your granddad is. That might win him over.'

'No thanks.'

'Are you still not talking to your Pop? Talk about stubborn.'

Before Maureen could respond, a third person joined their conversation.

'Those pans have cleaned themselves, have they, Nurse Bannon?'

Franny leapt down off the benchtop, grabbed a clean urinal bottle and squeezed past the substantial frame of Matron Kelly, leaving the door swinging behind her. Maureen stood fixed to the spot, unsure of what to do next. She finally turned towards Matron, hands behind her back, assuming the expected stance for another admonishment.

'I was just getting some background on Mr Smith, Matron. Franny – I mean, Nurse Patterson – knows him; or knows about him, at least.'

'Good. Then I'll expect to see him in a hospital gown some time this side of Christmas.'

'Yes, Matron.'

'And fix that cap, Nurse. You look like you crawled in through the window.'

'Yes, Matron.'

At least I could fit through a window, Maureen thought to herself as the sound of Matron Kelly's court shoes faded along the corridor.

~

Maureen had finished her rounds and was heading back to the nurses' station when Matron called her into her office. Three encounters in one shift. Nothing positive could come from such a request. Maureen's hands were trembling. She tried to hide them by putting them in her pockets.

Since starting her training, Maureen had been in old Kelly's sights on numerous occasions. Mostly for her slack standards of dress, it seemed, but also because of her obvious lack of enthusiasm for certain aspects of practice. Maureen had thought nursing was going to be better than high school. A nice, fun job for a little while – or, as her mother was fond of saying, 'something to fall back on until you meet Mr Right'. But as she entered her second year and found herself mostly in the company of elderly men like Mr Smith, she wasn't quite so sure.

'Mr Right-Over-the-Hill,' she would say whenever she recalled her mother's optimism about her finding a potential husband. Not that she was searching. Maureen had things to do, places to go – like Sydney, or even London – before she followed the path of most local girls into marriage and children. Besides, the pool of local males was more like a very small and stagnant pond.

'Nurse Bannon, we are not in the playground. Please stand like a grown-up.'

Maureen stood up straight, fingers interlocked behind her back, trying to blow away the stray lock of ginger-blonde hair that escaped her cap. Conscious of her shoes being less than pristine, she discreetly rubbed each foot several times down the back of her stockinged legs, all while keeping her eyes fixed on Matron, whose face looked set like stone.

'Mr Smith is still in his clothes,' said Matron. 'Is there a plan to get him showered and into a clean gown any time soon?'

'Yes, Matron. It's just that, well, he told me to bugg— to leave him alone. I've tried several times, but he tries to fight me. Even the ambos struggled with him.'

'I see. Well, we'll just leave him then, shall we? Sitting in his street clothes, smelling like a hobo.'

Nurse Bannon was not the fastest to recognise sarcasm, despite finding herself on the receiving end of it more than often, and now she could not hide her confusion.

'Follow me,' said Matron, gesturing with her all-powerful, beckoning finger.

When they entered the ward, the patient appeared to be sleeping, yet his hands moved back and forth over the blanket in some strange exercise.

'What do you think he's doing, Matron?' whispered Maureen.

'Dreaming, probably,' replied Matron.

Matron Kelly leaned in and placed her hand on the patient's shoulder. 'Mr Smith, are you alright?'

On finding Matron's face suddenly so close to his, Bill put up his defences once more, the bedclothes becoming a moat around his personal castle.

'Doctor will be around shortly to examine you, Mr Smith,' said Matron in a voice reserved for the public. 'It really would make things much easier if we could get you out of your clothes before then.'

'No, no, no. I told that one before – bugger off,' replied Bill. 'I don't need any doctor poking around where they don't belong. I just need to get out of here.'

As if to contradict him, Bill Smith's body suddenly lurched forward into a coughing fit, his voice becoming staccato and thick with phlegm. Matron repositioned the pillows behind his head, while Nurse Bannon instinctively turned on the oxygen cylinder and fitted the mask to his face.

'Pull the curtain, please, Nurse,' said Matron Kelly sharply, before resuming a gentler tone. 'Mr Smith, the sooner we get you better, the sooner we get you home.' She placed her hand over the white-knuckled fists that clenched at the sheets. 'You took a nasty fall. We need Doctor to examine you properly.'

'I've taken plenty of falls in my time, Lass,' Bill said, pulling the mask off. 'Don't you worry about me.'

Lass. No one had ever called Matron 'Lass'. By any measure, Maureen thought, it must have been a very long time ago if they had. Maureen's body stiffened as she waited to hear the patient inevitably get given what for. Instead, old Kelly just patted his hand and refitted the oxygen mask.

'Alright, Mr Smith. Relax for now, then. We can get you sorted later.'

Stepping outside the curtain, Matron conceded to Nurse Bannon that they could leave Mr Smith to settle for a bit, but there would be no excuse if he was not in a hospital gown by the end of the shift. 'No need to rush,' she added. 'Doctor is still busy in casualty. Get a phone order for some fluids in the meantime. Ask Nurse Patterson to give you a hand, but only if she has everything in order with her own patients first.'

'Yes, Matron.'

Maureen returned to the bedside to make sure the rails were up and the mask still in place. She studied Mr Smith, his gaunt and leathered face, his eyes wishing her gone. She was relieved that Matron had no more success with the wayward old bugger than she had. As she considered the troublesome patient she'd been allocated, the tiny figure pulled off his mask once more and poked out his tongue. Maureen reflexively poked hers out in return, before recomposing herself. She straightened the front of her uniform and righted her cap.

'Can we at least leave that on for now?' she said, indicating the mask. 'I'll be back later to get you changed, okay?'

'No, it's not okay. You go annoy somebody else now, Missy.'

'It's *Nurse* to you,' she countered. 'Why do I always get the difficult ones?' she said, not quietly enough, as she turned to go.

'Like attracts like, most probably.'

Maureen stopped mid-turn, ready to respond, but could not help smiling instead. She kept walking, planning her next move in the battle of Smith vs Bannon.

3

Nursing notes: 2/5/78 19:00. Pt refusing to get changed. Combative. Monitor until Dr available. Vitals: R 12, P 96, refused BP and temp. Positioned in High Fowler's. O_2 *via mask. Bedrails up.*

Some time after dinner, Maureen was finishing her observations of her other patients when she saw Matron standing once again at Mr Smith's bedside. Gawd, Maureen thought, what is she still doing here? Anticipating a further dressing-down about her lack of progress since the last directive, she hurried over to join her.

'Nurse,' Matron said to Maureen, 'do you know how much I was looking forward to going home after a day like today?'

'No, Matron,' said Maureen, who had never envisaged old Kelly in any setting but the hospital, before realising it was not a question to be answered.

On doing her final sweep of the wards and seeing Nurse Bannon's patient still in his own clothes, Matron had apparently decided to take matters into her own hands. Maureen, scanning that all was in place

– oxygen, pillows, bedrails secured, hospital corners executed neatly – stood patiently waiting for Matron's instructions; but with a wave of her hand Matron dismissed the junior nurse, stepping forward to take on the challenge herself.

'Mr Smith, you really must let me help you out of those clothes,' she said, reaching across the bed. Maureen could do little but watch as Matron began unbuttoning the patient's coat, until her attention turned to the old man's fist, which was suddenly in a tight ball. Before Maureen could sound any warning, Mr Smith delivered an uppercut that sent Matron's head whiplashing.

'Get! Get away from me! Get off me, ya bastard,' he shouted.

Nurse Bannon saw the blow hit its mark. The diminutive patient had caught Matron off guard, causing her to stumble momentarily before regaining her balance. Maureen was immobilised with indecision. Should she reach out a hand? Call for help? She had seen some aggressive patients since starting her training, but she had never seen anyone take on old Kelly. Big, strong men usually turned into little boys under this woman's directions. Everything stilled in agonising anticipation as Maureen waited for Matron to respond.

'It's okay, Mr Smith,' Matron said finally, gently placing her hand on his hands. 'It's okay. No one is going to hurt you. You're safe here.' She turned and retreated a short distance, Maureen instinctively following.

It was not the response Maureen had expected, but then neither was that powerful punch from this frail, geriatric patient. The effort had clearly drained him. Maureen saw his body go slack, his breathing slow and laboured, eyes scrunched shut. She turned then to study the woman who was normally so in control.

'Are you alright, Matron? Can I get you anything? Do you need to sit down?'

'I'm fine,' Matron Kelly responded, testing out the movement of her jaw in a fashion that reminded Maureen of a fish gasping for air. Maureen studied the Matron for a moment longer than comfortable, noting something she had never seen before. The redness in her face wasn't from the punch. It was embarrassment.

'What do you think is wrong with him?' Maureen asked, trying to divert her attention from the image of Matron's flushed face. 'Every time we get near his clothes, he lashes out.'

'Yes, something's not right. He's wearing an extraordinary amount of clothing for this climate. What did the ambulance fellows say?'

'He fought them as well. They couldn't listen to his chest – couldn't really do much of an exam at the house. Took a bit to get him here, apparently.'

They were now speaking as though in church. If Bill could hear, he wasn't letting on. His eyes were shut, his face finally relaxed, and there was even some quiet snoring.

'What about next of kin?'

'None known. His neighbour found him and called for help.' Remembering what Fran had told her, she added: 'Nurse Patterson reckons he was a jockey, years ago.'

Matron Kelly studied the patient with new interest.

'Of course,' she said, more to herself than to Nurse Bannon. 'Girly Smith. Didn't recognise him.'

'Yes, Girly. That's him.'

'Doctor Cunningham will probably know him. His father was a race caller here. Perhaps he'll be more forthcoming with a man, anyway.'

Matron Kelly had not looked directly at Maureen since being caught off guard by the frail little fellow now seemingly unaware of all the chaos he had caused. She turned to address Nurse Bannon.

'He could have dementia, or one fall too many, I suppose. Just be careful.'

'Yes, Matron.'

'Call Nurse Patterson in to help you. Let him rest for now, but try again when he settles. We can't have this go on much longer. Any more issues, let me know immediately.'

'Yes, Matron.'

~

'You should have seen it, Franny,' Maureen said, balling up her own fist to demonstrate. 'Whack – right in the kisser! And she just stood there and held his hand! Can you believe it?'

'She held his *hand*? *Matron*? *Our* Matron Kelly?'

'She thinks he might have dementia,' Maureen continued. 'I don't know. All I know is I was waiting for the explosion,' she stuffed her fingers in her ears and closed her eyes in mock anticipation, before opening them again cautiously, 'but – nothing!'

'Nothing?' repeated Fran. 'She didn't rip him a new one or anything? She just copped it?'

'Patted his hand like he was some sweet little schoolboy. Anyway, she recognised him when I told her who he was. So you have to help – Matron said.'

'Bloody hell, Bannon, you slack tart. You owe me then.'

'Put it on my account,' Maureen said, grabbing her friend in a bear hug.

~

'Hello again, Mr Smith,' said Maureen, with a guarded cheerfulness.

After a lengthy silence, she placed her hand on Fran's back and pushed her forward. 'I've got someone here who reckons they know you – or knows of you, anyway.'

Mr Smith opened one eye to check out the newest recruit in Nurse Bannon's army.

'Hi, Mr Smith. I'm Nurse Patterson – Fran, if you like. You used to be a jockey, eh? Our family is big into racing. We go all the time.'

He was unmoved by the introduction.

The sound of Mr Smith's fist connecting with Matron's jaw still echoed in Maureen's ears. She made sure there was at least an arm's length between her and the patient. But this time there was no resistance, as Franny pulled the curtain around the bed and Maureen set the washbasin on the trolley. In fact, there was no response at all.

'My granddad won a heap of money on you once,' continued Franny finally, while pulling the patient forward in the bed. 'At Tolga, years ago. Reckoned you were always good for the long shots.'

Maureen removed the old man's oxygen mask and started to take off his coat. He gave nothing in return, but he didn't resist, so they pushed on. 'Bit hot for this one – let me hang it up for you,' she said, draping it carefully over the back of the chair by the bed.

Bill was silent, compliant, done. It was more worrying than pleasing to Maureen, who sensed a change in the old man. She pressed on cautiously.

'Nurse Patterson tells me you were quite the rider in your day.'

'And trainer, too, eh?' said Fran, as she helped remove his vest. Bill stared straight ahead.

'I love horses,' continued the effervescent Nurse Patterson, who never let an unresponsive patient stand in the way of a good chat. Maureen had once observed that a patient could be intubated and Franny would still carry on chatting. 'I'd have given anything to be a jockey, like you.

That was never going to happen, though, being a girl. They still won't let women register. So much for women's lib, eh?'

A curious smile spread slowly across Bill's face. His eyes regained some light, and he nodded slightly.

'You could be like me,' he said.

Maureen stopped what she was doing, waiting for further comment, but there was none offered. The two nurses looked at each other, Fran shrugging her shoulders at the remark. After a brief pause to catch their breaths, they resumed their challenge to get Mr Smith out of his clothes and into a hospital gown.

'Let's get this shirt off, eh? It could definitely do with a wash.'

'As could old Girly,' whispered Maureen, a little louder than intended.

'Who said you could call me "Girly"? I never said you could. I told you – it's *Mr Smith*, thank you very much. No bloody respect these days.'

Maureen's face reddened.

'Sorry, Mr Smith. I thought that was your racing name,' she said, turning to Fran for support.

'I told Maurs that's what you were called when you were riding,' agreed her friend.

'Doesn't mean I liked it. Joe Grech called me that and it stuck like shit to a blanket.'

'Grech? Was he a mate?' asked Fran, trying to take the heat off her friend.

'No mate of mine. Just a little man with a big mouth. Thought he was top dog of the jockeys, but he was just a mean mongrel bastard.'

As if suddenly aware of his surroundings again, the old man grinned sheepishly at each of the young women and said, 'Oh, pardon my French there, Sisters – I forgot where I was for a minute.'

Maureen and Franny laughed. Being called 'Sister' was not uncommon

– it was a hangover from the days when most nurses were also nuns – but it was his apology for the colourful language that struck Maureen. It had not been the worst language to come from Mr Smith since he'd arrived, nor the most worrying aspect of his behaviour. On a scale of behaviours requiring apologies, she thought clocking old Kelly on the jaw might have been higher up the list, but their patient seemed unconcerned about what had gone on earlier.

Maureen leaned over and began carefully unbuttoning his shirt. 'Do you know where you are, Mr Smith?' she asked him, casually trying to check his awareness.

'Course I do. I've been kidnapped by you lot and held against my will.'

'Not quite. But you *are* in hospital,' said Maureen, going back to using her singsong voice.

'Fair dinkum!' said Bill, his impatience running high. 'What gave it away now, Missy?'

Intervening deftly before Maureen could respond, Fran asked him, 'What were you all dressed up for, Mr Smith? Were you going somewhere when you had your fall?'

Bill didn't answer. They continued their task, Maureen supporting the old man to lean forward as Franny gently removed his shirt, folded it, and placed it on the chair.

'Gawd, a singlet as well,' said Maureen. 'Weren't you hot in all this?'

As the last constrictive layer came off over his head, Nurse Bannon involuntarily let go of her hold and Mr Smith fell like a ragdoll onto the pillows. Franny stepped back. The pair stared at the half-naked figure, before locking eyes with each other across the bed. Their patient's eyes fixed only on the ceiling.

After a prolonged pause, Maureen continued gently easing off the trousers that had been so gallantly fought over. This surrender gave her no joy. After placing them with the rest of the clothes, she picked up the sponge and dipped it into the warm, soapy water on the trolley. Slowly, tentatively, she worked her way around the fragile body. Fran followed up with a gentle towelling-dry – a synchronised tending to the physical that swallowed the unusual silence between them all.

Now with her patient in a fresh, clean gown, Maureen straightened the bedclothes and pillows and secured the bedrails, before she spoke.

'I'll just put these things away, Mr ... um ... Smith, yes. I'll be back shortly.'

Her words were unattached to any movement, until Fran nudged her friend into action, guiding her out through the curtains and into the corridor.

4

Bill Smith lay motionless, staring at the ceiling, waiting for it to come crashing down. Was that movement? Surely, it was about to fall. He had fought most of his life to avoid this moment. But now it was done. The world had changed, yet only he seemed to have noticed. His roommates appeared unaware. And what about the nurses – the little ginger miss and her horse-loving mate? They were witnesses to it happening, but there had been no ridicule, no anger – not that Bill could feel, anyway. Instead, there were clean sheets and the scent of Pears soap to mark the end of a lifelong battle not to be seen for who the rest of the world would deem him to be. Now that it had happened, it felt like quite an unremarkable event. The memories that flooded his thoughts, however, were less so. All the near misses, the vulnerable moments, the threat of violence never being far away.

'Girly'. 'Girly' Smith, he'd been called back then. He knew it was generally meant with affection, and not meant to be taken literally – a lot of jockeys had nicknames, and most assumed his was just a reflection of his stature and his high-pitched voice. Bill took a while to take to the name, however. When he'd first heard it from Joe Grech, the number-one hoop in the north, his face had flushed with anxiety.

'Just keep out of my way, ya girly-lookin' bludger.'

What had been worse was how quickly it took hold. Trainer, Charlie McInnes found it a great laugh and used the nickname from then on. Bill Smith didn't care for it at all, but it was a choice between protesting too much and hiding in plain sight, in a way. So the name 'Girly' came to represent a large part of his life, when he'd got to fulfil his passion to ride. And ride he had, over a career spanning decades.

In the racing fraternity, Bill had mostly found decent, hardworking people willing to give a bloke a go – especially one with the horse-handling skills he soon became known for – but still, it paid to keep to himself. The horses were all the company he needed, and they asked no questions. Now, though, in this hospital bed, there was no more hiding. His mind filled with images of those he had worked with over the years. What would they think? How would they react?

He could hear a train being shunted over at the Leichhardt railyards, and he recalled the days before horse floats, when trainers, jockeys and strappers would all travel together up or down the line from Cairns to get to race meets. The faces of the men he'd travelled with back then were all vivid to him still. He recalled one such trip from Cairns to Mareeba, not long before horse floats became the way to go. He closed his eyes and drifted off in the memory.

~

As the train snaked its way over the Macalister Range, some of the horses would become a little unsettled by all the hairpin bends near Kuranda. The trainers and riders would congregate in one of the carriages, leaving the young strappers to care for their mounts, but Bill preferred to look after his own.

'Hey, Girly – come and have a drink with us,' one of the jockeys would say.

'In a bit,' he'd usually respond. 'I think the mare's a little travel sick.'

'Jesus, Girly, it's like you're chained to that bloody nag. Sit down and relax. Jacko's got a bottle of Bundy he's happy to share.'

'In a bit.'

But it was well known that 'in a bit' would never come. Most just put it down to shyness, but there were a few, like Nev Newbury, who weren't so understanding. Bill's pleasant recollections shifted, as did he, subconsciously tossing the bedclothes off in readiness for an altercation from the past.

~

'They're holding steady at the start of the 1940 Cannon Park Handicap for three-year-olds. The starter is taking up his position. There's some movement at the line – he'll have to hold them until Lady Walter settles. Lady Walter's in a cantankerous mood today – she's dislodged her rider. Newbury won't like that. The jockey is down between the horses. There's a hold-up here with Race Five. The starter has climbed down, and they'll have to line up again.'

Race caller Kenny Cunningham tried to entertain the crowd with fascinating facts about the race's history, as the mounts were backed up and made to go to the line a second time. Nev Newbury dusted himself down. He was fuelled with embarrassment and agitation. When he got Lady Walter up to the starting rope again, he put the boot in several times to let her know who was boss. Bill hated that kind of handling of a horse. He gave Nev a mouthful as the rope dropped away, causing them both to miss the start.

'Ya mongrel, Girly!' yelled Newbury as he moved up alongside Bill. 'You'll pay for that!'

With that, Newbury urged his horse to the inside, pushing Bill and his mount, Autumn Shadow, up against the railings. Bill used his boot to push back against a ton of horseflesh, as Newbury walloped his opponent's knuckles several times with his crop. With the rest of the pack furlongs ahead, the two horses bumped heavily at the first turn, causing both to stumble. Bill tried in vain to fight gravity as his animal staggered but, inevitably, he and his horse spilled across the track.

Autumn Shadow took a while to get back onto her feet. When she did, she bolted riderless towards the rest of the pack. Lady Walter had managed to stay upright, with Nev Newbury peering over his shoulder to view the consequences of his actions that had left his fallen opponent collapsed, motionless, the wind knocked out of him.

The clerk of the course, Danny Bolton, was soon with Bill, while the ambulance – two volunteers in a ute – made its way onto the track. Danny got down close to check that he was breathing.

'You okay, mate? Can you hear me, Girly?'

He put his ear to Bill's chest to listen for breathing, and squeezed his hand a few times.

'Bill? Bill? Can you hear me, mate? You've taken a pretty hard tumble. The first-aid boys are here to check you out.'

As the young ambulance attendant started to pull on Bill's shirt and unbutton his pants, the injured jockey's hands reached forward to stop him.

'Fuck off! Fuck off, the lot of ya!'

Bill's eyes stayed closed as he struggled to sit up, but his hands remained resolutely wrapped around the top of his pants. He tried again to sit up. The gathered men looked at each other. Girly Smith was not one for rough language, as a rule. They stood back and gave him room.

'I'm alright. Help up's all I need.'

'But you might have cracked some ribs there, mate. You really should let us check you out.'

'No, get off me. Leave me alone.'

~

'Leave me alone!'

Bill's shouting in his sleep was enough to wake the man in the bed next to him.

'Steady on there, mate. No one's even near ya,' came a raspy voice from the other side of the curtain.

Bill opened his eyes. The crowd had disappeared. The smell of the dampened dirt track, Danny Bolton – all gone. There was just the hospital ceiling, with its curls of paint hanging forlornly in the breeze of the ceiling fans, waiting for some attention.

'Sorry, mate, sorry. I must have been dreaming.'

'Well, dream quieter – don't you know there's poor sick buggers in here?'

Bill didn't bother responding. He wasn't sure he could be bothered with anything much anymore. He just wanted to get home.

5

Nursing notes: 2/5/78 20:00. Pt changed. Bed bath given. O_2 *via Hudson's. Commencing rehydration per phone order. Matron contacted re social/psych issues; assessment pending.*

In the pan room, Maureen emptied the washbowl and Franny placed the used towels in the laundry bag. It was Franny who spoke first.

'He's a *she*. Bill Smith. *Girly* Smith. A *woman*. I always thought that name was a joke. Everyone did.'

'Well, what are we meant to do now? We'll have to tell Matron. We'll have to—'

The words were firing out of Maureen like a Gatling gun. Franny stepped forward to grip her by the shoulders.

'Calm down, Maurs. Of course we'll have to tell Matron.'

'What's everyone going to say when my male patient ends up in the female ward?'

'I know what my granddad would say. He'd blow a gasket if he knew. Not that I'd tell him, of course.'

'We can't tell anyone. Can we? No. We can't. He obviously didn't want anyone to know – or *she* – gawd, it's giving me a headache!'

'Me too,' said the normally unflappable Franny. 'Come on, let's go tell Matron. She'll know what to do.'

'She did say to phone her any time if we needed to. Doubt she'll be expecting this one, though.'

Maureen went through a mental checklist, hoping to give Matron nothing else to criticise. She had her patient changed, at least, but still she hesitated. 'Hang on a sec.' She grabbed her scissors, cut some Elastoplast off the roll, pulled up the front of her uniform and pressed the tape along the hem that had been hanging down since her last lot of running repairs. 'That's better.'

~

If Matron was as shocked as the two young women now standing in her office, she didn't let it show. Having been called back to the ward with some urgency by the perplexed Nurse Bannon, she simply began studying room allocations. Maureen, in turn, began studying Matron. Now dressed in a yellow, sun-patterned shift and sandals, her dark auburn hair let loose, this woman seemed much younger and more approachable – until the no-nonsense voice of Matron Kelly broke the silence.

'Right, we've only got the TB room available, but it's not made up. I'll have to get someone to prepare it. We won't be able to move Mr Smith until later, so keep the curtain drawn for now. I'll be down before Doctor comes to examine him.'

'*Her*,' said Maureen, not intending to contradict Matron, but trying to get it sorted in her own head.

'*Mr* Smith, for now, Nurse. Until *he* tells us otherwise. Understood?'

'Yes, Matron.'

'And not a word to anyone. This is a small community. We need to protect Mr Smith's confidentiality.'

'Yes, Matron.'

~

'She's full of surprises, old Kelly, eh?' said Fran as they headed back to the ward.

'Not the only one, now, is she?' said Maureen. 'Have you ever come across something like this before?'

'In Leichhardt? Hardly. I did see *Les Girls* in Sydney once. With my cousin. Only they were blokes dressed as women. It was in Kings Cross – gawd, you see all kinds there. We had these fake IDs, but no one even looked at them. And we drank cocktails. It was bloody fantastic.'

'You have to take me some time – to Sydney, I mean. Not too fussed on seeing a bunch of men in frocks, myself.'

'Some of them were drop-dead gorgeous – you'd never know. And all the singing and dancing. You'd love it, I reckon.'

'If you say so,' said an unconvinced Maureen. 'Anyway, just when I thought this was going to be another boring shift on the oldies' ward ...' With that the two friends parted ways, as Maureen returned to her patient and Fran to hers.

~

Mr Smith was finally sleeping comfortably. Maureen was reluctant to disturb him. She studied the dryness of his lips, his sunken eyes and blanched skin, before putting her hand gently on his.

'Sorry to wake you,' she said, softly. 'We need to get you started on some fluids – you're a bit dry.'

Bill opened his eyes and stared back at her with an expression she had not seen before. It frightened her. She held her breath as his face contorted with anguish. Maureen realised he was trying to speak, but no words were coming out. She jumped back a little as he flung the sheets off and wrestled with his hospital gown, still unable to produce any sound. When he finally stopped struggling, she leaned in close to his ear and spoke discretely.

'It's okay, Mr Smith. Your secret's safe with us. We're going to move you to a private room. But for now, we'll just keep the curtain drawn. Let me get Matron for you,' she said, hoping Kelly was still in the hospital.

Bill Smith made no sound at all, and yet Maureen could hear a scream that reached into her core.

~

When Matron stepped in through the curtains, Bill made no effort to acknowledge her, still staring blankly ahead.

'You're safe here, Mr Smith. No need to worry,' said Matron. 'We can limit the number of people involved in your care. No one else needs to know.'

Maureen observed their interaction. Mr Smith nodded, still staring into the distance, before his face finally relaxed a little. He reached out and grabbed Matron Kelly's hand. 'Promise me,' he said, 'only those looking after me will know? That little ginger nursey' – he nodded towards Maureen – 'and her mate? Promise me they'll be the only ones?'

'There may be other staff I need to involve,' replied Matron Kelly. 'Some of the seniors. But I promise you, we'll respect your privacy as best we can. You have my word.'

Bill Smith released his hold on Matron's hand. He closed his eyes, as Maureen and Matron spoke around him.

'See to Mr Smith's belongings, Nurse. Make sure his clothes are washed and his personal effects locked away.'

'Yes, Matron.'

'Don't forget to check the pockets for any valuables.'

'Yes, Matron.'

~

Maureen was careful to check everything before placing the patient's clothes in a laundry bag and labelling it. This was a part of the job she really hated, especially when dealing with elderly patients.

'Oh, lovely,' she said to herself. 'An old man's hanky. Yuck. That can go in the laundry bag as well. Reading glasses – he'll be needing those. He—' she hesitated. 'Yes, he. Mr Smith.'

She continued working her way through every pocket, talking quietly to herself as she went. 'What in the world—?' She turned one of the pants pockets inside-out and a half-eaten digestive biscuit crumbled onto the floor.

'You right there, Maurs? Having a little chat to yourself, are you? You know it's the first sign of insanity?' said Fran, who'd popped her head in through the curtain.

'I know what's insanity,' Maureen responded, giving a nod to the now-soundly sleeping patient they would soon move to a private room.

'Not insanity. Courageous, I reckon. Imagine how hard it must have been, all these years.'

'I guess so. But I just don't get it'.

She continued her search through Mr Smith's clothing. A few dollars, a folded piece of paper – and a pocket watch. 'What's this?' she asked, turning over the tarnished silver timepiece in her hand and showing it to her friend. 'It's beautiful.'

'It's a trainer's watch,' said Franny, leaning in for a closer inspection.

'There's something on the back,' said Maureen, squinting to read the worn engraving: 'Norman Ridge Guineas, 1939.'

'Wouldn't those old racing fellas have a fit if they knew they were beaten by a woman?' Franny said.

'Yeah, I imagine they would.'

Maureen placed the watch carefully on the bedside table, before reaching into another pocket to find one more used handkerchief.

'Nice. Another heirloom,' she said. 'Reminds me of my grandfather's house and his old man's hankies.'

'How long has it been since you've seen him – old Pop Bannon?' Fran asked.

'Don't start.'

But Fran wasn't letting her off that easily – she left the silence for Maureen to fill.

'He's not the same since Nan—' Maureen said eventually. 'I'm sure he doesn't want to see me. He's a bit like this one,' she gave another nod towards Mr Smith.

'How's that, exactly? Stubborn, like all Bannons?'

'Very funny.'

'You need to make things right with him, Maurs, before it's too late.'

'Don't you have other patients to attend to? I think I'll be fine from here.'

'If stubbornness was worth money, you'd be a bloody millionaire,' said Franny, wrapping her arms around her friend and giving a gentle squeeze.

'Love you, too,' Maureen called after Franny as she left the room.

Maureen gathered the few possessions Bill Smith had arrived with and locked them in a secure cupboard. But something about those items caused her to picture Pop Bannon. She felt her throat tighten as she remembered their last meeting. It had been the day of her grandmother's funeral and, although things were civil during the proceedings, Maureen could still feel the pain of having been told she was not welcome back at his house.

Her parents had told her it wasn't her fault that Nan Bannon had died – it was a heart attack. It's just the grief talking, they'd told her. Pop just needs time, they'd told her. But one thing was certain: Maureen Bannon did carry some guilt for her grandmother dying alone, when she should have been with her. Still, she could not yet bring herself to say that aloud – especially not to Pop Bannon.

~

The hospital's doctor, Dr Cunningham, was still dealing with the traumatic road incident from earlier in the day, so an elderly GP, Dr Marcus, had been called up from Cairns to help with the ward patients. When he finally got to Mr Smith late in the evening, he stood at the end of the bed, trawling through the patient's file. He studied the notes, then the patient, and then scanned the men in the other beds in the room. Now in a clingy white gown, all external symbols of masculinity stripped away, the patient in this bed seemed to the doctor to be an elderly woman. It wasn't unheard of at times when beds were tight to have male and female patients in the same ward, but the files didn't normally dispute that.

'Nurse, I think you've given me the wrong file,' Dr Marcus said to Maureen. 'This is for a *Mr* Smith.'

'It's the right file, Doctor,' said Maureen with exaggerated cheeriness, raising her eyebrows up and down in the hope that the medic would crack the code and catch on. Instead, he rolled his eyes and turned to address the patient.

'Smith? There used to be a jockey called Bill Smith from around here. You're related to that Smith, are you, Madam? His wife, perhaps?' Turning back to Nurse Bannon, he added, 'This can't be the correct first name. Make sure you amend this file for Mrs Smith.'

Maureen leaned over and whispered to the doctor: '*Mr*. He prefers *Mr* Smith.'

'What? Don't be ridiculous,' said Dr Marcus dismissively, before placing the stethoscope to his ears. 'Now, if you could just sit forward, Mrs Smith – or Miss, whichever it is – I need to listen to your chest.'

Maureen caught the pained expression on Bill's face.

'Mrs Smith, I need to listen to your chest,' the doctor repeated, irritation dripping from his voice along with the sweat from his hands.

At that moment, Matron Kelly stepped into the room with heroic timing.

'Dr Marcus, I was hoping to catch you when you arrived. May I see you outside? Won't be a moment, Mr Smith,' she added, throwing Bill a smile.

'Don't worry,' said Maureen quietly to Bill once they'd left. 'Matron will word him up. Even the doctors snap to when old Kelly tells them.'

'They'll all know soon enough,' said Bill.

'Not if we can help it. You came in here as Mr Smith, and it's nobody's business to be saying otherwise.'

6

Nursing notes: 2/5/78 22:00. Pt reviewed by Dr Marcus. Privacy concerns. Move to single room when available. Specialling required. All visitors and staff to check at nurses' station prior to entry.

Maureen moved her patient to a private room towards the end of shift. Petra would be doing a double and looking after Mr Smith overnight because, of all the workers on the ward, she was the one who could be relied upon for her discretion and her ability to remain unfazed, no matter what was presented to her.

But the other staff were curious.

'What's so special about that one? Why's he get a private room? He's not contagious, is he?' asked Jen, who had a reputation for being able to deal with the grossest of wounds but would become highly anxious around anything she could catch.

'Yeah, I thought he just had a fall. What gives?' asked Di, one of the enrolled nurses.

'He's not contagious,' said Maureen. 'He was stuck on the floor for days. What do you think, at seventy-six? Matron wants to make sure he gets some peace and quiet.'

'Why can't anyone else go in there?' asked Jen, unconvinced.

'You've got time to wonder about rostering, have you, Nurse?' came Matron's voice from behind them.

How does she do that? Maureen wondered. She moves like a ninja when she wants to. She could have been a spy during the war, the way she can creep up on people.

Matron Kelly was supposed to have left hours ago. Normally, everyone was a bit more relaxed in the evenings after she had clocked off, but today had been unusual on many levels. Now here she was, dressed in her yellow shift and with her hair loose, still patrolling the ward late into the night.

'I – I was just about to go and do Mrs Fairbright's pressure care,' said Jen.

'Well, best you move then before Mrs Fairbright develops an ulcer.'

'Yes, Matron.'

Maureen was relieved that, for once, she wasn't the one scurrying away, but it was a short-lived feeling as the civilian-clad figure turned and directed her gaze towards her in the same way as the starched-stiff version. Maureen held her breath, waiting for what was to come.

'Nurse Bannon,' said Matron. 'Good job with Mr Smith. Keep it up.'

It took Maureen a moment to unclench her body and comprehend what had been said.

'Thank you, Matron.'

~

When Maureen and Franny finally got back to the nurses' quarters that night, they headed to Franny's room for their usual debrief.

'Pinch me,' said Maureen, holding out her arm. 'Go on, pinch me.'

'What are you on about, Maurs?'

'"Good job", she said. *Kelly. To me.* "Good job with Mr Smith."'

'I might have to pinch you. It does sound like a dream.'

Fran flopped back on her bed and kicked off her shoes. Maureen turned on their contraband kettle. Private kettles and toasters were forbidden in their rooms, as there had been one too many incidents of overloaded sockets or burnt toast setting off fire alarms. It was also suspected that some of the girls might occasionally have helped matters along just so the local fire brigade boys would have to pay a visit. All food and drinks were meant to be prepared and consumed in the common kitchen, but having your own facilities made late-night cups of tea taste that much better. Maureen reached into her uniform pocket and pulled out some crackers.

'Here, courtesy of Leichhardt Memorial Hospital,' she said, throwing a couple of packets Franny's way.

'Girly Smith, eh,' said Fran. 'Bill "Girly" Smith, a *woman*. I wonder if anyone ever knew?'

'I'm glad it's Petra staying with him tonight,' said Maureen. 'She won't let anyone get past her. Didn't even bat an eyelid when Matron told her about Mr Smith. Was he really a big deal? How come I never heard about him?'

'Why don't you ask old Mick?'

'Stop trying to fix things between me and my grandfather. You know we haven't talked since Nan died.'

'That's two Bannons being Bannons. Besides, Maurs, you can't keep feeling guilty. Nothing would have changed the outcome, and I'm sure your Pop knows that.'

'Who said I feel guilty? I don't.'

Maureen stirred the tea more loudly than necessary, hoping Franny would take the hint. She passed her a cup and sat on the opposite end of the bed so they were facing each other.

'If Mr Smith *feels* like she's a man, would she ever have had a girlfriend, or ... would that make her a lesbian?' Maureen was whispering now, as she broached previously uncharted subjects.

'Maurs, you're deadset funny! If she did have anyone, they'd pretty soon work out she was no bloke.'

'Don't you want to know, though? There must have been someone. But if she liked men – how would that work? Wouldn't that make her gay, because she's, like – a man?'

Franny, who had just taken a mouthful of tea, spat most of it out again, fortunately catching it in her cup.

'I'm serious,' said Maureen. 'Don't you want to know? I mean, if she only dressed like a man so she could be a jockey, then why is she still dressing like one?'

'Maybe she's a transvestite.'

Maureen leaned back against the wall. A *transvestite*. She wasn't sure she knew what that meant.

'How do you know all this stuff?' she asked.

'You'd be surprised what I know,' replied Fran, taking a long, satisfying sip of her tea. 'Shocked, even.'

Maureen studied her friend's face in the low light of the naked 20-watt globe on the bedside table. Franny's eyes were closed, but she grinned with the mischief of a life spent seeking out adventure. The poster above her bed of rock band Cold Chisel at a Sydney pub was further evidence to Maureen that her friend was more hardcore than she would ever be. She still had pop idol David Cassidy on her wall.

'Promise me you'll take me to Sydney one day,' she said. 'I want to be shocked, and I want to know just half of what you know.'

Fran reached her hand out to Maureen without opening her eyes.

'You're on, Bannon. Now bugger off and let me get some sleep. It'll be morning before you know it.'

~

Maureen found it hard to sleep after the day she'd had. There were so many questions running through her head that just wouldn't be quiet. She wondered whether her grandfather did know the jockey known as Girly Smith. Mick Bannon had been the chief steward for Cairns District for a long time – not that she really knew what that meant. Why didn't she? They used to be close, but that was before she'd broken his trust and very possibly both their hearts. Perhaps it *was* time to try to make things right again. Maureen wondered whether her grandfather would be ready as well and, if he wasn't, how she would handle being rejected a second time.

She lay awake thinking about Mr Smith. She found it hard to get the image out of her mind of those scarred breasts. What had happened to cause such disfigurement? she wondered. Who was Bill Smith, when the name seemed to contradict the evidence? Was Mr Smith really a *he* or should they now say *she*? And what did it all mean? Maureen felt a sudden flush of shame at her ignorance about the world beyond her small place in it. Now she couldn't wait to get back to the patient she had tried so hard to unload on her workmates.

7

Over the days that followed his admission to Leichhardt Memorial, in the privacy of his single room, Bill Smith drifted between bouts of semiconsciousness and fitful slumber. It was as if his life was playing on a cinema screen and he was detached from it, an audience to his own story. Thundering hooves and clattering barriers punctured any efforts to completely rest. The nights were full of memories and sensory hallucinations. Sometimes he would sit bolt upright, certain he could smell the mix of horse piss, manure and damp hay of the stables. It wasn't unpleasant; it smelled like home.

One afternoon, Bill was lying back with a smile on his face when Nurse Bannon interrupted his thoughts.

'What are you grinning about?' she asked him as she entered the room.

'I was thinking it must be time for that cheeky one to bring me my clothes and let me go home.'

'Is that right? Well, sorry to disappoint, but all I've brought are your meds,' she said, checking his armband. He allowed her to take a set of obs and noticed her uneasy expression as she recorded them on the chart.

'You look like you lost a shilling and found a penny,' he said.

'Not too many of those old coins around these days. Nan used to put sixpences and threepences in her Christmas puddings – but she passed away a few years back. Anyway, it's you I'm worried about,' Maureen said, plumping up the pillows and straightening the bedclothes. 'Don't want you to end up with pneumonia.'

Waving away her concern, Bill said, 'You couldn't kill me with a stick. Now why don't you go fuss over someone who needs it?'

'Since you seem so chirpy, then, a Mrs Jenkins keeps asking after you. Wants to know if she can visit.'

'Gawd, no!' said Bill, a hint of panic in his voice. 'Tell her I'm contagious or something. I don't need old Ivy sticking her nose into my business.'

'She seems genuinely concerned for you,' said Maureen. 'We could make sure all your bedclothes are in place, keep her at a distance – since you really are quite sick, you know. Sure you wouldn't like a bit of company? Is there nobody we can get in touch with for you?'

'Only company I miss is my dogs and my horses, and you can't exactly bring them back from the dead, now, can you? Anyway, I've got your sparkling company – what more could I want?'

The attempt at a toothless smile seemed to disarm Maureen.

'At least let me give your dentures a clean,' she said.

'Good. I need those choppers for all that lovely mush you're feeding me.'

Bill watched her leave, carrying his false teeth in a jar like they were something nasty she'd found on the roadside. He had begun to enjoy their banter and gamesmanship, and he suspected 'Missy' did as well. The thought of anyone else seeing him in hospital, on the other hand, was something that kept him on edge.

~

Despite repeated requests for everyone to 'bugger off', and to just let him go home, Bill Smith found himself still in Leichhardt Memorial Hospital a week later, his chest stubbornly congested and his pressure sores failing to respond to treatment. On occasions when sleep was impossible, he would become animated and happy to share with Maureen stories of his beloved horses, of shifty jockeys and trainers, of money squandered by clueless punters who loved you when you won and booed you when you lost. Some nights Maureen needed to insist that it was time for her to see to other patients, because she was worried that all of Bill's reminiscences, with their associated actions, would be too draining for him. But the truth was that whenever he was up for a talk, Nurse Bannon found herself wanting to know more about Mr Smith.

'You told us before that you didn't like being called "Girly"', she said to him one night. 'So that name, it wasn't because anyone knew your – situation, then?'

'No, they didn't,' he replied. 'They might have suspected, but I was stronger than I looked, at least. Done all sorts of work before I got into racing. Horse breaking, farm labouring, working on the steamships – but it wasn't till I turned up in Cairns that I became "Girly" Smith. Depended on who was calling me that, whether I minded or not. It started with that jockey, Grech. Little Italian fella, or Maltese, maybe. He was a nasty bast—' he stopped himself and turned to Maureen. 'Sorry, Missy, I forget where I am sometimes.'

'I'm not so delicate that I haven't heard the odd swear word,' she smiled.

'All the same, I never like to swear in front of a lady,' said Bill, before continuing. 'It was when I went looking for race work, first time I met him. I'd slide under the cyclone fence round Cannon Park Racecourse and stand near the 6-furlong mark most mornings when they were doing trackwork. I had a job at the brewery, but all I really wanted was to ride, so I'd go at dawn when all the trainers were there.

'One day there was this horse pigrooting and arcing up every time the bloke put the boot in. It wasn't the horse's fault – beautiful, 16 hands he was, chestnut boy – it was the rider trying to boss him. The more he shoved his heels into the poor thing's guts, the more he bucked about like a rodeo horse – till he unseated the fella, who landed right in front of me. I didn't have time to say much. The horse was going to jump the rails, so I ran over and grabbed the reins to steady him.'

'Was the rider okay?'

'He was alright. Pride hurt more than anything.'

Bill's face furrowed as he struggled to call up a memory that should have been readily accessed. He slapped a hand to his forehead in frustration.

'How did it start, exactly? Gawd, I should know this.'

'It's alright, Mr Smith. You're probably just exhausted. It'll come back to you in the morning, I bet. I'll check in on you later, eh?'

Bill tried to rest, but now he started to hear Grech, to see him sat there in the middle of the track, wiping dirt from his face. The picture was coming back gradually. He recalled looping the reins of the big thoroughbred to the fence and going over to check on the fallen rider.

'You alright, mate?'

'I'm alright, but that bastard horse needs a flogging.'

'Could be how you were riding him.'

Bill knew who he was talking to. He'd seen him at the track and in the newspapers. Joe Grech was one of the gun jockeys in Cairns District. But

Bill Smith didn't care. He'd been watching him and the trainer Charlie McInnes most mornings, and he wasn't going to let Grech blame the horse for him ending up on his arse.

Grech eyed the smart-mouthed young stranger up and down.

'What are you doing round this part of the track? You probably bloody spooked him,' he spat.

'I was hoping to get some work.'

'Work? You don't look like you could stand up in a stiff breeze. The track's no place for girly types. Reckon you better beat it before old Charlie sees you—'

'Who you calling girly?'

The jockey had hardly got his final words out before Bill pushed him in the chest with such force that he ended up back on the ground. With that, Bill unlooped the reins and flung himself up into the saddle, leaving a stunned Grech sitting in the middle of the dusty track.

'Come back here, you little shit!' Grech yelled after him. 'Get off that bloody horse!'

But Bill was long out of earshot. He was headed back to the saddling yard, where he could see the trainer, Charlie McInnes, calmly rolling a cigarette, binoculars tucked under his arm, waiting for his horse. The old man had been watching the proceedings from the enclosure.

When he rode in, Bill stayed in the saddle, waiting for McInnes to speak. He was prepared for a lathering. The trainer didn't lift his focus from his cigarette, until he was satisfied with its shape and tension. Then he ran his tongue along the paper, rolled it one more time between his fingers and stuck it behind his ear. Bill dismounted and reached out his hand towards the man, who made no effort to reciprocate.

'He was going to flog the horse,' said Bill. 'It wasn't the horse's fault he came off.'

When the trainer finally spoke, his voice was slow and thick like molasses.

'No one should ever be flogging an animal. Especially not one of mine. Can't see how that's any of your business though ... lad.'

The pause did not go unnoticed by Bill. He was used to it. He knew he was a peculiar looking fellow. A lot of people thought he was much younger than his age.

'I'm after some work,' he said to the trainer. 'I know a bit about horses. You wouldn't be sorry if you took me on.'

'I'll take you on, you little fairy,' said Grech suddenly from behind. 'I'll kick your arse so hard it'll make your nose bleed.' The words struggled to come out as he doubled over to catch his breath.

McInnes stepped between the jockey and the young man, keeping his back to Grech.

'Where did you learn to handle horses?' he asked Bill. He took the rollie from behind his ear and stuck it into the corner of his mouth, where it hung precariously, moving up and down as he spoke. 'You got a decent pair of hands for such a little fella.'

'My father was a breaker,' Bill said, running his hand along the mount's neck. 'I worked at breaking, myself – through New South Wales and out west. Last few years I been on the coastal steamers. Decided to stick to dry land for a change. Got the idea to give racing a try after I had a few rides in bush meets down south.'

Bill was mesmerised by the way the trainer held his cigarette on his lower lip. He tried to recall how his father had held his smokes. He hadn't thought about Albert Smith in a long time.

'Try this, ya bloody little upstart,' Grech snarled, shaking his fist in Bill's face before wresting the reins from his grip and launching himself back onto the horse.

Grech gave the young stallion a few quick kicks in the guts, trying once again to assert his authority. McInnes barely looked at Grech, yet instinctively managed to grab his heel and flip him out of the saddle. For the third time that day, Joe Grech found himself on his backside, nursing his pride.

'Can't promise anything, but let's see how you go,' McInnes said to Bill. 'I'll give you a week to show me what you got. Stablehand to start – everyone starts there.'

'Jesus, Charlie! You're not seriously going to take this girly bludger on!' Grech stared at the young man who had managed to win over McInnes. 'Look at him!' he sneered. 'He looks like my little sister!'

'I can see the resemblance,' shrugged McInnes. 'Same bumfluff moustache.' He gave a wink to Bill, who suddenly became conscious of his obvious lack of facial hair.

'What's your name, Son?' asked McInnes, breaking the tension.

'Bill Smith, Sir.'

'Fucking *Girly* Smith, more like it,' the wounded rider yelled over his shoulder as he retreated a distance to sulk. 'Just keep out of my way.'

'Fair enough. Girly Smith, then, eh? Don't make me regret pissing off my best rider, now, will you?'

Girly Smith! Bill was horrified at the name, and was about to say so when he thought perhaps he shouldn't protest it too much. It was always the way with nicknames, wasn't it? They wouldn't call him that if they really thought he was a girl. No, better to just take it in good humour.

'I won't, Sir.'

~

The nickname had stuck, much to Bill's chagrin. Some thought it was because of his thin voice, some thought it was because of his shyness around the other jockeys. Either way, around the racetracks, Bill Smith became known as Girly to most. He got used to it and stopped reacting by and by. Most of the time, at least.

That had been how it had started. The Bill Smith who was lying in Leichhardt Memorial Hospital more than fifty years later felt a sense of relief at finally being able to recall that scene, but now there was no one there to hear his story.

'That's it!' he called out to Maureen when she next walked past his door.

'That's what?' She popped her head in the doorway.

'Grech said it first, and McInnes went along, just to shut him up. I wanted to ride, and so that was it – I was "Girly" from then on,' he said.

'They really didn't know?' said Maureen. 'It was meant to be – what's that word – ironic?'

'Pretty ironic alright. But I've been called worse,' said Bill, with a laugh that turned into a convulsive cough. 'Plenty worse.'

8

Nursing notes: 10/5/78 19:00. P 92. Resp 24. O_2 *94% on 6 litres via Hudson's. Slight disorientation ...*

'Are you up for another story, Mr Smith?'

Bill studied the young woman with some confusion, as if he didn't know who she was. Maureen picked up his chart and scanned it. She would have expected her patient to have made better progress after a course of antibiotics, but his condition still waxed and waned. Maureen wondered whether something more was going on than had yet been detected. The pressure sore on his right hip was slow to respond, but there were also definite signs of disorientation at times. She reminded herself to check his urine again for any other indicators.

'It's me, Maureen. Maureen Bannon – your nurse.'

It took a moment for Bill to respond. Maureen felt her patient's pulse and watched the rise and fall of his chest.

'What's your name again, Missy?'

'Maureen Bannon.'

'Bannon? I knew a Bannon once. Lovely fella.'

'That was probably my grandfather. Franny thought you might know him.'

'I knew a Mick Bannon. Chief steward at Cannon Park.'

'That's him.'

'Eh? You're joking. Can't be.' Maureen saw her patient's eyes light up. 'Is he still – is he still with us?'

'Gawd, yes. He's a tough old bugger – bit like yourself! He's eighty-three this year. Lives back at Tinaroo Dam, in one of those aged care villages. I bet he'd love to see you – talk about old days.'

Maureen had said it before considering the implications. Now she saw her patient's interest turn to panic at the thought of a visitor. Her grandfather would only have known Bill Smith, the man, not the vulnerable, exposed Bill Smith lying in a hospital gown. And for Maureen, as well, putting the two of them in touch would mean contacting the man she had not seen since her grandmother's funeral.

'I wouldn't tell him you're here, though,' she tried to reassure him. 'We're strict on patient confidentiality. Especially in a small place like this.'

Bill nodded and offered a faint smile. 'He was the best stipe in the business,' he said.

'Stipe?'

'Stipendiary steward. That's what we called them. Stipe, for short. Don't ask me why – I can't remember. Something about being paid, I think, not voluntary. He was always fair, but firm. A lot of blokes tried to put things over, but Mr Bannon could see through them.'

Maureen checked the corridor for any sign of Matron Kelly, before pulling up a chair next to Mr Smith's bed.

'Tell me more about Pop Bannon – unless you'd rather have a nap?'

'Nap? Plenty of time for napping when I'm dead. Help me up a bit, Missy,' he said, trying to get into a good storytelling position. 'I remember when he caught Nifty Peters with a box of bicarb in his kit. Have I told you about Nifty? Nifty tried to tell him it was for his indigestion, but Mr Bannon knew.'

'No, I haven't heard you mention Nifty. What was the bicarb for?'

'Nifty was a good name for that one. Shifty Nifty. Some of those jockeys – not only the jockeys; some trainers and owners, too – did anything to get an edge, especially when the odds lengthened. Give the horse a little bicarb breakfast and it'd go off like a firecracker – or so they believed. They'd try all sorts of things to spark a horse up, or slow it down – depending on what fix was in. Didn't really make a difference, but those drongos thought they were putting one over. Mick Bannon couldn't stand cheats – especially useless ones, like Nifty.'

'That's horrible. What did my grandfather do?'

'Nifty was all, "No, fair dinkum, Mr Bannon – I got the worst guts today," all that bullshi— bull,' he corrected himself, before continuing. 'Bannon eyed him up and down and said, "Well, Son, you better get some into you right now, then." And Mick took a few big tablespoons and mixed it up in a glass of water for him and stood there till Nifty drank it all down.'

Maureen could easily imagine her grandfather making someone drink a whole glass of bicarb. He had made her drink castor oil once – just one of Pop Bannon's many disciplinary battles with his headstrong granddaughter. The memory made her gulp.

'Have you ever tasted it in water?' Mr Smith went on. 'Wretched stuff to swallow. Supposed to settle your guts, but it's god-awful to drink. Right before a ride, too. Don't reckon he ever tried that again.'

'Did you ever get up to any tricks?'

'If a horse doesn't run for the love of it, flogging it with batteries, filling it with bicarb or any other loathsome act is not going to make it a winner. It'll hate you for it, and it'll hate racing. My horses ran because they wanted to, and every now and then you'd get one that just wanted to be in front – that's all the trickery you needed.'

'Sounds like you loved your animals.'

Maureen thought she noticed his eyes moistening at the memory of his horses, but she was eager to hear more about her grandfather.

'Tell me more about old Mick.'

'I can tell you he saved my life. I don't think that's an exaggeration to say. Not long after I started riding at Cannon Park.'

Maureen leaned forward in her chair.

'The stewards didn't like suspending anyone,' he continued. 'Racing had taken a while to pick up again after the War. That "war to end all wars"', he shook his head at the irony of the phrase. 'Between that and the Spanish flu that had come back with the soldiers, there were a lot of men gone – a lot of families devastated.'

Bill's gaze was off in the distance, the mood suddenly sombre.

'So how did Mick save your life?' asked Maureen gently.

'I got into a bit of trouble with one of the other riders, and we were pulled up before the stewards. Copped a two-week suspension, both of us. Well, Newbury – that was the other jockey – he was none too happy about that. We were still butting heads with each other twenty years later. He really liked to hold a grudge, that one.'

'Was it Mick who suspended you?'

'Lucky that's all he did. They reckon the stenographer recording the hearing was red as a beetroot at the language coming out of Mr Bannon that day. But we deserved it. Anyway, I was heading back to collect my gear from the jockeys' room when the boys went quiet all of a sudden.

I knew they'd been talking about me. Newbury had them all stirred up, and they were out to get me – but Mr Bannon walked in before things got out of hand.'

'Seriously? They were going to beat you up?'

'God knows, but you can imagine if they – if any of them found out – well, you know. Anyway, Mick Bannon got up 'em and they pretty much left me alone after that.'

Maureen sensed there was more to the story, but Mr Smith had closed his eyes. It had become the signal that they were veering into territory where he was not prepared to go. Maureen got up from the chair and checked that everything was in order.

'I'm glad my grandfather stood up for you,' she said as she turned to leave.

'Me too,' he said. With his eyes still shut, Bill reached out a hand to the young nurse. 'And now another Bannon's come to my rescue.'

9

There was indeed a lot more to the story but, as he started to relate it to Mick's granddaughter, Bill realised not all was for the telling. He loved recalling the old days, and no one had really shown an interest before – although he had hardly encouraged any, keeping himself secluded the way he did. His horses and dogs had proved good listeners, and he didn't have to worry about any judgement from them. Now, this 'little miss' with a connection to Bill's own life was interested. But not all were light and pleasurable memories. Bill could still feel the events of that day in his body all these years later.

~

Nev Newbury had always had it in for Bill Smith, and now, after their joint suspension for careless riding, he left no doubt about who he blamed. As Bill gathered his belongings from the jockeys' room after the hearing, he heard someone say, 'I reckon we should pull his dacks off – see what he's got to hide. Then we'll know for sure.'

'Yeah, let's dack the little twerp. Who's he think he is, anyway – not getting changed in here with the rest of us? What's he got down there? That's what I want to know.'

Bill tried to back out of the room, but found the door shut behind him and Nev blocking the only exit. His heart rate quickened, and his muscles tightened as he prepared to defend himself, hands balled into fists ready to land the first blow on anyone who got close enough.

'Don't try it, you bastards. I'm warning you – don't you try it.'

'Or what, Girly? You'll cry on us?'

With that, the would-be gang dissolved into laughter, before Nev stepped up from behind Bill and grabbed him in a bear hug. Bill kicked out and wrenched at Nev's arms around his chest, but he was unable to prevent himself being lifted off the ground.

'Quick! Dack him!'

The other jockeys were looking to each other to decide who would be the one to do the deed, while Bill thrashed about with his legs, making sure it would be no easy task, when suddenly the door behind them was flung open. Chief Steward Mick Bannon filled the doorway, like a titan filling the void. Nev and Bill still had their backs to the exit, so were oblivious to the shadow that fell across the room until an unmistakable voice boomed out from behind them.

'Lay a finger on that fella and I'll flog the lot of you from arsehole to breakfast.'

Bill stopped struggling as Nev loosened his grip. Mick Bannon was not one to make idle threats. Immediately the gang dispersed, all the jockeys grabbing their gear and fixing their helmets, no one daring to make eye contact as they inched past Mr Bannon to the weigh-in before heading out for the last race.

'Go on – get, the lot of you. You ought to be bloody ashamed of yourselves. And you, Newbury, piss off home, before I— You're already on thin ice, Son.'

Bill remained where he was, bent over, struggling to breathe again, trying to steady his nerves before he could meet Mr Bannon's gaze.

'You right there, Girly?'

'Thanks to you, Mr Bannon,' nodded Bill. 'I thought I was done for.'

When everyone else was out of the room, Mick Bannon closed the door and indicated to Bill to take a seat next to him on the bench. Bill sat, fighting to still the trembling that coursed through his body.

'They were only doing what stupid young blokes do – a bit of roughhousing, that's all,' said the chief steward. 'Don't tell me you've never been dacked before? It's all just a bit of fun, really – not that I'd tell them that, eh. They've no business playing silly buggers on race day.'

Mr Bannon put a friendly hand on Bill's knee.

'Girly, you gotta admit – you're a funny bugger. Coming and going in your colours, never getting changed here. People are bound to wonder. What's the problem, Son – you embarrassed about your ... equipment?' he said, with a nod towards Bill's lap.

'No, I just don't like getting changed in front of everyone. I want to ride and be left alone, Mr Bannon. I didn't start this.'

'Well, some might say you did, some might say you didn't, but you don't make it easy on yourself with this little peculiarity of yours – coming and going without changing with the boys, always keeping to yourself.'

Bill was suddenly conscious of Mr Bannon's hand still lying on his knee. It was friendly – nothing more – but Bill felt something more. He studied Mr Bannon's face: tanned, and recently shaven. He noticed the flecks of grey in Mr Bannon's sideburns, and the shape of his jaw. He found himself staring way too long. Mick Bannon removed his hand and stood up.

'Look, Son, you're a smart little rider. Just try and attract less attention, if you know what I mean. I might not be around the next time.' He left the room.

Bill remained sitting there, focusing on the place where Mick Bannon's hand had lingered. It had evoked something he didn't dare contemplate. A tenderness, a longing to be close. Something not felt since another's touch so many years ago. He shook his head, trying to dislodge the confusion of dangerous thoughts.

Mick Bannon had left without a look back, but for Bill, the encounter had just amplified the long-time loneliness that he himself had chosen. A life without intimacy – of resisting any kind of attraction. How could it be any other way? There had only ever been one love, and that would have held even greater risks.

As Bill drifted off to sleep in his bed in Leichhardt Memorial Hospital more than fifty years later, another name was spinning in his head. Catherine.

10

By the time Maureen was due days off, she was reluctant to leave her special patient. She found herself thinking about the intersection of her life with Bill Smith's – about her grandfather's relationship with someone who was, by all accounts, an outsider. The man that Maureen called Pop seemed the very definition of conservative, and yet he was owed a debt of gratitude by Mr Smith. Maybe this was a sign, she thought, that she should finally try to heal the rift that lay between grandfather and granddaughter.

It wasn't going to be easy, making that long-overdue call. When she went for Sunday dinner at her parents' house over in Tolga, Maureen thought she'd make some casual enquiries.

'Dad, did you ever go to the races with Pop when you were young?'

Charlie Bannon glanced across the table at his wife, and then forked up a load of mashed potato and gravy.

'Uh-huh. Nearly every Saturday. Why?'

'And you used to go a lot when you got older as well, eh?'

'Yep.'

'How come you never took me to the races? Because I'm a girl? You took the boys.'

'Your brothers were just a little bit older and, well, to be honest, you didn't seem that interested. I did take you once, when you were about seven. Remember? I took you over to pat the horses in their stalls, and you stepped in some fresh horse shit and squealed like a banshee. Your mother had to take you home, you were so beside yourself.'

'What's this about, love?' asked her mum, Joan.

'Nothing. I was just thinking about Pop, and how he was a big name in racing, and I wondered why we didn't go to meets. Like Franny's family – they still go to the races most weekends.'

'Your grandfather became a steward fairly young,' said her mum. 'He was a jockey for a brief time, but he grew too big. Which was a good thing, really. Any other part of racing is a mug's game. Why the sudden interest, Maurs?'

Charlie was shovelling food into his mouth, saying little.

'Doesn't matter,' said Maureen.

'If you want to know anything about racing, you should talk to your grandfather,' said Charlie.

'She doesn't need to know anything about racing,' said her mum, shooting a sideways look Charlie's way before turning to her daughter. 'But I do think it's a good idea for you to talk to your grandfather again, love. It's not right that you haven't visited since Nan died.'

Maureen regretted opening this particular topic.

'Any more gravy?' she asked.

'That's right, change the subject,' sighed her mother. 'You're your father's daughter, that's for certain.'

Charlie Bannon winked at his daughter. It was true. Maureen was like her father, in both looks and personality, while her two brothers, Jack and Michael, were more like their mother. The boys were also a lot older than Maureen – not just the 'little bit older' that her father had suggested. Maureen knew that she was what her parents called their 'happy little surprise package', having come along when Joan was in her early forties.

After dinner, as was the routine, Charlie Bannon drove his daughter back to the nurses' quarters in Leichhardt. The radio in her father's Holden station wagon was playing 'Stayin' Alive' until Charlie fiddled with the dial, trying to find something more to his taste.

'What did you do that for? It's disco, Dad.'

'It's fellas who sound like their undies are too tight,' said Charlie with a grin, finally turning the radio off altogether.

Maureen rolled her eyes but didn't argue with her father's description.

'Anything interesting happening at work?' Charlie asked.

'Hardly,' said Maureen. 'Still gag when I have to empty the sputum cups.'

'You're just a regular little Florence Nightingale, aren't you, love?' laughed her father.

They drove on in silence for a time. Maureen was about to try to find something on the radio again when her father, his eyes fixed on the road for any roos, started to speak.

'I stopped going to the races when you were still little. I had to. Your mother would have left me if I hadn't.'

'What? Why?'

'I got mixed up in some bad business. Almost cost your grandfather his job.'

Maureen had never heard her father be so open with her before. She didn't need to say anything. The story came tumbling out. How Charlie liked a bet, how the bets got bigger and the stakes higher. How certain people had pressured Charlie to use his relationship with his own father to access information that ordinary punters were not privy to. Maureen watched Charlie Bannon's face as he spoke, his eyes remaining steadfastly on the road.

'I got into some real strife, love. Nearly lost everything – including my life. There was this bunch of thugs from Townsville that had a fix on a certain race. You know how I used to love a drink, as well as a bet. I was spouting on about how my old man was the chief steward, and I was talking a bit too loose about how I knew a good bet because I was Mick Bannon's son. Well, these blokes pulled me aside and wanted me to get old Mick to turn a blind eye to certain things. They threatened to take me for a ride if he didn't go along. Mick wasn't having a bar of it, of course, and the police rounded 'em up quick smart. But I ended up being sworn off all racecourses for a number of years – a complete ban across Queensland tracks. I was lucky I didn't end up worse off. That's why your mother's so deadset against the whole business.'

'Geez, Dad. I never knew.'

'Course you didn't. We Bannons keep our skeletons well locked up,' he said with a smile. 'But now you know, and now you know why your granddad is so tough on certain matters – like honesty and trust.'

'You can turn off the guilt-trip highway right here, thanks,' said Maureen. 'Anyway, I'm thinking of going to visit him soon, if you must know.'

'Good, love. For both of you.'

With perfect timing, they had arrived at the nurses' quarters. Before Maureen got out of the car, she leaned across and kissed her father's cheek.

'Thanks, Dad. I'm really glad you told me.'

'What made you ask about racing?'

'Can't tell ya – if I did, I'd have to kill ya,' she said, laughing.

'Good on ya, Nurse Bannon. Love ya guts!'

'Love you too, Dad.'

~

Maureen was already asleep in her room when Franny finished her evening shift and came in for a catch-up. None of the girls locked their doors inside the quarters.

'Wake up, you slacker. If I'm awake, you should be, too,' said Franny, jumping on Maureen's bed.

'Piss off, mole.'

'Nice. You kiss your mother with that mouth?'

'I do, in fact. What's got you so cheery at this hour?'

'Your favourite patient was asking for you.'

'Really?'

'Yep. Don't know why, but he seems to prefer you taking care of him these days.'

'Probably because of Pop. He told me my granddad saved his life somehow. I haven't got the full story yet, but he seems to hold old Mick in pretty high regard.'

'Really? I told you they'd know each other. Have you asked your Pop about him yet?'

Maureen turned over and buried her head in her pillow.

'Not you, too. Give it a rest!'

'Well, I think when we're on shift again, we need to get old Bill into a steam bath. That chest is still nasty.'

'He's not doing so well, is he?'

'A few steps forward and a couple back,' said Franny. 'But he'll come good.'

'You think so? I hope he does. I've become quite fond of the old bugger for some reason.'

~

Maureen's hopes of an improvement in her patient's health took a battering several days later. His lungs remained congested, and when she came to get him up one evening, he was not interested in talking. Uncharacteristically, he didn't even resist her suggestion of some steam therapy. He now appeared increasingly frail in his hospital gown, and less like the feisty Mr Smith she'd first met.

She got him to sit up, and carefully swung his avian-thin legs over the side of the bed while Franny pulled the hospital gown closed around his slumped shoulders.

'Not up for an argument tonight?' said Maureen. As she said it, she caught herself in a disheartened smile, realising that wasn't necessarily a good thing.

'What's the use? You lot'll do what you want anyway,' Bill said, gazing at the floor.

Maureen had no answer. She knew it was not going to be a good day. If they could loosen up his lungs, at least he might be more comfortable. Franny helped Maureen get him onto a shower chair and into the bathroom. When Maureen removed his gown, she noticed clearly defined bony protuberances that now showed through his almost translucent skin. Both nurses watched as the hot water ran over his emaciated shoulders and back, saying nothing but catching each other's concerned expressions. Swirling steam filled the bathroom, as Bill sat staring at the image reflected in the mirror, watching it slowly disappear in the mist. Breasts – misshapen and atrophied– hung from his frail chest.

'Bloody useless bastards,' Bill said, loud enough for the girls to hear.

'You mean us?' asked Maureen, with hurt that her face couldn't disguise.

He didn't answer. The young women continued gently bathing the body that felt like it might snap if they applied any pressure. It was no time for talking. Maureen lingered carefully over the deep grooves and distortions to the breast tissue, until she noticed Bill's hand on hers.

'I used to bind them,' he said. 'With strapping tape, mostly. Nearly sixty years trying to flatten the bloody things. Don't really need to these days.'

Maureen looked down at Mr Smith's hand as he tightened his grip.

'Promise me when I go, you'll put me back the way I was,' he said, staring intently into Maureen's eyes until she met his gaze.

'What do you mean, when you go? You're not going anywhere if we can help it, Mr Smith.'

'That's right, darling girl. *Mr* Smith. That's who came in here – that's who they need to see in the box when it's time.'

The smiles that the nurses had tried hard to hold fell away in a moment of shared understanding.

'We promise,' said Maureen. 'We'll make sure you look right when the time comes. But let's hope that's not going to be any time soon, eh.'

As she was gently patting her patient dry, Maureen ventured the question she'd been longing to ask.

'What made you want to live your life as a man?' she said. 'It can't have been easy for you.'

'You think living as a woman would've been easy? Not in my day. Not as a woman alone. I'd have ended up on the streets – or worse.'

'So, have you always gone about this way?'

Bill didn't reply. He was more than happy to talk about racing, and about some of the other jobs he'd done over the years. Steamship crewman, farmhand, canecutter, horse breaker. All of the heavy jobs that men did, Bill Smith had done – and held his own with the best of them. He'd lived so long this way, he didn't know how to be otherwise. But there were times when it felt like the price he'd paid was greater than Bill could bear. When the memories became too painful, as they had just now, he turned in on himself and became unreachable to those around him.

11

After the steam treatment, Bill slept comfortably for several hours. Dreams swirled through his head of the days when he and every other jockey had sat cooking in sweatboxes, trying to shed those final pounds before race day. He thought for a moment that he was back in the homemade sweatbox he had created for himself, behind the rented stables in Cairns, when he'd first gone out on his own as a registered jockey. He'd never had trouble with his weight until he got older, and his body lost the litheness of his younger days.

He had rigged up a small firebox beneath an old boiler and stoked it with enough wood to burn for about half an hour. A hose ran from the bottom of the boiler bucket into the box to produce steam. On the top of the box there was a hole he'd cut just big enough for his head.

Jockeys had all kinds of techniques for dropping weight before race day, and few of them were any good for the body. It was a fine balance. There was one time when Bill had almost expired in his rigged-up sweatbox. He hadn't eaten since lunch the day before, and had been sitting in the box for about fifteen minutes, listening to *Dad and Dave* on the radio, when he started to feel drowsy. One of his mares, Nor East, seemed to know Bill was in trouble when his head fell forward and he slipped further into the box. He had bought Nor East from a station on his way back from Brisbane one time, and she'd never let a closed stall get the better of her. The horse lifted the latch to the makeshift sweatbox with her nose, got up close to her semiconscious friend and vigorously nuzzled his face, shaking him back into action.

'Holy ghost, girl – you frightened the living daylights out of me!'

When Bill realised what had happened, he opened the lid and stepped out into the fresh air, wringing wet in his underwear. That afternoon Nor was treated to a special thank you when a grateful Bill opened a bottle of Cairns United beer and let the horse guzzle it down. Nor was partial to the taste, and whenever Bill did a shift at the brewery, he would ride Nor East there and back and let her feed on the grain while she waited. Bill swore it was the secret to his success with Nor East, who won her share of races, especially around the Tablelands tracks.

~

Fully awake now in his hospital bed, Bill could almost taste the brown ale he had shared with his horse, and vividly remembered the feeling of being almost cooked in his own contraption all those years ago. It felt so real. He could feel himself wringing wet, exactly as he had been that day. He was shivering now, doubled over, unable to stop the shaking. He pulled the sheet up to his mouth and coughed into it. There were rust-coloured stains on the white linen.

Bill was relieved to find Nurse Bannon quickly in his room, as his coughing had broken the silence of the ward, now in darkness except for the low lights behind the beds. He was still shaking uncontrollably.

Maureen put the side rails down and felt his forehead.

'You're burning up. I need to get you out of these wet things. I'll be back in a sec.'

Bill lay back in his bed, and barely noticed when one of the night wardsmen, Kevin, put his head around the open door to the private room.

'You right there, mate?'

'I'm right, I'm right,' he said. But the convulsive coughing had started again. With the rails down, Bill was in danger of falling out of bed as he lurched sideways, wracked by the cough.

Kevin charged forward. He flung his arms around Bill's tiny body and in one movement lifted him back into the bed, holding the patient tightly against his own chest, just long enough for a question to form. Bill noticed the hesitant step backwards as the wardsman cast a confused eye over *Mr* Smith. Bill's hair, grey and curly, was no longer plastered down in the short, mannish style it had been on his arrival, and the wringing-wet hospital gown no longer hid the breasts beneath. Kevin was still standing in uncomfortable silence when Maureen returned.

Bill watched Maureen push her way past Kevin and secure the bedrails. She swiped the curtain in front of the wardsman's face, leaving him outside the sanctuary Bill desperately wanted restored.

'Right. I'll leave you to it then,' said Kevin.

Maureen stopped straightening Mr Smith's pillows long enough to pop her head back out through the curtains.

'Didn't you see the sign on the door? No one is meant to be in here except nursing staff.'

'The door was open, and the old bugger was practically hanging out of bed. What did you want me to do, Maurs – let him fall?'

'Sorry, Kev, mate – it's just no one else is meant to come in here,' Bill heard her say.

Smart little miss, he thought to himself. She's looking out for me. Then the conversation became a strained whisper that he struggled to hear but seemed to understand all the same. He recognised the tone in the man's voice. He had heard it before.

'He's a bloody *she*! I thought he was a jockey!'

'Shoosh, Kevin, please. It's none of your business.'

'No problem, love – *it*'s all yours.'

12

Nursing notes: 14/5/78 19:30. R 30, P 126, T 38.4, BP 90/50. LLL pneumonia, crackles r side. PAC 4 hrly. Abscess r hip, packing dressing in situ.

Maureen felt annoyed with herself for having left the bedrails down and exposing Mr Smith to Kevin's reaction. How many such responses must he have experienced in his lifetime? she wondered. Her thoughts returned to her grandfather, Mick Bannon, who had saved Bill Smith from a previous hurt and humiliation – one that most likely would have ended his beloved career.

She felt a sense of pride that Mick Bannon had been protective towards Bill. She recalled the sweet and funny Pop of her childhood, and the revelation about her father fracturing his trust. The urge to talk to her grandfather was strong – to tell him she was sorry, and that she missed him – but the last words spoken between them were still so raw.

That evening, when her shift was finished and the nurses' quarters were quiet, Maureen went down to the public phone at the end of her corridor.

Pop Bannon had moved into a little aged care unit after his wife died. Maureen had gotten his new number from her dad but had not been able to bring herself to use it until now. What if he hung up on her? Or told her again that she wasn't welcome? The youngest of his grandchildren, she had been so close to him. And now Bill Smith had made Maureen realise that some people had no one to love or be loved by in their lives. She had both, and yet she was letting it slip through her fingers.

Maureen dialled the number and waited, holding her breath as the ringing seemed to echo down the line. She was about to hang up when a familiar, raspy voice answered.

'Hello?'

'Pop.'

The pause was excruciating. Maureen wanted to place the receiver down, but stopped herself.

'Who's that?'

'Pop, it's Maurs.'

'It's not. Maursie? You don't say.'

There was no malice in his voice. If anything, it was warm, as it had been before the freeze. Maureen felt her emotions about to overwhelm her. Why had she taken so long to make this call?

She told her grandfather that she hoped to come for a visit on her next day off. That she hoped they would be able to sit down together and talk. That she had something she wanted to say, face to face. That was all that was needed for now. Pop Bannon promised to have some of his famous johnnycakes and jam ready for when she came.

She had finally made that long-overdue contact. Perhaps their relationship could be repaired after all.

Her patient, on the other hand, seemed to have no one. He had made it that way. Maureen had started to worry that this isolated individual, who lived in constant fear of exposure, would leave this world with no one knowing the truth of his remarkable life. She wanted to do something to ensure that didn't happen. She determined to get more stories from him, and decided to start with a scrapbook about Bill Smith's racing career.

~

Two days later, Maureen caught the train down the Ranges to visit Cairns Library, searching for some information on Mr Smith's horseracing past. The librarian suggested she might want to use the microfiche collection to look up old newspapers. There was not a lot to start with. Bill Smith – or 'Girly' Smith, as he'd been known – seemed to have been as big a mystery to the press as he was to the other jockeys. Unlike some of the other characters on the track, who loved to see their pictures in the paper, there were none of Bill Smith to be found – except for the winning photos, which were always taken at a distance. In any close-ups, it seemed he would artfully fall into the shadows or happen to be holding something in front of his face. There were no clear images of him to be found.

Even so, Maureen managed to compile a lively collection of highlights from his days on the track. She spent several evenings putting it all together and, when it was finished, she couldn't wait for her next shift to share it with him. She was bursting to surprise Mr Smith with her efforts to capture just a little of what had been a largely untold story.

~

'Well, who's this, sitting up in bed all bright-eyed and bushy-tailed?' Maureen remarked as she next entered her patient's room. 'You must be feeling a little better tonight. You've got a bit of colour back, finally.'

'Funny you say that,' Bill replied. 'I was just thinking about Mr Bannon, and wondering if he remembered me.'

'I haven't told anyone you're here. I wouldn't – unless you want me to?'

'No, no. Don't bother Mr Bannon. I just wondered if he ever mentioned me. You could ask him if he remembered any jockeys in particular?'

'Sure – in fact, I'm going to see him next week,' said Maureen, not wanting to explain that she had only just spoken to her grandfather for the first time since their falling-out. Keen to change the topic, the anticipation of her surprise got the better of her.

'I've got something for you. I hope you won't mind. I did some investigating to see what I could find about your riding days.'

'Oh, yes? How did you do that, then?'

'I looked up some old newspapers and race books and, well, I put this together for you. I thought it might make you feel better – about being stuck in here.'

Maureen pulled the scrapbook from beneath the patient file in her hands, with the flourish of a magician having achieved some incredible feat. Bill's eyes tried to focus on the book she held in front of him.

The Amazing Bill 'Girly' Smith: Champion Jockey and Trainer, 1922 to 1968, it said on the cover. Bill ran his fingers over the text and down onto the photograph. It was the 1952 Marsfield Bracelet. The grainy black-and-white image showed a triumphant horse and rider garlanded in the winner's circle. He pulled the book up close to his face and removed his oxygen mask. His expression was hard to read. Staring, staring into the past. Saying nothing, showing nothing. Maureen began to panic.

'I – I thought – I hope you don't mind,' she ventured.

'Mind?' A tear coursed its way down Bill's cheek unimpeded, then dropped on the page. 'Gawd, look what I've done! Quick, wipe it off,

Missy!' He held the book out to her to wipe, then brought it close again. 'Mind? That's the kindest thing anyone's ever done for me.'

Bill slowly turned the pages to see a series of old clippings, names, faces, horses and events, all rushing back to him through time and memory. Maureen pulled up a chair and asked him if she had them all right.

'Perfect, young Miss,' he said, lifting the oxygen mask again and speaking directly to her. 'Maureen, I mean. Just bloody perfect.'

It was the first time he'd used Maureen's name. She'd been Miss, Missy, 'that cheeky little miss', 'that little ginger nursey' ... The significance wasn't lost on her.

'Tell me about the Bracelet. That must have been exciting.'

'The Bracelet? That was really something special. Everyone wrote us off – Starlight Miss and me. She was a nine-year-old by then, and I was getting up there too. They reckoned we were past it. I didn't mind – I knew that old girl better than anyone.'

Bill's fingers caressed the photograph, as if the mare's mane was there to run them through, her neck there to scratch. He took a deep breath.

'Everyone had all but given up on her. The original owners wanted to send her to the knackery. She kept suffering shin splints, and she was getting up in age – but I knew. It was how they worked her. So I said, "I'll take Star off your hands." They were ready to turn her into pet mince, but they still wanted a price for her when they saw I was interested. I didn't care. I knew Starlight girl could do it.

'We trained hard, Star and me. When stinger season was over, we'd exercise along the beach, in the water and out. And she seemed to know when it was a big event. For the Bracelet, I took her up a few days early, let her settle into the place. Did trackwork there to get her used to things. The Bracelet was a big field that year, and some of the best horses came up for it, so we were longshots – both of us. Old horse, old jockey, old trainer,' he grinned. 'But we got a good barrier draw on the inside, and we were set. That was my first big win as jockey and trainer.'

'And that was the prize – the watch?'

'That and a nice bit to put in the pocket. They were all slapping me on the back that day. "Good on you, Girly." "Have a beer with us, Girly." Now everyone knew I didn't drink, as a rule, but I had to celebrate that one. Got proper pie-eyed and rode Star into the main bar of the pub, apparently. I don't remember too much, but the local constable let me and Star sleep it off out back of the police station.'

'Gawd, did you still have your prize money in the morning? You could've been mugged!'

'Yeah, I know. But it was all good fun. I think it was probably the most fun I ever had – but it was risky, too. Imagine if anyone had found out, about— Well, I didn't touch a drop for years after that. Not that I drank much before.'

Bill began sucking hard, trying to get air into his lungs. Maureen refitted his mask, and suggested they go through the book later. His oxygen sats remained poor, and the slightest exertion or excitement drained him. His eyes were overwhelmed with tears.

'How about we take a break for now? Is that okay?'

He gave her a nod. Maureen felt her own eyes glisten and blinked to stop her own tears from tumbling out.

'I'll be back later with a cuppa for you,' she said over her shoulder as she left the room.

~

Over the coming days, Maureen looked forward to talking through the scrapbook with Mr Smith. From the time he'd received it, it was as if he was on a mission to share as much about his life as he could. The book brought his racing life vividly into recall. He remembered the names of every horse and jockey, the times, margins, weights, what they won, both in prize money and in hardware.

'The bracelet itself was a beautiful piece. A rose gold ladies' watch, made from gold they got from the Marsfield digs at the turn of the century. It was tradition. They'd been using gold from there for the bracelet since it first run.'

'Have you still got it?'

'Somewhere – in a drawer at home. I got a few other lovely pieces of jewellery as well – brooches, pins. Some silverware, too.'

Bill suddenly went silent. When he spoke again, he looked directly at Maureen.

'I was thinking. What's going to happen to all those keepsakes? Who's going to take care of them? You've got to get them and give them to someone – the Jockeys' Club? Do you think they'd want them?'

'I'm sure they would. There's a lot of history there.'

'Not the bracelet, though. I want you to give the bracelet to ... Catherine.'

'Catherine?'

'Catherine was my ... best friend. In the home.'

He was speaking in a whisper now, with a reverence of sorts that Maureen felt. Why had he been in a home? And when? She had only known about the Bill Smith who'd tried hard to keep himself from getting too close to anyone. Now she saw a Bill Smith who had had a best friend. Had there been others who'd managed to break through the barricades?

Maureen was dying to ask more about Catherine, Mr Smith himself, and the home. She was unsure of which question to ask first, when she noticed Mr Smith had closed his eyes. The signal had been given.

Whenever he wanted to end a conversation, he would feign sleep until he was left to his more private memories. If Maureen had learned anything about her now-favourite patient, she had learned to wait.

~

With no talk yet of a discharge date, Bill started to doubt he would ever get back home. He became increasingly anxious about his house. There were no longer any animals to worry about, but he wanted to make sure he'd left his home in order just in case there was no chance to return. He wasn't afraid of death – he was more afraid of what people might find, and what would happen to his cherished possessions. He began to think about the small treasures he had acquired throughout his life – not worth a great deal materially, but for Bill, they were evidence of a life that was, in his mind, richer than he'd ever imagined it could be. Mrs Jenkins had called the hospital several times to find out how her neighbour was, but Bill was adamant that he didn't want any visitors – especially not while so exposed in the hospital attire. And he certainly didn't want old Ivy poking around his house.

For most of his life he'd been deliberately solitary. There had, from time to time, been a few who'd got close – but Bill or circumstances had always pushed them away. And so, when the chance arose, he asked Matron if the two young nurses might be permitted to collect a few belongings for him, and check on his house and garden. Matron gave permission, and the pair were happy to go at the first opportunity. His life story had been drip-fed to them over his weeks in their care, and they hungered to learn more about the recondite Mr Smith.

13

Anticipation and a little anxiety bubbled through them both as the two friends stood outside the half-timber, half-tin miner's cottage that seemed resistant to modernisation.

'What do you think it will be like inside?' said Fran.

'I just hope we don't find any false teeth,' her friend replied. 'You know they freak me out.'

'Mr Smith's got his teeth with him, you goose, and I know you offer to clean them for him every shift, so who's kidding who? I don't think anything freaks you out, really. Anyway, I bet it will be neat, everything tidy. It says a lot that he asked us to do this. Just imagine, Maurs – we might be the only people he's ever let in his house.'

'True.'

They surveyed the garden at the front, and agreed it was managing fine with the occasional downpours. Some effort had been put into making it self-sufficient, such as directing the run-off from the roof onto the garden beds below, but it was otherwise free to roam where it desired. They climbed the front steps of the old cottage and Fran felt around in the power box for the key, as per Mr Smith's instructions. But before they could get inside, Ivy Jenkins popped her head out the kitchen window of the house next door.

'Yoo-hoo, ladies! Yoo-hoo! Can I help you? Mr Smith isn't home, I'm afraid.'

'Yes, we know,' said Franny. 'We're from the hospital. We're here to get a few of Mr Smith's things.'

'I can help. Give me a minute and I'll be right over.'

'Don't need any help, thanks, Missus. We know what we're looking for, and we'll be out of here quick sticks,' said Maureen.

But Mrs Jenkins was not put off easily.

'Don't be silly, dear. Mr Smith and I are old friends. I'm the one who called the ambulance. Be over in a jiffy.'

'Come on,' said Maureen to Fran. 'Let's be quick. I don't think Mr Smith would want her in here.'

The first thing they noticed when they got through the door was the lovely old squatter's chair on the enclosed verandah.

'Oh, I love these chairs. Get a load of this – these bits swing out to put your legs up. It's so cool,' said Franny, sinking into the hessian seat to demonstrate.

'Let me have a go,' said Maureen, pulling her friend up before she got too comfortable. 'Oh, yeah. If I had one of these, I'd never get out of it,' she said, putting her legs up and dropping her head to one side, feigning sleep.

Fran was already busy scanning the tools and half-finished leather projects on a worktable further along the verandah where the light was optimal.

'Looks like he did leatherwork – pretty good, too,' she said, turning over a stockwhip that was ready to be attached to its wooden handle.

'Wait for me,' said Maureen, springing up from the chair to peer over her friend's shoulder. 'I love the smell of leather,' she said, inhaling deeply, only to get a nose full of dust instead.

As they ventured further through the house, they noticed there were piles of newspapers scattered around the floor of the shuttered verandah, most of them opened to the racing pages. The lounge room, however, was cosy and neat with framed photographs of horses filling the walls, mesmerising Maureen with their detail. In fact, the whole house was remarkably tidy apart from the newspapers on the verandah floor.

Mrs Jenkins' high-pitched 'Helloo-oo!' broke her contemplation.

'We can't let her in,' said Maureen, and went back to meet her at the front door while Fran continued to study each photo.

'Mrs Jenkins, is it? Sorry, we're here under strict instructions from Matron Kelly – we can't let anyone in without permission from Mr Smith,' she said, keeping the door open only a crack.

'But we've been neighbours for nearly twenty years! I'm sure he wouldn't mind—'

'Would you like me to give him a message when I see him, then?'

Ivy Jenkins was stuck with one foot wedged inside the door and the rest of her on the step below. She wobbled, trying to retrieve her forward foot so that she could stand up straight.

Eyeing the young woman with irritation, she said, 'Tell him Ivy Jenkins sends her love. I've been trying to see him, but they keep telling me he's not allowed visitors. Is he really that unwell?'

'Yes. Yes, he is, I'm afraid,' said Maureen.

'Are you sure he can't have *any* visitors? Since my husband died, and with Mr Smith being a widower, we like to keep an eye out for each other.'

'A widower? Really? Did he tell you that?'

'Oh well, I assumed – I mean, a gentleman of his age and all.'

'Fancy him a little bit, do you, Mrs Jenkins?' said Maureen with a wink.

'I beg your pardon?' said the older woman, taking a step backwards. 'You tell Mr Smith that Ivy Jenkins was enquiring about his health, and hopes he'll be on the mend again soon.' And with that she turned and marched back towards her own house.

Maureen came in, chuckling to herself.

'I think that old biddy fancies Mr Smith,' she told Franny. 'She'd be in for a shock if she knew, wouldn't she?'

The memorabilia on the lounge room walls still had Fran's attention. The framed photos started from one side of the room in sepia and ended in gaudy coloured prints of the same subjects: finishing-post shots, sashed winners, trophies and satin horse rugs. Each frame was carefully laid out, with the names of specific events, horses, riders, trainers, owners, prize money, winning times and lengths written in beautiful calligraphy. Bill Smith was variously named as jockey, trainer, owner or all three.

'This must have been when he was young,' said Maureen, studying one photograph closely. 'He wasn't bad looking – not that you can really see him that well. He either has his hat down low or he's looking away in most of them.'

'I wonder if anyone else knew his secret – or suspected.'

'Here's one of him as a trainer. In a coat and tie and a little felt hat. He looks just like my uncle Fred.'

In the bedroom there was an array of seamen's memorabilia that took the pair by surprise.

'Oh yes, he told me he'd worked on the steamships. SS *Mandura*, is it?' Maureen said, squinting to read the writing on the sepia print. 'He must have done it for a while. How on earth did he manage to get away with it for so long – that's what I want to know.'

They checked briefly in each room. Nothing of concern. A neat, gentleman's home, it appeared. Some small evidence of the ambulance crew's activity was left behind in the bedroom, from tending to the superficial wound on his head. It was a man's room, but there were some feminine touches, both observed.

'Look at this lovely old dressing table,' said Maureen. 'He kept everything very neat, didn't he?'

'He did,' said Fran.

'Do you think he ever dressed like a woman in private, or do you think he always dressed as a man – at home as well?'

'I don't know. It must have been hard to keep up all those years.'

As they checked drawers and wardrobes for anything needing attention, there were no signs of women's clothing anywhere to be found.

'I guess that answers that question,' Maureen said. 'I suppose it would have been too big a risk – especially with the old bird next door watching everything like a hawk'. She paused, before continuing with a thought that surprised even herself. 'Or maybe that's who he was – who he'd become?'

'Listen to you. I think my little Maurs is growing up,' said Fran affectionately, wrapping her arm around her friend's shoulder and squeezing her close.

'Bugger off,' said Maureen, pulling out of the hold.

The bed was an old wrought-iron four-poster with a large mosquito net suspended from a ring above. As they surveyed the room, they finally saw an embossed tin that Mr Smith had asked them to retrieve. Inside was not only the rose gold watch that was the Marsfield Bracelet, but an assortment of other pins and brooches, each engraved with a race, year and placing. There was also a small newspaper clipping in a frame. It looked like a piece from the social pages of quite an old publication. Maureen took it to the window to study the image and the caption.

Mrs Catherine Stimpson of Sydney, enjoying the Townsville Race Meeting.

'Hey, it's Catherine!' she said, waving the framed clipping as if she had found the map to the lost gold. 'Well, it's *a* Catherine – but how many could there be? What's the date – 1966? It's got to be her, don't you think?'

'Let me see. Wow. She's quite the lady.'

'He won't talk about her, though. He clams up every time – but he did say he wants her to have the bracelet. It's got to be her, don't you think? The Catherine he was in the home with?'

'He might open up more if he sees this again.'

'Maybe.'

Maureen carefully placed the picture and the tin on the kitchen table to take with them, as Mr Smith had asked.

When they'd finished in the house, Fran peered out the back door.

'Let's go look at the stables. Mr Smith said there's a blacksmith's forge down there too.'

They walked down through the backyard to the two stables and the feed shed that had, like Bill Smith himself, seen better days. Battered by the odd cyclonic storm or two, there were loose boards letting the light and the rain through the roof. The feed room would need some attention if it were ever to store chaff again. The blacksmith's forge was in a corrugated iron shed, tucked away behind an enormous mango tree. With no one there to pick the harvest, rotting fruit filled the air with a sickly sweet cocktail. Inside the shed, a leather bellows cradled years of dust and cobwebs. Across the top of the wall, horseshoes of assorted sizes formed a collage of rust, all hanging upright so as not to let the luck run out. An anvil had a half-finished shoe hanging from its nose, waiting for the maker to return, hammer and pliers at the ready.

'It's like a museum, this place,' said Franny.

'Yes, but what's going to happen to it all?'

'It's sad, really. There's no one to hand it on to. All those memories, trophies.'

'It is sad. What about the mysterious Catherine? We could try to find her? There's got to be someone who cares about Mr Smith, besides Mrs Nosy Parker next door.'

'What if Catherine doesn't want to see him? What if she never knew about ... *Mr* Smith?' said Fran. 'But then again, why does he have that photo from 1966? They must have met up again after the home.'

'But the Catherine in the photo is married, according to the caption – it says *Mrs* Stimpson. You're right. It's probably a bad idea.'

'Since when did you ever let a bad idea go untested?'

'That's true,' said Maureen with a smile.

Before locking up, the pair noticed another small, framed, colour photograph of Bill with a family, at the Tolga Races in 1969, which they decided to take back with the other items.

'This is unusual. He's actually with people in this one. I wonder who they are?'

'Maybe he does have a family,' said Fran. 'Let's put it in with the rest.'

~

'I hope you don't mind,' Maureen said to her patient that evening, 'but we found this photo at the house and thought you might like to keep it by your bed?'

Bill took the photo and held it close to his face, trying to remember.

'That's little George,' he said, as if that explained everything.

'Little George? Did you have a son?' asked Maureen.

'Good grief, Missy. No, that's my little mate from up the road and his parents, June and Alan Fisher.'

'Are they still around? Would you like us to contact them for you?' Maureen said, tentatively.

'You really want me to answer that? His parents divorced, and they moved out of Leichhardt a couple of years ago. I couldn't tell you where they are now. Besides, *little* George is a soldier now – soon as he was old enough he joined up. He was always upset that he missed out on Vietnam. Bloody mad, if you ask me – look how we treated those poor bastards that did go. I reckon he was lucky. He said he wanted to be a jockey, but he grew like a beanstalk.'

'Do you know if he's okay, or where he is now?'

'I don't know. He stopped coming round as he got older. Don't think he'd be too fussed about seeing his old neighbour again now, especially – well, you know.'

'But you must have cared about him to still have this photo?'

'He was alright. He helped me a bit with things, and his mother would invite me for a Sunday roast now and then. They lived the other side of old Ivy.'

'What about this one? Is this your friend Catherine? We can put them both here on the side table if you like?'

Bill studied the woman in the black-and-white newspaper cutting until his eyes became moist, and he turned away. Maureen was about to take them to store with his valuables when she heard a whispered response.

'If you insist, Missy.'

Part 2

South Australia, 1911–1918

He let me ride the stallion …

14

> Welfare report: Wilhelmina Smith, age 9. Mother: Deceased. Father: Horse breaker, boundary rider. Frequent school absenteeism. Monitor ...

When Wilhelmina was nine years old, she still loved to prod her father to tell her the story of how he'd come to marry her mother. She knew to pick her days, though. Sometimes, it was after he'd had a few ales at the end of a long day but was still in the happy drunk phase, before the night dragged in melancholy and silence.

'How did you get Mother to say yes?' she asked him one night, as he nursed his third ale. 'What did she think when she saw the block the first time?'

'Gawd, Willie. I must've told ya a hundred times now,' he complained as he always did, before relenting at the sight of his daughter's big, calf-brown eyes. 'The railway made all the difference. Your mother didn't want to be too far from her folks, so having the train come all the way to Quorn meant the world to her.'

Albert leaned back on his kitchen chair, as he recalled aloud the slow pace of development back then. Not like the hastened growth of the past few years, as the region became the main supplier of bran and pollard for horses. The town of Quorn, beyond the Pichi Richi Pass, had been full of promise when Albert had asked Flora to be his wife. It was still isolated by city standards, but the world was changing and Albert's rural block close to town was a good place to put down roots. Albert didn't care for too many people himself, and any family he had were back in England. Not that they had been in contact since he'd left. It was like that with the Smiths.

Flora, on the other hand, had never ventured far from home in Port Augusta in all her twenty-one years, so Albert thought it might sweeten the deal to know she wasn't going to be too remote. The railway line from the Port to Quorn meant that Flora could always go home to visit her parents whenever she felt the need. By the turn of the century, Quorn had a postal service, a police station and – although not needed at the time – it didn't escape Flora's attention that it also had a sizeable school, should they be blessed with children before long.

Albert's idea of close to town, however, meant that life on the block was still relatively isolated and lonely for the newlyweds. Their nearest neighbour was a good half-hour buggy ride away, and town was at least double that. Not that Flora ever complained.

'She must've really loved you.'

'Must've. Probably got too much sun and was delirious when she said yes,' he said, with a wink.

'And she must've loved me, too?'

'You were the light of her life. She was never so happy as when you were born, let me tell you.'

He reached across the table and drained the dregs of his third ale.

Willie crossed her fingers behind her back and wished he might be done for the night. She uncrossed them when he pushed the empty bottle towards her and asked her to grab him another from the cellar.

'Don't you think we should have dinner first, Dad?'

As soon as the words were out, she wished she could fish them back in. Albert's face twisted, and spit flew from the corners of his mouth. 'Get me a drink or get yourself to bed. Asking all this shite about your mother. Your mother died because of you.'

And there it was.

Albert had read the tracks that morning, seven years earlier, piecing together the terrible event. The overturned washing basket, the half-hung sheets and the unmistakable pattern in the dirt leading towards where Albert knew his wife would sit their baby while she hung the laundry. But what did a baby know of snakes, or a mother's sacrificial instincts?

Willie knew her father would be sorry in the morning for the venom his own mouth had sprayed that night but, no matter what peace offering might be made, some of it had got in. Wilhelmina was fundamentally a problem, she had sometimes told herself. The cause of her father's drinking, the reason for his being stuck alone with a kid – a girl, at that. Yes, it was Willie who was wrong. She was not a boy. A boy would've been able to help his father more, would have been better company for him. Her father wouldn't have had to be embarrassed taking his boy along to buy some new clothes. But a girl. What was he supposed to do with one of them?

He did his best for the first little while, but soon realised he would need help. He hoped Flora's parents might assist with raising their granddaughter, but those hopes were dashed when Willie's grandfather took a fall from a sulky that left him an invalid in need of full-time care. How was a man meant to work a block and look after a toddler too?

For a time, Albert would bundle Willie up and drop her off at the blacks' camp, where the old ladies and younger girls would fuss over her for a few hours, until he returned with a couple of roos or rabbits for their trouble. He thought it a good solution, and Willie always seemed happy, giggling away as the children played with her fair hair and ran their hands over her pale skin, as if touching something otherworldly.

It wasn't long, however, before the do-gooders stuck their noses in, asking questions about the child and how Mr Smith was managing. It was one thing to have native women as domestics in one's home, it seemed, but entirely another to leave a white child in a blacks' camp. Welfare had started a file on Wilhelmina Smith, and Albert had to rethink how he would continue to care for her.

By the time Willie was three years old, she had become a fixture in front of her father whenever he was on horseback, or propped up with her own pretend horse in the corner of the breaking yards. Her 'horse' was a barrel with a blanket over it and some old reins, and Willie would sit on it for hours, mimicking her father's movements. She was fearless around horses – mesmerised by their stature, their smell and their individual personalities. She didn't so much learn from her father as absorb by osmosis, since Albert, for the most part, gave far more attention to the animals than he did his growing daughter.

Albert Smith was the first to admit he had no idea what to do with a little girl with no mother. He fed her, clothed her in a fashion – although nothing like the other little girls in town. He didn't want to set foot in the women's clothing section of the general store, so he would grab whatever he needed from the boys' side. When some of the town women offered him a selection of hand-me-downs from their own girls, Albert would accept them awkwardly but never put them out for his daughter to wear. What good were they around the horse yards, anyway? They would only get dirty in a minute. No sense spoiling pretty frocks like that, he would think, as he packed them away in the back of the cupboard.

Willie couldn't have been happier. As she grew older she wanted nothing to do with the frilly impracticality of girls' clothes. If she was to be of any help to her father, it would not be with her dressed in such ridiculous fashion.

It was their shared love of horses that eventually pulled the pair together. Willie relished watching her father work them. That she was there when she should have been at school was another problem, made more apparent by the fact that Wilhelmina still could not write her first name without an error or two. It was a tricky one, after all. Willie was a much better name for a motherless child whose father didn't have time to take her into town five days a week and bring her back again. And better suited to a child who got around dressed like a lad, anyway.

After she outgrew her barrel horse, Willie would climb onto an old saddle slung over a low rail and sit for hours taking everything in. She mirrored her father's every move as he turned a newly broken horse this way and that. Never rushed. Never rough. Albert had all the patience in the world for a horse in need of love and attention. The more damaged and discarded, the more time Albert would spend working to salvage what others had deemed hopeless.

While common sense should have made her wary of the excitable brumbies Albert would spend days breaking in, she couldn't wait to be allowed to ride by herself. She had been on horses since before she could walk – cradled in front of Albert and, as she'd got bigger, pulled up by one arm and swung on behind him – but never in the saddle alone. She would beg her father to let her try her hand.

Albert's standard response to her pleas was usually unvarying, until one still spring morning brought a different reaction. Willie was caught off guard when her father, standing there with the rope over his arm, his eyes focused on the cigarette he was rolling between tobacco-stained fingers, said instead, 'You don't need to grab him – let him come to you. Don't rush him. Let him get to know you. And when you're up on his back, no reins – squeeze with your knees.'

Willie was not looking at her father when he spoke, so it took her a moment to understand what was being said. When she did, she had to hold herself back from showing her excitement. She slipped under the railing and stood in front of Albert, who gave the rollie paper a good lick of his tongue before flicking the finished cigarette deftly into the corner of his mouth.

'Call him up.'

Willie had learned a lot sitting behind her father, sensing the way he used just his legs to direct a horse, and she had rehearsed over and over, perched on her old saddle on the rail, waiting for the day when it was just her and a horse. It came not long after her twelfth birthday, in 1914.

For Willie, this was the best day of her life. Albert did not need to praise her or cuddle her or pat her on the head. His hand beneath her bent knee, lifting her up onto the bay stallion, was everything she needed. The view from the back of the 16-hand giant she called Boy made her feel like a warrior princess parading before her adoring followers.

Round and round the yard she rode, first one way, then the other, stepping the horse over and around various obstacles that her father positioned for her to practise with. There was no lavish praise from Albert. The silence was praise enough – that and the nod of his head, before telling Willie to brush down Boy, give him some chaff and then turn him out into the big paddock. That job alone was all the praise she needed.

'Come on, Boy. Good boy, Boy. Have some breakfast while I make you handsome,' she said, running the curry comb over his black mane. She had to stand on a little wooden stool to reach.

'*More* handsome, I should say, Mr Boy,' she corrected herself as she stood back admiring her work, before pressing her nose to the stallion's, who snorted in agreement. Willie headed back to the house, contemplating the enormity of her father's gesture. Boy wasn't a quiet little mare or pony. He was a large animal with a big personality, and her father had chosen him for her first solo ride.

Getting ready for bed later that night, she recalled the feel of the stallion – the way she had managed to control him with just her knees and the trust that her father taught her. She lay down on her pillow and stared out the window at the night sky, wondering if her mother was out there somewhere, watching all that had happened today. Wilhelmina closed her eyes and felt something she thought must have been real happiness. When sleep came that night it was sound and untroubled.

15

Lessons continued for several weeks, until one day in late August 1914 when Albert told Willie to roll her swag and pack the tuckerboxes. She could hardly contain her excitement when she realised she was going with her father to Wilpena Pound to help muster the brumbies – which would mean a big pay cheque this season. Willie didn't care that she would be missing school, and Albert was more than ready to see off those do-gooders who reckoned they knew better what his own child needed.

'Being out in the bush is the best education you could have,' he'd say whenever a letter arrived about Willie's frequent absences from school. 'They can bugger off, telling a man what's what with his own child.' He'd utter the same refrain before using the letter to mop up his spilled tea or tossing it into the stove to watch the words shrivel and burn. Willie agreed wholeheartedly. She didn't enjoy going to the school at Quorn. Especially not when the teacher made her change out of her breeches and work shirt to put on a hand-me-down frock.

The trip was the greatest experience of Willie's short life so far. Albert didn't talk a lot, but it was enough for his daughter that he wanted her with him – that she was useful and hardworking, and that he could see that. She could stand up to the long days in the saddle, and she knew how to be around the skittish wild horses that had made the Pound their home. And the highlight of their time together was that Albert didn't touch a drop of grog while he was on the job. At night, by the campfire, she studied her father's face adoringly, and every now and then he would catch her gaze and give her a wink and say, 'You did good, sweet girl. Better than good. School couldn't teach you that, eh?'

~

The day after they got back from Wilpena, Willie rose early, eager to go and check on Boy and the skittish mob now secured in the settling paddock. Her excitement was soon tempered, however, by an absence that marked this day as different from others. There was no smell of burning toast from the kitchen. The house was unusually quiet.

'Dad? Daa-aad?' she called out, making her way to the kitchen, as she jammed her fingers into both eyes to loosen the crusts of sleep that always arrived mysteriously overnight. She saw the newspaper spread open on the kitchen table, shouting headlines about the looming war on the other side of the world. So far away, nothing for them to worry about on their little patch of earth, he had assured her when they were in Quorn one day – but then things had seemed to change. She recalled her father becoming quite animated about it all before they'd left for the Pound, suggesting there might be a need for good horses, and how the Army might want his brumbies for breaking. Maybe that was what had happened.

Willie was used to being left alone for prolonged periods as she got older, but Albert had always let her know when he would be gone, and for how long. Now she wandered from room to room, noticing only what wasn't there. Her father's razor from the bathroom sink. The money jar. The greatcoat from his time in the British Army before he'd emigrated. She walked into his bedroom and stared at the space where he usually kept his wife's small but precious jewellery collection, from a time when she'd enjoyed a different life.

Willie's heart began to pound unevenly in her chest. She tried to think of an explanation. Could it be that he'd packed up and was going to take her on a holiday? No, he'd never taken a holiday in his life. Could it be that he'd taken her mother's jewellery to sell, because of the other night when she'd asked if she could get some new boots and he'd told her that a man wasn't bloody made of money? No. It had to be the brumbies. He must've gone to see if he could sell off some of the brumbies. There was probably a note somewhere.

Willie opened the kitchen chest to see if there was anything to eat. A bit of porridge and some condensed milk. When she finally went to look outside, she saw a line of dust approaching from the distance. It wasn't a sulky – it was moving too fast and too smoothly. After some minutes, a black car drove in through the bottom gate. Cars were not common around these parts. Only rich people and government workers had cars, and it was not likely that a rich person was coming to visit. Willie studied the vehicle until a glimmer of recognition hit her.

When Albert was in the grip of the grog, he would sometimes tell his daughter that he would get Welfare to take her away, because what was a man meant to do with a bloody girl around the place with no mother? She knew it was the grief talking – the pain that her father tried so hard to drown in his beer and, when it was really bad, in whisky. She never thought he meant it. But the only time she had seen a similar car at the property was when some of what Albert called 'those bloody do-gooders, bloody busybodies' had sent Welfare to check on the 'poor wee mite with no female company out there in the bush'. Albert had chased them off quick smart, telling the round-faced woman at his front door that if he needed help raising his own bloody kid, he would ask for it. Had it finally come to that? Had he asked for it?

In an instant, Willie retreated inside the house, locking the door behind her. She knew what had to be done. Whenever strangers approached the house, it was usually by horse or carriage, and the dust could be seen a good ten minutes away. Albert would sling one of the donated frocks at Willie, whisk the broom across the floor and hide the dirty dishes in the meat safe. When the knock came, the scene was one of domestic order. She knew what role to play.

But this morning, after the high of her father taking her on the muster, there had been no warning, no Dad and no time, what with the new vehicle covering the distance to the house so smartly. She'd hardly had time to take in the fact that Boy and the brumbies were also missing on her first scan across the paddock. They could have been moved over to the spelling paddock, she thought, but her rationalising and hopes were soon interrupted. The knocking was heavier and more insistent than she'd heard before. Willie opened the door just a crack, to see Welfare's Mrs Martin, the woman Albert had called 'that potato-faced old fart' after he'd sent her on her way last time.

'Wilhelmina, dear. You need to open the door, my darling – we need to speak to you.'

'Dad's not here now. I mean – he is here, but he's gone to the paddock to work the brumbies. Best you come back another time,' Willie said, trying to push the door closed.

The large hand of the police officer standing behind Mrs Potato-face reached around and stopped its progress. Willie began to panic. She pushed harder against the door, but found herself sliding backwards on the floor. Mrs Potato-face stepped forward, with the marble statue of a police officer behind her. She put both hands on Willie's shoulders and crouched down to face her.

'Your father called us, darling. You need to pack your things and come with us.'

'No. No, he didn't. He's down with the mob. He's waiting for me to go help him. We're just back from Wilpena with some horses, and I slept in is all.'

'Now, Wilhelmina, your father has gone. He's gone to enlist. The Mother Country has put the call out for our men, and your father is keen to get among it. He also knows that you need to be with young girls your own age and get some female influence in your life, so he's organised a place for you at Cranbrook. He wanted the move to be easy for you, so he asked us to arrange it all.'

'Liar! Liar! Bugger off, you old Potato-face! It's Willie, not Wilhelmina. No one ever calls me that. Anyway, there's no war here. He wouldn't leave me. He wouldn't!' Willie cried, twisting this way and that, trying to release herself from the Welfare woman's grip.

'Listen to the mouth on her,' said the officer. 'Now, you get your things, and be quick about it. Sounds like you needed to be in that home sooner, speaking like that. Get moving, girly.' He placed his hand in the middle of her chest, forcing her to stumble backwards and out of the Welfare worker's grip.

Willie scanned the room for an exit. When she noted her father's good hat also missing from its place by the door, she felt something break inside her. Was it because she had pestered him to ride the stallion all the time? She'd thought that he had been pleased with her, proud of how she'd done on the muster. She felt her knees begin to crumble. It was real. Albert was gone, and he had arranged all of this without saying a word. Albert had said goodbye, only Willie hadn't heard it until now.

She gathered the few items of worth to her in an old suitcase and threw the donated dresses on the floor. Mrs Potato-face asked, 'Will you not put on one of those lovely frocks, dear? You would look so much nicer. You look like a little tomboy in those clothes.' She was trying to be kind, but Willie wasn't interested in anything she had to say.

'They're not mine,' she said. 'These are mine.'

The Welfare worker nodded. Today was a big enough defeat for Wilhelmina Smith.

16

The lettering on the cast-iron gate read 'Catholic Girls' Reformatory', but Mrs Potato-face referred to it as Cranbrook Home for Girls. It didn't look like home to Willie. Willie's home had been a simple wattle-and-daub hut, with a couple of corrugated tin extensions built over the years and a cellar cut into the hard stone beneath. This looked like a grand house from the outside, although inside, she would discover, it was more spartan.

When the black car pulled up at the entrance, Willie noticed the row of small faces staring down from the upstairs windows. She sat back further in her seat, keeping a grip on her meagre belongings. Why was she here? She had a home. Who was going to feed the horses? And the chickens? Then she remembered seeing the empty paddocks as she'd been driven away. The horses were gone, with her father. The chickens would have to fend for themselves. At least there was an abundant supply of grasshoppers, with some warm weather about. She tried to picture the chooks running around in circles, squabbling over whose grasshopper it was, until pieces of leg and wings went in various directions, to the satisfaction of none.

It had become apparent that Albert had planned for this day, but he surely hadn't meant for her to be taken to the girls' home. This was where bad girls went. Murderous types who'd lost their minds and had to be locked up. But the faces staring down at her didn't seem so scary. They appeared more scared than anything else – or sad, perhaps. It did not feel like somewhere she was supposed to be.

Mrs Martin got out of the vehicle, where she stood with an encouraging hand outstretched, the bottom of her grey dress covered with the fine red dust of Willie's farm.

'Come along, dear. Don't be frightened. Think of all the lovely new friends you'll make here.'

Willie didn't move from the car.

'Dad will be wondering where I am. He's probably back by now, and he'll be sick with worry.'

'Come, Wilhelmina dear. I already told you, your father instructed us to bring you here, since you have no other relatives who could take you. It's not a punishment, you know. I told you – he's gone to enlist. He just couldn't bring himself to say goodbye to you. You need to be brave, like your father – so come along.'

'But he'll come and get me when he gets home, won't he? It's only till they give those Huns a hiding, and then he'll come to get me.'

'That's right. While he's away at the War. And the War will be over quick smart once our lads get there.'

'Must be why he took me to Wilpena,' Willie said, stepping hesitantly out of the car.

A man in a long black dress was eyeing Willie up and down. The person standing beside him was also all in black, with big heavy men's boots and a stiff veil covering all but a small, plump circle of her pale grey face. The Welfare woman called her Sister Perpetuata. When she responded, the

Sister moved her mouth in a way that Willie thought looked like she was about to belch. But she quickly realised with the strangled laughter that followed that it must've been a smile.

'Thank you. We'll take her from here. She's in God's loving embrace now,' said the grey oval to Mrs Martin. Even she pursed her lips at the nun's suggestion, which sounded more like a funeral message than something to comfort a little girl.

'Here's her paperwork then, Sister. Her father's gone to join the Imperial Forces, and—'

'Yes, yes. I'm sure it's all there in your comprehensive files.'

With that, Willie was shunted towards the heavy front door of the large sandstone building, barely catching another glimpse of Mrs Potato-face, who now seemed not so bad after all. Willie suddenly felt guilty about calling her names. She tried to give her a smile, hoping that it might compel the woman to run back and admit that it had all been a terrible mistake. But Mrs Martin was already in the car, taking the remnants of the farm with her, and Willie had entered her new life.

The man in the black frock ran his bloodshot eyes once again up and down the length of Willie's tiny frame. She was transfixed by the glow of his nose – all spidery red and purplish veins.

'Sister, you do realise this is a home for girls?'

'Yes, Father.'

'So what do we have here, then – this little ... ragamuffin?'

'She is a girl, Father. Wilhelmina Smith. But neglected, clearly. No mother. Just a father who did what he knew best, I suppose.'

'Do you think you're a lad, then, Missy?' the man said, peering down at Willie. 'Did your daddy want a little boy and got you instead? Is that why you're here with us now – unwanted by anyone but God?'

'My dad does want me. He loves me.'

'Does he, now? Well, where is he? Welfare brought you here because you were abandoned, child. Abandoned. But we will make sure you're not abandoned again. Here at Cranbrook Home for Girls, we are all God's children – and God abandons no one. No matter how strange or queer their disposition. Sister, make sure you find something suitable for Wilhelmina to wear before I see her again.'

'Yes, Father.'

Willie stood staring at where the nose had been. She didn't dare look around in case the tears tumbled out. He does love me, she thought. He does. He let me ride the stallion on the muster.

'Come, child,' said a younger nun who was waiting to take charge of the new inmate. It wasn't Sister Perpetuata, at least. This one was softer and less grey. She pulled Willie in close to her side and wrapped an arm around her thin shoulders.

'It's because your father loves you that you're here now,' she said in a low whisper, as if she were sharing a magical secret. Willie turned her face towards the young nun's.

'What do you mean?'

'I know that your father loves you so much, that he had to make a great sacrifice. Like God did with his only son. Your father wants you to become a young lady – to learn the things a young lady needs to learn. He couldn't do that for you on his own, you see. And now he has to do his duty for King and country. He couldn't just leave you there alone, now, could he?'

'He did say we might need to help out the Mother Country,' said Willie, suddenly sick at the thought.

'Yes. That's why, I believe, he's intending to join the mounted units – being so good with horses. He is, isn't he? That's his special skill, as I understand.'

'We went to get horses for the Army, but I didn't think he was going to go away. How do you know? Did he tell you?'

'Not me directly, child, but I heard Sister Perpetuata talking to him when he came to make arrangements.'

'When? When did he come here? Why didn't he tell me?'

Willie pulled away from the young nun's hold and stood face-on to her, imploring her for an explanation, with tears now running freely down her cheeks. The woman put both hands on Willie's shoulders and crouched down so her face was directly in front of hers, just as Mrs Potato-face had earlier.

'I don't know why he didn't tell you, child. I suspect men are not particularly good with such things. And knowing how upset you would be ... But you need to know he did it because he loves you. Father, and Sister Perpetuata – they sometimes say things that, between you and me, are less than godly. I think they feel they have to be strong and stern all the time, to keep control of all the emotions this place stirs up. But you must know that it is all done in love. Now, come and let's get you sorted – get you some better clothes.'

Willie looked down at what she was wearing – what she always wore. Long brown calico shorts and a blue grandfather shirt. Good working clothes, and all she needed. Even her schoolteachers had given up trying to get her to wear a frock. And any boys who'd dared comment had soon stopped as well, after finding themselves pinned face-down in the dirt until they promised to 'shut their pie-holes'. But Willie had a feeling she wouldn't be winning this fight.

'What's your name, then?' she asked the young woman.

'Constance. Sister Constance Mary, but you can call me Connie – when we're on our own,' she said, with a wink.

17

Connie turned out to be one of the good ones. It was Connie who buddied her up with Catherine on her first day at Cranbrook.

'Catherine, come say hello to Wilhelmina. That's quite a mouthful, isn't it – or do you prefer Willie?'

'Willie. Dad only called me Wilhelmina if I was in trouble.'

'I thought so. Willie shall do just fine, then,' Connie said with a smile.

'Hello. Welcome to Cranbrook and the loving arms of the Sisters of Grace,' Catherine said, mechanically. She barely glanced up from her job of preparing the vegetables for the evening meal, but Willie couldn't take her eyes off Catherine. She was the most beautiful girl she had ever seen. Olive skin, glossy hair the colour of pitch, tied back with a red kitchen scarf. When Catherine did look up, her eyes were a kind of hazel that Willie hadn't known existed.

'No need for the formalities, Catherine,' said Sister Connie. 'Stop what you're doing and make a proper introduction. Willie needs a friend, and I have a feeling you two little rebels will get along just fine.'

Rebels? Were they? Willie supposed she could be rebellious at times, but could the same be said of the compliant-looking girl conscientiously doing her chores? She seemed, as Willie's teachers would sometimes say, as sweet as pie.

Catherine suddenly took more interest. She put down the vegetable knife and wiped her hands on the front of her apron. Sister Connie had given the signal.

'So, Willie. Where you from?'

'Quorn – well, outside of Quorn. My father breaks horses.'

'You got a father? How come you're here then?'

'Now girls, you've got plenty of time to get to know each other's stories. Why don't you take Willie up to her room, Catherine? She'll be in the bunk next to you.'

'Good,' said Catherine. 'You've come at the right time. Little Miss Prissy got herself a new family just this week, so I won't have to listen to her farting all night anymore. You don't fart, do you? No, you don't look like a farter.'

'Catherine! Good grief. I hope I haven't made a mistake putting you two together.'

Willie stared in wonder at the girl who appeared so innocent and yet could start talking about bodily functions without any sense of embarrassment. She felt a smile edge its way across her face and, for a moment, she stopped feeling that ache that would keep revisiting her no matter how long she stayed or how funny her new friend would be.

Although Willie was from an area close to the home, she soon found out that most girls who passed through Cranbrook were from the city. Country air was believed to have a positive effect on the wayward ones, and the remoteness was intended to have a similar effect on any tendency to try to abscond. Apparently, the Catholic Girls' Reformatory had quite a record of failed escapes. Catherine assumed responsibility for giving her new roommate the full story of the home.

'Escapes?' said Willie. 'Is this a prison?'

'Of course it is, silly. What do you think "reformatory" means? You're not here because you've been a good girl.'

'But I am. I haven't done anything. My father couldn't take care of me, because he's gone to fight for the King. I'm not a criminal. Are you?'

Catherine smiled and gave a wink.

'The worst kind,' she said. 'An orphan.'

'So why are we here, then? We don't need reformatoring.'

'Oh, you are funny. It's "reforming" – haven't you been to school? Anyway, that's why they changed the name to Cranbrook Home for Girls. All the terribly bad girls are sent to Peterborough. We're a mix of orphans and paupers, waiting to be adopted by rich families.'

'Well, I ain't – isn't – am not,' said Willie, suddenly aware of her many days of missed education. It wasn't easy getting into town for school, even when the neighbours offered to meet partway and let her go in their buggy. The days were just too short to prioritise schooling, when there were chores to do and horses to deal with.

'Stop worrying. Like I said, it's now called a home – especially after the suicide attempt,' Catherine whispered.

'Suicide? Strewth. What happened?'

'You met Sister Perpetuata? Well, the last matron of the home was her evil twin sister.'

'Really?'

'No, not really. But she could've been. She was as cold as a witch's tit.'

Willie, who had been up close to Catherine, sharing in the secrecy of the tale, pulled herself back a distance to study the angelic face with the shocking mouth. She would not have expected her new friend to have any knowledge of how cold a witch's tit would get, but she now leaned back in agreement that it must indeed be icy.

'What did the matron have to do with the suicide?'

'*Attempted* suicide,' said Catherine. 'Well, I'll tell you, but not now. Anyway, you're lucky, because they got rid of that matron. She was cruel to anyone she took a dislike to. Drove poor Ethel to her limits. Some say she went to an insane asylum, but – later. I have to introduce you to the other girls. There's twenty of us inmates – I do beg pardon – *residents*, I should say. You make twenty-one.'

As Catherine moved around the dormitories, with everyone engaged in their after-school chores, she introduced each of the girls, and shared a snippet of their history. The two new friends moved from room to room, meeting each occupant as they went, with Catherine explaining the rules and routine along the way.

'You got your little 'uns – Martha and Maggie. They're still babies, really. They can be clingy and, you being new, they're sure to try it on with you. They're supposed to be looking after the chooks, collecting the eggs every day, but half the time they get distracted and come back empty-handed. You gotta keep on them.'

'They make the little ones work?'

'Maggie, Martha – have you got the eggs for our breakfast tomorrow?'

Two freckled faces turned to look at Catherine from their windowsill perch, where they were busy plaiting each other's hair. With a well-rehearsed look of 'Eggs? What eggs?' they giggled nervously.

'Get on with you, before Sister Pep spies you sitting there doing nothing.'

With that they skipped off, holding hands, down the stairs and out towards the chook pen.

'I'll wager my boiled potatoes that they'll get sidetracked before they get there,' said Catherine. 'Everyone works. Everyone gets given a job. Up at seven o'clock, breakfast at eight. School from nine to three, and supper at five o'clock. I'm in the kitchen from four o'clock every day to help Mrs Sangionne with the cooking. And it's strict lights out by nine o'clock for us older girls.'

'Are there any horses here?'

'They got a big old Clydesdale for the field, and two sulky ponies.'

'Can I work with them?' asked Willie.

'Sister Perpetuata will give you your work assignment. If I was you, I'd tell her you'd rather do anything than work with smelly old horses. That way she might make that your job. But if she thinks you want it ...' She shook her head to indicate that it would be unlikely.

'She sounds mean.'

'Sister Pep's not just mean – she's the devil's daughter hiding out in a habit.'

Catherine studied Willie's face before touching her lightly on the shoulder.

'Don't worry. They're not all like that. Sister Connie is a doll, and the new matron is a good old stick, really. You'll be right.'

Willie wasn't so sure. She didn't want to be here, no matter who was good or who wasn't. She wanted to be back on the farm, watching her father shoeing Boy, collecting her own eggs from Blacky and Speckles and all the other chooks. Why had her father sent her to this place? So what if he did have to go and fight in a war? She could've kept things running on the block, she was certain. Willie tried to think of what she might have done to upset her father, but she couldn't think of anything. She'd kept the house clean. Helped with the chores. Her teachers had never found fault with her – other than to say she was too quiet at times, and that she missed a lot of school. No. It didn't make sense for her father to have just up and left her like this – even if she was a girl, or the King needed him.

Not prone to crying, Willie found herself quietly sobbing in her bed that first night at the home. Catherine got up from her own bed and slipped in beside her new friend, wrapping her arms around her from behind. She said nothing. She just held Willie, who realised in that moment that she had never been held like that before. Not that she could remember. Certainly not by Albert, whose main show of affection was to ruffle Willie's hair as he went by.

Willie lay there in the warmth of Catherine's arms. For the first time since Mrs Potato-face had arrived with the constable, the knot in Willie's chest loosened, and she was able to fall asleep.

18

The first weeks at Cranbrook were hard on Willie. She cried most nights – a silent, internalised crying that others didn't notice, except for Catherine, who seemed to know Willie in a way she'd never known possible. Catherine also proved to be a reliable informant about all matters Cranbrook, especially the staff. Her advice about hiding any desire for certain jobs around the place was especially helpful.

'Everyone at Cranbrook must earn their keep, and you, Miss Smith, will be no different,' Sister Perpetuata informed her. 'Your father was not especially generous to the church or to the home when he signed you over, you know, so when you are not at your studies, you will be working. Now, let me look at you. I need to see what your physical suitability might be. Having been motherless for so long, I can't imagine you would be much use in the domestic realm – but perhaps that's exactly what you need.'

Sister Perpetuata wasn't really talking to Willie so much as talking about her. As she studied her tiny frame and rattled off various work options, Willie remembered what Catherine had told her on her first day.

‘I really don’t mind, Sister. As long as I don’t have to shovel any more horse shi— manure. Or try to get another knot out of a pony’s tail. Please, Sister – just don’t make me do anything with the horses, like my father made me do. I’ll do anything else.’

‘You will do anything else? You will do exactly as I say you will do. And with that mouth of yours, shovelling manure seems perfectly suited.’

Willie tried to drag her feet as Sister Pep marched her over to the stables. The oversized grey sack that was the Cranbrook tunic hung like a chaff bag from Willie’s narrow shoulders, and the black lace-up boots were completely impractical for working in stables. They would be impossible to clean, with all their hooks. Willie wanted her own workboots back, even if the soles were almost worn through, but everything she owned had been sent away for what Sister Perpetuata called ‘fumigation’. What that was exactly wasn’t clear, but Willie felt she should take some offence.

When they got to the stables, Sister Perpetuata stood with her hands tucked in opposite sleeves of her tunic. A scrawny, blonde girl, maybe a few years older than Willie, was attempting to rake out one of the stalls but succeeding only in choking the air with dust and hay.

‘Ahem,’ said Sister Pep.

The young worker was oblivious as she continued to back out of the stall towards them, swinging her loaded rake around and dropping its contents onto the startled nun’s shoes.

‘Good Lord, you idiot child!’ snapped the Sister, grabbing the rake from an equally startled young girl. ‘Mary Edna Philpott, are you not the most useless dolt God ever put breath into?’

Mary Edna Philpott might have been clumsy, but what she did next shocked Willie, who wondered whether this wasn’t one of the girls who would soon end up in Peterborough.

‘Maybe I am,’ said Mary Edna, ‘but I’m not a sour, old, lemon-faced crone, like you.’

As soon as the words were out, Mary Edna started to shake. Sister Perpetuata wrenched the rake from the child’s hands, lifted it above her head and brought it down sharply where the girl had been, but where there was now only air. Mary Edna had taken off in the direction of the home’s gates. Sister Perpetuata thrust the rake at Willie, lifted her dress to near her knees and set off after the girl, blowing on a silver whistle so hard it was a wonder the pea didn’t shoot out.

Willie found herself in charge of the stables without any further discussion. She took the opportunity of Mary Edna’s escape attempt to get to know the horses – two little ponies and the big workhorse. The ponies were in their stalls, while the workhorse was out in one of the paddocks. Each had a halter with its name on, which Willie appreciated since it didn’t seem there would be a handover from the last stablehand.

‘Who have we got here?’ said Willie, putting her fingers under the nose of the first little Welsh pony, a motley, butterscotch-and-cream-coloured horse, about 11 hands, called – not surprisingly – Butterball. The pony snorted and stomped a hoof, as if to give her approval of the change of management. At least, Willie liked to imagine that’s what she was saying, giving a brief thought to what would happen to Mary Edna and whether she would ever see her again.

In the next stall was a black pony, also creatively named Sooty. Sooty was too absorbed in her nosebag to investigate matters further, but Willie was confident they would become fast friends.

‘That’s perfectly fine, Miss Sooty. I also like my tucker and would not want to be interrupted,’ said Willie, rubbing the pony’s ears. ‘Now, who’s the big boy over there?’ From the halter hanging in his stall, it appeared his name was Titan. ‘Well, of course.’ She couldn’t believe the size of the iron shoe hanging over his stall door. She walked across the paddock and approached the animal without hesitation.

One thing she knew about draught horses was that they were truly gentle giants. Not that she'd ever found a horse she was scared to get up close with, but the size of this boy shocked her still. Willie stood a little past Titan's belly. She hoped there would be a stool of some kind to help her with his bridle and harness. She couldn't wait to tell Catherine that their plan had worked, and about the incident with Sister Pep and Mary Edna, if she had not already heard the commotion.

~

There were many nights when sleep didn't come easily. Willie would lie awake, recalling each sensory memory of the block and her father. His tobacco, his hair cream, the leatherwork he would leave on the kitchen table. She thought also of Boy, and the feel of his soft, sloppy lips as she offered up a piece of carrot. Catherine was surely a great help to Willie, but nothing could make up for the way in which Albert Smith had left, or the place he'd chosen to leave her.

Catherine's job was in the kitchen, but their friendship grew fast and staunch and, when they weren't working or in lessons, they were inseparable. While most of the residents hoped that their way out of Cranbrook would be through finding new families, neither Catherine nor Willie wanted to be adopted. Catherine had become jaded to the possibility and Willie, of course, had a father who would be coming back for her any time now.

In the months that followed, Willie overheard many of the adults at Cranbrook speak of the War and Australia's pending involvement. Men from all over the country were making the trek to the cities to join up for what was expected to be all over in a flash once our lot got there. Not by this Christmas, but surely the next, or certainly the one after. That had to mean that Albert would be strolling through the gates one day, asking to collect his daughter and heading back to the block. Until then, Willie would have to try to make the best of the circumstances in which she had callously been placed. Her work in the stables at least reminded her a little of home. That helped make her days at Cranbrook a bit more bearable. Being able to work with the horses – and having Catherine as support, of course.

As she settled in to the routines and regimen of life within the confines of Cranbrook, Willie became obsessed with news of the War, which was in full swing by the end of the year. 'When the Empire is at war, so is Australia at war,' the prime minister had told the nation, and even the Cranbrook girls were expected to do their bit, sewing sandbags and putting together care packages for men on the other side of the world.

Catherine would often sneak the newspapers back to their dormitory for Willie to pore over at night. They were weeks old, however, as she came by them only after the Sisters had finished with them, or when certain grocery items arrived at the kitchen wrapped in old papers. While some of the early stories of heroic deeds were uplifting, the growing lists of dead and missing men from the region were a stark contrast. Catherine could see her friend's anxiety as she took a deep breath before turning to the notifications page, so she would begin to screen the newspapers before sharing them with Willie.

'No Albert Smiths,' she would reassure her with a touch on the arm.

'He will come back for me, won't he?'

'I'm sure it'll be the first thing he does. He'll march right up to old Sister Pep and say, "I'm here for my daughter, so hurry that fat bottom of yours and bring her to me forthwith."'

Willie collapsed laughing onto her pillow. She knew her friend was trying to cheer her up. 'And while you're at it, fetch that Catherine O'Connell girl. She's peeled her last spud for you sour-faced lot,' said Willie, tears streaming down her cheeks. 'I know you don't have anyone to come for you, Catie dear,' she said, using the affectionate name only Willie was permitted and reaching for her friend's hand. 'But you will always have me, friends forever.'

'Friends forever,' Catherine said, squeezing her hand in return.

Willie wasn't sure which might be worse – having a family who'd left you without a word and never knowing whether they were still alive or ever coming back for you, or losing your family in a freak accident and knowing they could never return. Catherine's parents had died in a buggy accident when she was only a baby. She was lucky to have survived herself, but the memory of her parents had long dimmed. Her memories instead were of a series of foster families until she finally ended up in Cranbrook.

'I just wish we could find out something – is he dead or injured? He could have got that shellshock and not even remember me,' said Willie.

'I've got an idea,' said Catherine. 'We've been asked to knit socks for the soldiers, and Sister Connie said we'd be sending the next lot to the Light Horse battalions. Why don't we put a letter in with one of the pairs, asking whoever gets them if they could pass the letter on to Albert Smith of Quorn?'

'But we don't know which lot he's with. Sister Connie said she thought it was the Light Horse, but how do we know?'

'It's worth a try. I'll make the socks especially. I know you can't knit to save yourself,' said Catherine.

Willie didn't mind the tease. She was too excited by the idea of finding her father. Every time she asked Sister Perpetuata if she could write to him, Sister swatted her away, saying the cruellest things, such as, 'If Mr

Smith wanted to communicate with you, child, he would have done so by now. You need to accept the possibility that he is likely lying in a field, with his soul in heaven.' She seemed to take delight in thinking up the unkindest words to say to everyone around her – including Sister Connie, who was also often on the receiving end of her most unchristian ways.

'There are many ways to do God's work, if you find the rigors of our Order beyond you, Sister Constance Mary – the public school system, for example,' she was heard to say one day when she found the young nun's art class a scene of joyful chaos rather than the dull discipline expected. Willie thought she saw tears in Connie's eyes after Sister Perpetuata walked away.

Willie carefully practised writing her letter over and over, before Catherine told her the knitting packages were almost ready for sending. She finally settled on a version and read it to her friend.

Dearest Father,

I am writing in the hope that this may find you safe and well. I want you to know that I understand why you didn't say goodbye that last morning. I could not have stood a goodbye any more than you, I imagine, and you must have believed this a kindness. I am well, and I do not want you to worry about me. The Sisters are all so loving (just like the ones you told me about when you were a boy!). I could not be anywhere better, except for back home, when you are ready. I have grown quite a lot, Father, and will be a strong hand to help you when we go home to the block.

You will be happy to know I am looking after the horses here at the home, and learning quite a lot about maintaining the sulkies and the farm equipment. With so few men available now that they, like you, are engaged in fighting for the King, the women and girls are having to step up, so I will be well-skilled for when you return.

And you will return, my dear Pa. We are hearing about the bravery of our men, and especially of the Light Horse, and I long for the day when you can tell me some of your own stories.

Your loving and ever-faithful daughter,

Willie xxxxxxxxxx

'Perfect,' said Catherine, wiping away a tear. 'If you don't hear back, it will be because he is simply not able to respond, and you must prepare yourself for that, but in all honesty, it is a beautiful, heartfelt letter.'

They placed the folded pages inside the package, with a request on the envelope to whomever received the socks to please forward to Albert Smith of Quorn, with an expression of gratitude and a wish for their own safe return to loved ones. Willie was so happy she could barely sleep that night, picturing her letter finding its way into Albert's hands, mortar shells raining down and Albert declaring to all around him, 'Let's finish this thing, lads, and get home to our loved ones, eh.' That was how she pictured him, night after night, until time finally eroded her confidence and she stopped searching through the newspapers and stopped thinking about him altogether.

19

When wealthy people arrived at the home in their flash cars, all the younger children would press their noses to the dormitory windows, the same thought passing through them like an electrical current: '*Pick me – please, pick me*.' For some, their wish would come true, but not for Catherine or Willie; nor the recalcitrant Mary Edna Philpott, who had been reluctantly returned to the home after her attempt to flee. It was hard to be cute, as you got older. Rich ladies wanted cute. If they didn't, they wanted strong. Strong wasn't so good. Those chosen because they were big and robust were not chosen to be part of a family, to have their own room, to be allowed to call anyone Mother or Father. They were wanted for work.

For those picked for more altruistic reasons, the dream didn't always work out, either, as evidenced by the number of children who were brought back to the home. Every now and then a familiar car or carriage would return, and a girl would be put out at the front door with the same meagre belongings with which she'd left. No hugs. Slammed doors and flicked-up gravel as the cars pulled away at speed or the carriages were given swift urgings onward. Whatever the reasons, the children knew it was their fault. It had to be their fault.

If they didn't, Sister Perpetuata would make sure they knew. Her cruelty was the subject of talk even among the other staff of the home. Mary Edna had long given up hope of finding a new family and, now that she was almost of age to be turned out of Cranbrook, her battles with the old nun verged on mutiny. One day, when Willie was taking the harness off Titan, she heard Mary Edna yelling from the roof of the main building. It was when the head of the diocese had just arrived for one of their supposedly snap inspections. Everyone knew when these would be occurring, however, as the meals improved dramatically, and bowls of fresh fruit were suddenly left out for the girls.

Mary Edna had apparently taken up a sack of potatoes with her, because as Sister Pep stepped forward to greet the bishop, a shower of spud missiles rained down. It was a calamitous scene, with the handyman ordered up on the roof to retrieve the girl, the bishop ushered quickly inside and the emergency bell rung, warning all residents to return to their dormitories immediately. Willie watched with a mix of awe and anxiety as Mary Edna led the handyman on a wild pursuit, then shimmied down a drainpipe and sprinted off towards the gate where a young man on a bicycle appeared to be waiting.

'Go, Mary Edna! Godspeed!' yelled Willie, before looking around to see if any staff had heard her cheers. Several days later, the escapee was yet again brought back through the gates, but not for long. Although no one knew for certain, Mary Edna was said to have been transferred to the reform school in Peterborough to serve out the rest of her time.

If that was meant to put an end to wayward behaviour at the home, it seemed to have quite the opposite effect on some of the girls, including Willie. It unsettled her more than ever. She longed for a life outside Cranbrook, even if it was not to be a return to the life she'd had.

~

Willie had experienced many bouts of extreme despair, even with Catherine there to make things better. Some days the weight of her abandonment was so great that darkness completely engulfed her, as it did at the time her fifteenth birthday came around. There had been no word of her father in three years. She had no idea whether he was dead or alive, and the thought of another three years in the home overwhelmed her as she sat on the shower floor. She didn't look up, even when Sister Perpetuata walked right into the cubicle and reached over her to turn off the fully running tap.

'You think this water is in such plentiful supply that you should splash around in it willy-nilly, you stupid girl?'

She did not even hear Sister's words until a gnarled, grey hand appeared in front of her face, waving to check if the girl was in fact still of this world. Willie dropped the large sewing scissors she was holding, her eyes tracing their path as they clattered and banged several times on the tiles before coming to rest over the drain. Pinkish water swirled around the scissors' shiny blades, before snaking its way out into the world, away from Sister Perpetuata, beyond her reach. In that moment, Willie felt herself envious of the blood's capacity for escape. She wrapped her arms tightly around herself, before turning her eyes up to face Sister's.

'What in heaven's name have you done, you vile little misfit? Show me. Show me now.'

Willie struggled to her feet, let her arms drop to her side and stood naked, except for the blood painting a river down her body from her left breast all the way down to the floor.

'What exactly were you trying to do, you idiot child?'

Willie wasn't sure she knew herself. She stood staring at Sister, trying to work out why exactly she had sliced into her own flesh with scissors from a sewing kit. But before any words could come out, someone else pushed their way through the cubicle door, scooping Willie up in a towel and carrying her from the bathroom.

'Sister, this child needs help. We need to get her to the infirmary. The time for ridiculing her would be after we stop this bleeding, don't you think?'

Miss Franklin was one of the new lay teachers who had arrived at the home that year. Willie had never heard anyone speak to Sister in such a manner. She was so engrossed in studying this angel's face that for a moment she forgot the pain she had inflicted on herself. She couldn't remember the last time an adult had ever held her in their arms. Where had she come from? Sister Perpetuata also stared, but not with shared awe.

'The child is a cretin, Miss Franklin. You do what you must.'

Willie was still fixed on Miss Franklin's face. It was beautiful. And familiar. Her mother might have looked like this. Willie couldn't retrieve her mother's face from memory, but she thought she could see it in the face of this woman. Now it was Miss Franklin who stared back in confusion at the smiling, naked girl clinging tightly around her neck who had just, it seemed, tried to remove one of her breasts.

~

Days lying in the infirmary brought Willie new insights. Her father was not coming back. Even if he had survived the War, he had made no effort to contact his daughter in several years, and she knew she had to plan for a life on her own. To that end, Willie's father had not left her entirely incapable. She had developed skills that other children might never accomplish. Although she did her best to keep it hidden from Sister Perpetuata, Willie knew a lot about horses, and she also knew how to keep out of the way while at the same time watching and learning all she could. She had applied much the same approach to her time at Cranbrook.

Her father had been a man with endless patience and love for his horses, but little of the same for his daughter. Willie had always tried to be the best she could be – eager to help, to please, not to get in his way, not to ask too much of her dad. He had his own troubles, as he had been fond of reminding her. She had never really understood what those troubles were, although she suspected that her being a girl had been one of them.

20

After the incident in the shower, Miss Franklin insisted that Willie be excused from classes and work for a period.

'Do you want another suicide on your hands, Father?' she asked the newly appointed Father Le Bron. Since Cranbrook had a history of young girls attempting to harm themselves – not to mention the latest incident with Mary Edna – head office had been forced to make some changes in the home's administration. First was the departure of the red-nosed, altar-wine-swilling Father Tully, who had made such an impression on Willie that first day. His early retirement brought a younger and more progressive Father Le Bron to oversee the running of the home. Miss Franklin found a willing ally in this 'new broom', which seemed to infuriate Sister Perpetuata.

'Ridiculous. The child is attention-seeking. Nothing more. Her father has abandoned her, so she thinks this will garner some sympathy – get her out of working in the stables,' said Sister Perpetuata.

'Yes, yes, I'm sure there will be an element of that, Sister, but I do think Miss Franklin is right. We can't afford any more ... incidents with the inmates – residents, rather. Let the child settle, and then we will get her back to work,' Father Le Bron said, signalling an end to the discussion.

~

Alone in the dormitory all day as her substantial wound healed, Willie's thoughts became increasingly preoccupied with getting out of Cranbrook. The tight dressings wrapped around her chest gave her the seed of an idea. She would need plenty of time to develop it but, with any luck, by her next birthday Willie would be somewhere well away from Cranbrook. She hoped Catherine would be by her side.

~

'Why did you do it?' asked Catherine, one night when it was safe enough to lie together in bed as they had often done in times of heartache.

'I don't really know.'

'Did you want to die?'

'No. I don't think so.'

Catherine snuggled in more tightly to her friend, holding her with a strength that Willie felt renewed by.

'Don't you ever do that again – promise me.'

'I won't. I promise.'

'Friends forever,' said Catherine, with a peck on Willie's cheek.

'Friends forever.'

~

Willie didn't share her plans for getting out of Cranbrook with Catherine until she was completely healed and feeling strong again. She had broached it before, but Catherine would dismiss it as an impossibility. Willie couldn't understand why her friend wasn't equally eager. They both knew that their chances of adoption by one of those families with the big cars were long gone. Willie and Catherine were more like workers for the home now than residents. There were people employed to do certain jobs, but a lot of them, more often than not, sat around the grounds, bullying the children into doing their work for them with endless criticisms and threats of the leather strap.

Mrs Sangionne, the home's head cook, had a particular fondness for making the girls bend over a chair, pull down their underpants and receive several blows of the strap that she kept behind the kitchen door. That was bad enough, because the strap could come out for the slimmest of reasons, but what made it worse was when Sister Perpetuata would come to observe.

'Caterinuh,' Mrs Sangionne would say to Catherine. 'You stupid or what? Look what you done to these potatoes. You think we can afford to waste all this, eh? Look how you peel. Like a monkey. Get me the strap.'

'But I tried to peel them finer. The knife is too blunt,' protested Catherine. 'Please, Mrs Sangionne, I'll try to use a sharper knife.'

Willie watched on from the doorway, signalling to Catherine to stop trying to make a case for herself, as they both knew that would only make matters worse. Better to get it over with and hope it would be someone else next time. But Catherine continued to plead for herself, to no effect. In fact, her tears only made Mrs Sangionne more agitated.

'Whose fault you got the blunt knife, eh? Whose job is that? Your stupid friend here, eh? No, it's your job. That's why you getting the strap. Now, be quiet and take down your pants.'

BOARDING PASS

Economy

NAME: EVERETT/BUNNIE MISS

DEPART: Sydney 18:00 FLIGHT: VA 874

ARRIVE: Melbourne 19:35 DATE: 28 Jul 23

ETKT

FARE: R

PNR: MTPNYY

CARRIER: VIRGIN AUSTRALIA

GATE: 44 AT: 17:35 SEAT: 19F

BAGS:

SYNC SITA SYSITAGL1002

BAGGAGE RECEIPT

DATE: **28 JUL 23**

GUEST NAME: **BUNNIE EVERETT**

PNR: **MTPNYY**

ITINERARY	BAGS
VA 874 MEL	6795229903
	6795229904
	6795229905

Incredibly, Sister Perpetuata always managed to walk in as one of these hidings was about to happen. Now she took the strap from the door and handed it to Mrs Sangionne.

'You heard Mrs Sangionne,' she said sharply to Catherine. 'Bend over, you godless, parentless fool, and think about what you've done.'

Catherine tried to keep her eyes fixed on Willie as she pulled up her dress, dropped her underpants and bent over the heavy kitchen chair. Willie held her gaze, nodding discreetly, encouraging her to get it over with. But Sister Perpetuata seemed to delight in dragging the event out as long as she could.

Her hand held up in a signal to Mrs Sangionne to wait, Sister left Catherine in a state of dread-filled anticipation while she cast her eyes over her adolescent bottom. Her gaze was sickening to Willie, who could not fathom what pleasure this could possibly give a nun – or anyone, for that matter. Finally, when it appeared that Catherine's legs were about to buckle beneath her, Sister Perpetuata's hand went down, and Mrs Sangionne made sure each blow left its mark as a reminder for later.

It was Catherine who'd felt the sting of the strap, but it was Willie who decided it would be the last time. As the pair snuggled up in bed after all the younger kids were asleep, she whispered something to Catherine that made her friend spin around to face her. It wasn't the first time it had been said, but it was the way it was said that provoked a response.

'What are you saying? What do you mean, you *love* me? You can't.'

As soon as the words were out, Willie desperately longed to reel them back in. The scene was not the one she had dreamt would play out when she finally got up the courage to tell Catherine.

'Gawd, had you going there, didn't I? Yeah, I love ya, ya silly goose. I was mucking around – playing a character. Because listen, I've got a plan to get us out of here, by me dressing up as a fella. If you come with me, we can pretend we're a young couple, or brother and sister. No one would be looking at us – they'd be looking for two girls.'

Catherine stared long and hard at Willie, as they lay together in the dormitory bed. They often cuddled up at night. A lot of the girls did. No one thought it odd – especially on those nights when Father Tully would choose certain girls whose souls needed 'extra effort' to save. When they were returned to their dorm, someone would silently turn back their blankets and make room for the newly 'saved'. Thankfully, Father Le Bron did not have a similar interest in the young residents of Cranbrook, but the girls still liked to hop into each other's beds when they felt like it.

Tonight was not like other nights, however. Willie felt different. Catherine looked different to her. Although Willie had tried to brush off the unguarded declaration, Catherine surprised her by leaning over and kissing her on the cheek.

'I wish you *were* a boy,' Catherine said. 'Then we could run away together and get married. But you're not.'

Catherine then laughed at the preposterousness of her wish, and then turned over to close her eyes and sleep. But Willie was not able to sleep.

'If wishes were fishes ... I wish I was a boy, too,' she whispered in Catherine's ear. Life would be easier, that was for sure, she thought as she held Catherine more tightly.

21

The beating of Catherine with the strap – and Sister Perpetuata's vile enjoyment of it – was more than Willie could bear. She was desperate to get out of Cranbrook and as far away as she could from the ugliness of the place. She lay in bed at night thinking about how and where and all the whats such a plan required. She hoped Catherine would come with her, but she dared not raise the idea again until she had it clearer in her own mind.

And so, in the early hours of the morning that marked her fifth year in Cranbrook, Willie pulled Catherine aside and shared her idea for escape.

'Catie,' she said, 'we have to get away from here – you and me. I know we've talked about it before, but I mean it now. We could, you know. I don't reckon anyone would even miss us.'

'And go where, exactly? And do what, exactly? At least we've got a bed here, and something in our stomachs every day,' said Catherine.

'Yes, but what happens when they put us out? When we come of age – what then? We'll be on our own then, and I'd rather go now than keep working like dogs for this lot.'

'You're such a dreamer, Willie.' And with a quick kiss on the lips, Catherine put on her work apron and headed downstairs. Willie stood fixed for a moment. She put her fingers to her mouth where the trace of Catherine's lips felt tangible. The strangest feeling of warmth filtered throughout the whole of Willie's body. She couldn't understand what it was that she was experiencing. She knew it caused her pain to think of not having Catherine with her when she had to go, but go she must. Her father was not coming to her rescue and, with no expectation of release from the home, Willie feared she would die if she could not soon see a life outside the gates. It had to be now.

Willie had succeeded early on in convincing Sister Perpetuata to allow her to work with the home's horses, but all that had changed one day when the nun had overheard Willie declaring how much she loved being in the stables with the sulky ponies. When Sister Pep realised she had been conned, she was furious, and Willie lost the one thing that had given light and purpose to her days. From that point on her days had consisted of domestic skills training, sewing and relentless mopping of floors for no other reason than to keep the girls busy. The jobs she wanted to do were not proper for girls, she was told repeatedly, and so Willie's dreams for the future became as dulled as the floors that had lost their shine from too much unnecessary cleaning.

She had been slowly acquiring the items she would need for her escape. She knew she would need to get far away once she left the environs of Cranbrook. Locals would be quick to recognise an 'escapee', she thought. Unless ... unless she was not so obvious. She had formed a picture in her head of the Willie who had arrived at the home five years earlier, when Father Tully and others had mistaken her for a boy, dressed as she was in the clothing that she'd always worn before coming here. As a resident of Cranbrook, her standard day wear these days was a grey tunic, which puberty had ensured Willie now filled out in all the 'right' girlish places. She hated it, hated her body, hated the limitations it put on her.

Now she pulled off the tunic and stood naked in front of the mirror, staring at her breasts.

'Why? Why do they have to be there? I hate them.'

She ran her hand across the prominent scar she had inflicted on herself with scissors some time ago. She grabbed an old sheet and began tearing it into strips. She wrapped a long piece around her chest, pulling it so tight that she could barely take a full breath. Then she pulled on her undershirt and stood back to consider herself from various angles. With her breasts flattened, Willie found herself standing differently. More upright. More like her father.

She grabbed a pencil from the table and stuck it into the corner of her mouth. She studied her stance with some satisfaction, before grasping the pencil-cigarette between two fingers and pretending to blow out a long, tantalising cloud of blue-grey air. She could almost smell her father again, almost taste the bitterness of his cigarettes.

She pulled on the trousers she had pinched from the home's laundry. The local publican often sent clothes and hotel linen for washing at Cranbrook. It was a side venture that Father Tully had offered on the inmates' behalf and Father Le Bron had chosen to continue, but it was strictly off the books, so if an item or two went missing now and then there was hardly going to be a big noise made about it. The trousers were a little baggy, so she would need some braces. For now, however, she would have to make do with the sheet she had torn up for a belt. She would turn the top of the trousers over to cover it. The shirt was pale blue, with a fine white stripe and a grandfather collar. Loose enough to hide the form underneath. The herringbone cap she'd taken from the gardener's cottage fitted well, but there was still the issue of her hair.

Willie held the sewing shears, pausing only for a moment before cutting away at her hair until there was hardly any left. It reminded her of how the nuns shaved the girls' heads whenever there was an outbreak of lice. She put the cap back on and, although it now sat a little roomier on her head, she felt happy with the result.

The boots had not been so easy to come by. She didn't have big feet, so finding men's boots in her size was a challenge. She had been trying to find a pair for several weeks. Her luck changed when she met a young workman doing repairs to the horse yards. Willie thought the young fellow couldn't have been much older than she was. She made a concerted effort to be nice to him over the few days he was around. She got her boots, but only after the young bloke got his 'pipe pulled'. Willie had no real idea what pulling his pipe was when she agreed to it. She had seen the stallions aroused, and how quickly it was all over for them when they mounted a mare, but she had never seen a man's erect penis before.

Her incompetence at the task resulted in the young bloke completing it himself. She stared in disbelief at the agonised ecstasy on his face, and thought how stupid he was giving away a perfectly good pair of boots in exchange. She hadn't particularly liked touching his private parts, and promised herself that whatever else might be available for such a price in future, she would have to find another way.

The trousers were long, and bunched up over the oversized boots, but she hoped that would do for now. She opened the door and made her way to the kitchen, where Catherine was doing the preparations for breakfast. Willie scanned the room to make sure they were alone.

'Hey, sweet cheeks. Wanna come for a walk?'

Willie leaned against the doorframe, trying to assume a casual but confident air, the way she had seen many a cocky young bloke do when they talked to the girls. Only her voice came out a little too squeaky. She felt the blood run to her face as Catherine swung around and eyed the stranger up and down with suspicion. Catherine stared hard at the skinny youth in the baggy clothes.

'You cheeky devil. Who the hell are you and how did you—?'

Willie tried to look unconcerned. Catherine put the peeling knife down and made her way towards the somewhat-familiar intruder.

'How about it, then?' said Willie, trying to speak an octave lower.

'What in the world!' said Catherine, as recognition dawned on her face. 'What do you think you're doing?'

'Shoosh. Don't go bringing attention to us. I'm getting out of here. I can't take it any longer,' she said. 'I'm going to head over east and get a job somewhere.'

'Dressed like that? Whatever for? It's queer! It's not natural!'

'How will I get any job that pays half decent if I go as a girl? What do you think will happen? I'll either be brought straight back here or somewhere worse. Come with me, Catie. Come, and let's travel round, see something more than this wretched place.'

'And what? Dress up like a fella as well? I can't. Besides, they *will* catch us, and then there'll be hell to pay. I can't, and neither should you.'

'You wouldn't have to dress like a fella. I can do that and get enough work to look after us both.'

'So, what then? I'd be your sweetheart, would I? I think you've lost your mind, Willie Smith.'

Willie's eyes moistened. What would be so wrong with that? she asked herself. But she could tell that Catherine didn't have the heart or stomach for it. Willie would be leaving alone. Leaving her best friend. There wasn't any going back now. She walked over to Catherine and planted a kiss on her cheek.

'Don't forget me, Catie. I won't forget you.'

'You're really going?'

'I can't do two more years. Come with me – please. Please, Catie. We can get on a ship to Adelaide and then we can go anywhere we like. I've worked it all out.'

'I can't, Willie. I can't go with you, looking like a fella. The police'll throw us in gaol. And Father Le Bron, Sister Pep – we'll be put away for deviancy. Please, Willie. Get yourself changed before someone sees you.'

'I can't. I can't stay here another day.'

'Wilhelmina, wait,' Catherine said, grabbing for her friend's hand.

Wilhelmina. No one had called her that since the day Mrs Potato-face had dropped her off on the steps of Cranbrook. But Wilhelmina didn't look back. Wilhelmina was no more. And neither was Willie.

The open kitchen door was a sign that now was the time. Stepping out into the crisp dawn air meant more than leaving a best friend. It meant leaving Willie, the girl no one wanted. It meant leaving her female self, which didn't feel so hard, but she would now have to start thinking, acting, *becoming* more masculine if she was to succeed. William, or Bill, perhaps. Just enough of a change to make a difference in how she might be perceived in the world. She would have to try them out on strangers to see what fitted.

With only the clothes he had on, it was now Bill who took a path via the stables to collect the kit he had secreted away over several weeks. But before he reached the perimeter of the home, Catherine came running after him with a sack of assorted foodstuffs from the pantry. She held out the calico bag for Bill to take, and then leaned in with a hug that never wanted to end.

'Friends forever, remember?' said Catherine.

'Friends forever.'

22

Bill walked as far as he could in the early light to get distance from the home. There was a risk that someone associated with Cranbrook might see him and – worse still – see *through* him. He had decided to keep his name as similar as possible so as not to come undone by failing to respond to an unfamiliar identity, but there would be many other ways to be exposed.

He kept off the main roads, barely stopping all day. By late afternoon, feeling the miles and the spent energy of his plans coming to fruition, he started looking for somewhere to bed down for the night. There was a hay shed close to the road, and Bill hoped no one would be back in the vicinity until morning. He took out the half loaf that he had lifted from the baker's cart when it came earlier that day, and the wedge of cheese Catherine had provided that was probably intended for Father Le Bron's dinner. He wondered whether anyone would be out searching for him yet – or *her*, at least. He peered out across the road and hoped that even if they were, this hay shed would not be on any expected escape route.

In the morning, he left before full light and made his way to the main road to town. It was a stroke of luck that the first passer-by he put his thumb out for was an old bloke floating a horse behind his carriage, and an even bigger stroke of luck that he stopped.

'Where are you heading, young fella?'

'I need to get to Port Augusta. Down the docks,' he said, a little higher pitched than intended.

The old fella scanned him up and down, pausing longer than was comfortable for Bill.

'Got to get to Adelaide – me mum's crook. Thought I could take a steamer tonight.'

'Hop up, Son.'

Bill felt the tips of his ears flush. Does he know? Bill was stuck to the spot.

'You want a ride or not, young fella? I haven't got all day.'

'Yeah, of course,' he said, drawing on a voice from further down than he had ever used before.

He was grateful that the old bloke wasn't the talkative type. There wasn't even an introduction from the gnarly character, and thankfully no interest in getting to know his passenger. The driver needed all his concentration to keep the old carriage rolling along. Frequently he would turn his head to check the feisty mare at the back. When they stopped for a break, several hours into their journey, Bill began to relax. He mirrored some of the old man's movements, arching his back and stretching like the driver had done.

'You smoke, Son?' the driver asked, offering the rest of his cigarette.

'No, no thanks – I mean, if you're sure you've had enough,' he said, taking it between his fingers the way Albert would. Bill took a hesitant drag, and exhaled a minuscule amount of grey smoke before handing it back. 'Not used to store-bought – mostly have bush baccy.'

The driver studied the young fellow more intently, until Bill felt compelled to take the focus off himself.

'Where you taking the horse?' he finally asked, giving the mare a nuzzle.

'Gonna give the old girl over to the constabulary. Can't afford the feed anymore, and she's too good a horse for the knackery.'

'They're all too good, I reckon,' said Bill, pulling himself up from sounding too soft.

'Can't disagree with you there, Son. I think she knows I'm leaving her, which is why she's a little toey.'

Bill felt a bit anxious when the old man mentioned the constabulary. He vividly pictured the heavy-handed sergeant who'd come that day more than five years ago, and had no desire to go anywhere near a police station.

'How much further to the Port?'

'We should be down over the Pass by midday, and then it's an easy two, three hours. Be there by afternoon, all going well.'

It was going to be several hours bumping along the road together down to Port Augusta, and the chance of discovery was high. Bill was glad of the silence. The fewer questions, the better. He pulled his cap down over his face, folded his arms, and stretched out his legs as he had observed so many men do when they took up space as passengers in carts or carriages.

Bill remembered his father talking about the steamships that sailed down the Gulf to Adelaide. Albert Smith, when in one of his more jocular moods – the stage between the beer and the spirits – would say, 'Let's take a steamer to Adelaide for a holiday. Would you like that? I bet you'd like that.'

'Yes, yes, I would, Dad. When? When can we go to Adelaide?'

'When me ship comes in, that's when. When me bloody ship comes in,' he'd say, laughing as he walked away.

It took quite a few years before young Willie understood the joke. Years of innocent hopefulness. Now, bumping along on a rickety dray, with one life behind him, Bill knew he would have to find his own ship.

~

Bill had planned his escape well but had given less attention to exactly what he would do after he got away from the home. He had thought about going back to the farm, but dismissed the idea as that would be the first place the authorities would look for him – or *her,* he supposed. Either way, it was too risky, and Bill couldn't even be sure that the farm hadn't been taken over by someone else. He thought if he could get to Adelaide he might be able to find his grandparents, but there had been no contact between his father and Flora's parents after they'd left Port Augusta years earlier. He couldn't even be sure they were still alive – and besides, he had no real clue where to start searching. Apart from where to go, his one big obstacle was money, or lack thereof, and so the idea of working his passage to Adelaide was formed.

The Port Augusta docks were bustling with people, produce and animals. Rail lines snaked their way to the waterfront, and cranes and pulleys danced across the unnatural sky. Bill thought the colour seemed like the end of days. He felt anxious looking back to the Ranges and wondering what would happen when he – *she* – was discovered missing. He hoped Catherine would not be punished for any assumed complicity in the escape.

Why couldn't you come with me, Catie? he thought to himself. He had been so certain that Catherine would be just as eager as him to get away from Cranbrook that he had never really thought about leaving her behind. But something had shifted when he saw her reaction to the idea. It had frightened her more than the thought of staying did, and Bill knew at that point he would be going alone. It was even more crucial then that it be in the guise of a male. A young woman travelling alone would raise many more questions and face greater risks, after all, and it felt quite natural to become Bill. What stung more than anything, however, was Catherine's suggestion that they might be considered deviants if discovered. How could that be? What did it mean? The plans he made now were only for one.

The impact of the War meant there was a shortage of young, fit men, so Bill hoped there would be few questions asked when he went hunting for a job. When he'd said goodbye to the old man, Bill sat down by the water, watching and waiting. He studied the faces of some of the returned soldiers as they passed by. The War was supposed to have been over by then, but still it dragged on. The only returned soldiers he saw were those the War had spat out – macerated or maddened by the experience. The faces of the men in uniform that the War gave back prematurely seemed anything but at peace.

One of them could be Albert, he thought. He tried to imagine what would happen if he saw him. Would he run up and throw his arms around him? Would his father be happy to see him, or would Albert Smith wonder why this young lad was behaving so? Then he asked himself, do I really want to see him again? He had left Willie without a word, had organised for Welfare to put her in that place and had never sent even a postcard of enquiry into her wellbeing. No, Bill Smith had no father, and Albert had no daughter. All that was left was ahead, on the possibility of a steamship to a new life.

23

Bill needed a job where he could be out of public view. He watched, fascinated, for hours as the light began to fade. Movement in all directions, shouted orders, echoed replies. On one steamship he watched a fellow, who he guessed to be a boss of some kind, put his head out of a door several times and check his watch. The ship was readying to leave. The SS *Winfield*, en route to Adelaide, according to the signage on the dock. The man's checking continued with ever-greater urgency and more colourful language.

'Where the feck is that bastard Maxwell? If he misses departure, he needn't bloody bother turning up at the next port this time!'

With one last scan of the docks, he put his head back inside and disappeared. This was Bill's chance. They were a man down. He jumped off the wall where he had been perched and made his way up the gangplank, pulling his hat down further on his head and his coat tighter around his shoulders.

'Hey, Mister, any work available?'

The man turned towards the sound of the high-pitched voice, took one glance at Bill and gave a dismissive wave of his hand.

'Go home, boy. I need a bloody man, not someone who looks like they'd blow over in a breeze. Bloody Maxwell. Leaving us in the lurch ...'

His voice trailed off as he ducked back down below for the umpteenth time. Bill stood in place, unprepared to leave the ship. This was his best chance of getting away from Cranbrook, and no one would be looking for him – her – on an Adelaide line steamer. At least he took me for a boy, Bill thought. This gave him the courage to press on.

He flung his pack over his shoulder and followed the fellow down the stairs, where the workers addressed the man as 'Chief'. No one really took any notice as Bill slipped in behind him, standing close as if he had every right to be there. The Chief started in full roar to the assembled crew, and all eyes were on the spittle and fury spraying out with every word.

'Right, now, you all know what an unreliable drunk Maxwell is. He's nowhere to be seen. This ship is embarking in exactly fifteen minutes, but even if he tries to slink aboard last whistle, he'll be shown the end of my boot and the black embrace of the Spencer Gulf. I won't tolerate it from anyone – you hear me? This company has a reputation to uphold. There's no room for any man that can't do his job – so now you'll all need to take up the slack.'

A slow murmur of discontent spread like a wave through the crew, before the Chief tried to shut it down with a loud, 'Right?'

Bill took the opportunity to step forward, conscious of the need to impress now. He tried to find the deepest register in his voice.

'I can lend a hand. I'm not as big as your other fellas, but I'm strong. Give me a go, Chief? I won't let you down.'

'Not as big? Boy, I'm surprised you're even off your mummy's breast.'

The crew sniggered and poked one another in agreement, until one wiry man stepped forward and they all fell silent.

'I'd rather a little bloke who's here than a drunken hulk who's not. Besides, Chief, need I remind you that the union expects safe staffing levels? If you can't provide 'em, then we might need to—'

'Hold on now, Dave. No need to be pulling the union card out. I'm on the same side, you know. You want the little fella, you can have him, but,' he turned to Bill, 'no excuses, lad. You pull your weight, or you could end up in the Spencer as well. No room for freeloaders here. Show him the ropes, fellas, and let's get going or none of us'll have jobs.'

Bill was on his way. His plan had worked, but he barely had time to bask in his success before he was pushed and bumped by men trying to get to their stations.

'Stow your stuff. You won't need that coat down here. Watch for a bit to get the rhythm. Ever been on a steamer before? Steamships run on steam, of course. You don't keep up the supply, we don't go nowhere – simple as that, so watch and learn. You a member, Son? You'll have to become a member – of the union. What's your name, Son? I'm Dave, Davo – or Boss to you, when we're on watch.'

'Bill. Bill Smith,' he tried to insert into the rapid-fire discourse.

The questions were coming so fast Bill barely had time to consider them let alone answer. Not that Dave was expecting any responses. They were directives more than questions. Bill was too concerned about the need to remove his coat to think about anything else. When he did take the coat off, he kept his vest done up tight. Dave looked Bill up and down and laughed.

'Shy boy, eh, Bill? No room for embarrassment down here. Most of the fellas work shirtless – you'll soon see why. Depends on whether you like freezing or frying better. The furnace'll singe the hairs off your chest, then the ventilator'll freeze your other bits,' Dave said with a grin.

Panic flooded Bill's body as he began to question his choice of jobs.

'It's a condition I got,' he said, thinking quickly. 'Got to keep covered up. It's okay – I don't feel the heat.'

'Really?' said Dave. Bill couldn't tell if he was convinced or if the disguise was about to come undone but, as the horn blasted on the great steamship, there was nothing further to do but as instructed. Everyone took their places, and a great piece of choreography brought the ship to life. Men moved in perfect combinations in response to bells ringing and captain's orders echoed throughout the bowels of the ship.

'Slow ahead.'

'Slow ahead.'

'Slooww ahead.'

The pistons rising began a rhythm that Bill swore was saying, 'Let's go now, let's go now.' Three long blasts of the horn and he could feel the ship moving slowly from its mooring.

'Half ahead.'

'Half ahead.'

'Half ahead.'

Machinery picked up the pace as more bells signalled actions that the crew were all ready for, with the chief engineer turning a large black wheel fully one way and then making adjustments, steam puffing from valves straining to contain the blow-by.

Bill was in awe of the musicality of it all, which meant there was no turning back now. He was on his way to uncertainty, certain only that it would have to be better than where he had been.

He took his turn with the other firemen, but Dave was kind enough to cut the new chum a break and only made him do two-hour stints instead of four, giving him a half-hour break. As the *Winfield* sailed south through the Gulf it was a surprisingly fast and smooth trip. If Bill's clothes were a little ill-fitting before, they were positively swimming on him by the time they got to Adelaide. The Chief studied the young fellow carefully from the doorway, seeing the scrawny arms jutting out from Bill's pushed-up sleeves and buttoned-up vest.

'Well, Davo, did the boy earn his passage or does he still owe us something?'

'Oh, he earned it alright. Strong little bugger,' Dave said, giving Bill a pat on the shoulder.

'Right. So do you want to do the return with us then, Son? Even if bloody Maxwell turns up in Port, he can go to buggery. If Davo is happy to vouch for you, that's good enough for me.'

'I – I can't, Chief. I have to go see my mum – she's poorly. Near dying, they say. But I'm grateful you gave me a go. Really grateful.'

'Suit yourself. Boss can see to your wages, then, Son – minus your fare, of course. I'll be in at the company office, trying to get a replacement for fucking Maxwell then,' he said, directing the remark to Davo. The Chief turned and headed back up the stairs.

'So, what now, little mate? You going to see that sick mum of yours?' Davo said with a wink. 'Don't worry, Son. I know a runaway when I see one. I was one meself once. Only I legged it by train, not steamer. Had to get away from me brute of an old man.'

Bill nodded in a sign of solidarity with Dave's story.

'Yep. Thought so. What are you going to do now, then? We turn around and head back in the morning. Up and down the Gulf. What's the plan? You going to stay in Adelaide?'

'I don't know. I've never been to Adelaide. Might need to earn some more money first.'

'You could get yourself on one of the other Adelaide Steamship Company vessels going east, if that's preferable. I gotta give it to you – you held your own, alright. So, no sick mother in Adelaide, I'm guessing?'

'No, she died when I was a baby.'

'And your father?'

'Left me in a home and went to fight the Huns.'

'And has he passed too, then?

'I've not heard a word since the day he sent me there. No one's come with a telegram to find me, so who knows? Anyway, they'd be putting me out soon as I come of age. I decided to take matters into my own hands.'

'Alright then. I reckon there's a vessel we can get you on,' he said, indicating another Adelaide Steamship docked nearby. 'You follow my lead and see if old Davo can't get you on one going somewhere nice and better suited to that "condition" of yours.'

24

When they got into Port Adelaide, Dave managed to talk his mate into letting Bill sign on with the SS *Mandura* heading for Townsville, leaving in a week. Townsville. It was further away than Bill could even imagine. Still, he was up for it. A new place. A chance to start over. The *Mandura* didn't have a big crew, but the captain, Hannigan, agreed that Bill could give a hand to the cook, because they seemed to lose a cook's assistant at every port. Bill thought the kitchen would be easier to handle than the furnaces. He had held his own on the trip down the Spencer Gulf but it had been tough, and he wasn't sure he would've been able to keep up for the lengthy trip to Townsville.

Davo knew the young lad had nowhere to go until the *Mandura* sailed so, after paying him his wages for the trip down, he pointed Bill in the direction of the seamen's mission.

'Just down the street there, Son. They'll give you a bed, a feed – and maybe even save your soul,' he said with a grin. 'And here's a little something to get you through until you sail.'

Bill opened his hand to see the notes Davo pressed into his palm as the pair shook their goodbyes.

'I can't take this, Boss. You've already done enough.'

'You can and you will. Now, I'm off to murder a pint. Best of luck to you, little cobber.'

~

The Sailors' Rest, as the mission was known, provided exactly what Bill needed – a place to stay and, importantly, somewhere no one would ever think to look for a runaway from Cranbrook Home for Girls. When asked to sign in, he thought about whether to use a completely different name, but the trip down from Port Augusta had given him confidence. The less to remember in a lie, the better, he convinced himself. And Bill was a perfectly common name – it wouldn't be at all unusual for people to know of other Bill Smiths, if any connections might be made. He filled out the mission's register as *WA Smith* – W for William, the formal version of Bill, and A for Albert, after his father. He was happy with the additional layering of male identity that it offered, and could easily explain any slip-up should he call himself Willie in an unguarded moment.

The clothes secured for his escape had served their immediate purpose, but in the town environment he felt conspicuous. They were ill-fitting and a hodgepodge of styles. Bill spent the next few days exploring Port Adelaide and the city. He couldn't believe the wide streets, the massive sandstone buildings and beautiful parklands, the abundance of grand churches, the size of the stores and the endless array of goods for sale.

In one of the shops there were ex-army boots on display. Bill bought a pair of blucher boots with a metal toe that made him feel taller. They were in exceptionally good condition because, as the shopkeeper explained, the previous owner, a lad not much older than Bill, had had his legs blown off in France and had no need for shoes anymore. Bill wished he hadn't told him that, picturing the young fellow sitting at home with stumps where his legs had once been; but then he thought there was no sense in letting good boots go to waste.

'I'll just wear them now, thank you, Sir,' he said, tucking his old pair under his arm.

'Is there anything else I can do for you today, young man?'

Bill also bought a long-sleeved grey flannel shirt, some tweed trousers, and a handkerchief for his neck. When he got back to the mission and tried everything on, he saw reflected in the mirror a young Albert Smith. It felt so right. All those years in the drab, impractical tunic of the home had made him feel like a freak.

Now Bill Smith stood taller in the world.

~

The week passed quickly and no one came banging on his door, asking after the Cranbrook inmate with a remarkably similar name. Bill wondered if Catherine was missing her friend as much as he was missing her, but wondering was all he could do. He had thought about sending her a letter – or perhaps a picture postcard would be safer. Even if Sister Pep suspected it was from the runaway inmate and noted the postmark, no one would be looking for a male employee of the Adelaide Steamship Company.

While waiting in the office to sign on for the trip to Townsville, Bill found it hard to steady his nerves. He'd been lucky with the ship getting to Adelaide, but that had only been a short journey. How would his disguise hold up over a voyage of such distance? But there was no real option otherwise. Bill could not even contemplate being returned to Cranbrook, despite the thought of never seeing Catherine again churning in his head.

He noticed a stand in the office with postcards of the company's ships. Would Catherine understand the meaning without it giving too much away? Bill chose a card depicting the *Winfield* and addressed it to his friend at Cranbrook. He held the pencil ready to write a brief message but couldn't find any words. There was no need. If it reached Catherine, she would know its meaning. If all went well with the new job, he would be back in Adelaide from time to time and, with any luck, she would know how to find him.

~

The *Mandura* was a small vessel considering how far it travelled each trip – round the south-eastern tip and all the way up the coast to Townsville. The ship's cook, 'Flatpan' Freddie Lewis, was a sour-faced character who always complained about the pantryhands. No one met his standards. When told that Bill would be sailing with them as an assistant in the kitchen, Flatpan eyed his new helper up and down and muttered to himself a string of indistinct commentary interspersed with some audible profanities.

'Don't worry, lad,' said one of the stokers, Harry Edmunds. 'His bark is worse than his bite. That's his happy face. Hard to tell, I know, since he was smacked in it by a flat pan. That's how he got his name, you know – Flatpan Freddie,' he said with a grin.

Bill looked at Flatpan and nodded, convinced of the sincerity of the story since the cook did have a peculiarly flattened facial structure. The crew was a good bunch of fellas, he soon found. They were like a big, rowdy family. Everyone had a nickname, and a story to go with it.

Harry Edmunds was 'Casanova'. Bill had never heard that name before and wasn't sure what it meant, until Harry explained that Casanova was a famous lover. Harry was a handsome man, Bill could see that easily enough, but it would take a few trips and a few heartbroken women left sobbing on the docks of various ports before the reason for the nickname became clear.

They called Sven 'the Swede', despite his protestations that he was Norwegian. That just stirred the rest of the crew into using his nickname more.

'Why they call me bloody Swede?' he would moan to no one in particular. 'I am not Swede. I am Norsk. What is so bloody hard about Sven, anyway? Everybody gotta have a bloody nickname in this place.'

'It's a sign of affection, matey,' said Casanova, slapping the Swede on the back as he pushed past him on the walkway.

'Affection my arse,' said Sven.

Bill made several trips between Adelaide and Townsville on the *Mandura* over the following months. He couldn't believe the things he saw on those voyages around the coast. Dolphins, seabirds, even an occasional whale. The *Mandura* was mostly a freight-carrying vessel but had a few passenger cabins. Bill was eventually offered a job as a steward, which he enjoyed more than being in the kitchen. He settled into life on the ship well and found the men of the *Mandura* to be hardworking, decent fellows. No one commented or looked twice at the shy young lad who never took off his shirt, even in the most humid of climates.

It didn't take long before Bill was given a nickname – 'the PM', in reference to the wartime prime minister, Billy Hughes, who was similarly small in stature. Bill liked the nickname when Harry first came up with it. It felt like acceptance. It felt like the family Bill longed for, and it helped ease the pain of losing Catherine a little.

He quickly gained a reputation for being a solid worker and had little trouble staying in employment. When they were back in Port Adelaide, Bill liked to spend his money on clothes and, most happily of all, on a horse of his own, which he stabled nearby. He had never stopped thinking about the stallion, Boy, from the farm, or about Titan, Butterball and little Sooty from the home. Just the smell of a horse was enough to evoke a sense of bliss in him like no other.

His first horse he came by unexpectedly. On his way into the city one time, Bill saw a milk cart being pulled by a feisty chestnut mare – not the right animal for a sedate job in city streets, Bill thought. The driver was having trouble controlling the young horse. There was an obvious clash of wills, which almost resulted in the milk cart being overturned. Bill raced up and grabbed the mare by the mane, before getting to the bridle and steadying her.

'Doesn't seem to like the job much, this one,' Bill said to the driver, who was clearly rattled by the incident.

'I should've known she was too good to be true,' the driver replied. 'Now I'll have to head back to the stables and swap in the old mare. Thought we'd move quicker with this one, but she's a little too quick for milk deliveries.'

'What's her name? Looks better suited to racing than pulling, I reckon.'

'She's called Addy – Adelaide – and you're right. She was from Morphettville, but they said she was too slow and was only good for pulling a milk cart. I took 'em at their word and thought I was getting a bargain, being a young 'un. I've given her a fair go, but today's the last straw.'

Bill offered to pay what the driver had paid to take the mare off his hands. What better than a horse of his own called Adelaide, for when he was back in the city of the same name?

Addy would always be his first visit on disembarking. Bill gravitated to horses like the rest of the crew to pubs and brothels. Initially some fellas would tease him for not coming with them, but eventually the joke wore off.

'You coming down the Royal for a tipple or two?'

'No thanks, mate. I got a special girl I'm off to spend time with.'

'That's right. Lovely chestnut hair, shapely long legs, eh lad? All four of 'em!' Harry Edmunds chimed in, playfully knocking Bill's cap from his head.

'That's right,' said Bill, 'and lovely big teeth too.'

'You're a funny bugger, Bill.'

Bill stood watching his mates head off up the road. He noticed he was right outside a barbershop and, with his cap still in one hand, he ran the other over his hair. He caught a glimpse in the window's reflection of himself in his well-tailored apparel, an improvement on the scrappy youth that first stepped out in Adelaide. Even his stance came more naturally than it did when he'd first tried it out at Cranbrook.

He wondered what Catherine would think of him now. Bill thought often of Catherine, and hoped she might do the same, but there had been no response to the postcard he'd sent before he started on the *Mandura*.

'What's it to be, Son?' called the barber, beckoning the young man to step inside.

'Tidy thanks, friend,' said Bill, taking a seat in the chair.

'For a shilling more, I can give you a shave,' said the barber automatically, draping a cape around Bill's shoulders, then scanned the young face and let out a laugh. 'Well, I can see I'd be wasting my time eh, cobber? Perhaps you'd be more interested in our studio portraits? Handsome chap like you must have a young lady you could send it to?'

Bill felt his face redden. The urge to flee from the chair and scrutiny was strong. But then he thought about Catherine. How could he be sure she had even received his previous postcard? Would she have known what it meant, with no name or message? He could send a portrait this time. If she could see Bill as he was today, and if she wrote back, he would know for sure whether their friendship could endure. He decided to give it one last go. He studied the portraits arranged around the shop and agreed that there was in fact a special young lady, but said he would come back after he'd had a chance to change clothes.

'Fair enough. I'll tell our photographer to expect you then.'

~

When Bill finally collected his photograph, he was shocked to see the resemblance to his father. Surely no one would recognise the runaway from Cranbrook in this portrait. Even so, he would need to be careful about what information to include. He doubted anyone would be searching for him with a view to returning him to the home now that he'd turned eighteen, but he feared there might be some charge of absconding that could be laid. It was a risk either way, as he didn't know whether Catherine would still be there either, but he thought it likely, as she was a few months younger than Bill.

He touched the tip of the pencil to his tongue and then hovered it over the cream-coloured postcard.

My dear cousin, Catherine,

I hope this finds you well, as it does me.

You might be surprised to hear from me. My work has kept

me quite busy, but I find myself in Adelaide from time to time. Should you ever wish to meet, I would be most pleased. You can leave a message for me at the Adelaide Steamship offices in Port Adelaide.

Your most affectionate cousin,

Bill xxxx

He studied the sepia photograph on the front. The clothes were smart. The fedora pulled low across one eye, the fine pinstriped suit. What would Catherine think? Would she be happy to hear from her friend? Would she understand the ruse, or would it repulse her? Bill hesitated. What if Sister Perpetuata intercepted the card? Catherine was not known to have any family – would this draw further scrutiny? He placed it in an envelope in the hope that Catherine would be the first to see it. When he finally mustered the courage to drop it in the postbox, he tried not to think about it anymore, but that was not easy. Catherine was never far from Bill's thoughts, and the pain of leaving her behind was still palpable.

He couldn't wait to get back to port after his next voyage, to see if there was a reply waiting for him. The first time, he was disappointed but still hopeful. He checked in at the office again every time he was back in port. The office clerk would check every piece of mail, calling each name aloud, alphabetically, before telling him there was nothing for Smith. Months later, the clerk would just give a shake of his head, mercifully shortcutting Bill's disappointment. Eventually he stopped asking.

Part 3

South Australia to New South Wales to Queensland, 1920–1978

… a strong and capable worker of sober habits and quiet disposition …

25

For the next year and a half, Bill settled into life on the steamer. He was grateful for the work, and no one had even raised a glimmer of suspicion that Bill Smith might have been a runaway from Cranbrook Home for Girls. Not even when a newspaper headline in March 1920 declared: 'CRANBROOK RIOTS AND AFFRAY!' Administration of the home would now be taken over by the state government, the article said, and major reforms instituted. Bill scoured the page to see if there was any mention of past absconders, but there were no names listed. Catherine would have been put out at the end of the previous year, but still he held hope for some hint, some indication of the fate of his friend – only to be disappointed once more.

He resolved to look only forward from here. There was no reason to look back. The *Mandura* was getting on, but she was still a fast vessel and the crew lovingly tended to her every need. They all expected to be sailing her for a long time, so it came as a terrible blow, when they docked in Port Adelaide near the end of August 1920, to learn that the Adelaide Steamship Company had gone into receivership.

'It's that bloody union that's brought all this on,' said Casanova.

'Bullshit. It's the bloody union makes sure we get a fair wage for a fair day's work. You should be grateful, you ugly bastard,' said the Swede.

'Well, no point having a fair wage if there's no company to work for.'

Bill sat listening to the to-and-fro, puffing on the Navy Cut cigarettes that he had grown accustomed to since his first awkward effort at smoking, but his mind went to what would happen next.

The captain stood at the gangway, shaking the hand of every crewmember as they left for the last time. When Bill stepped forward, the captain pressed a letter into his hand, saying, 'Well, Son, it was good working with you. You come back when things pick up, and there'll always be a place for you on any ship I command.'

As Bill lay on his bed back at the Sailors' Rest in Port Adelaide, he considered what to do next. He tentatively opened the envelope from the captain, and saw that it was a reference. The first written letter ever to come into his possession. He read and reread it as if it had come from the King himself, ran his fingers over the creamy paper and traced the fine lettering on the top right-hand corner.

The Adelaide Steamship Co. Limited
Adelaide
SS *Mandura*
Port Adelaide

22 August 1920

To Whom It May Concern: Regarding Mr William (Bill) Smith.

This is to certify that the above named served under my command as a ship's galley-mate and steward on the SS *Mandura* from the

12th day of September 1918 to 22 August 1920, and that he has given entire satisfaction in the execution of his duties.

I have pleasure in recommending Mr Smith as a strong and capable worker of sober habits and quiet disposition.

AF Hannigan

Captain

SS *Mandura*

~

It would be more than a year before positions on the coastal steamers would come up again. In the meantime, Bill had taken his chestnut mare, Adelaide, and an older packhorse called Missus and set off across country. He found occasional work droving and as a farmhand, but mostly as a horse breaker, like his father. It suited him to be away from the cities; even more so with the terrible flu epidemic that swept around the world after the War.

As he moved throughout western New South Wales, Bill became renowned for his considerable skill with horses. Calls for his services as a breaker kept him on the move. It suited him not to stay too long in any one place. The crew of the *Mandura* had made no business of Bill's shyness or need for privacy, but it wasn't like that everywhere he went. Rougher types he encountered in some of the smaller outback towns could make life difficult for anyone who didn't fit the mould of the hard-drinking, woman-chasing 'good bloke'. Anyone who didn't was considered a 'wowser', or worse. The work on the land also showed in Bill's strengthening body. When he did go back to the ships, he thought, he might even be able to work as a stoker. They made better money, but they earned it.

A lot of the time, as he moved across the outback of New South

Wales, Bill chose to camp out near the Aboriginal families along the rivers. They asked no questions of the wiry, tanned young fellow who hunted kangaroos with an ex-army rifle and would drop a few off at the old people's wurleys in appreciation of their acceptance of his comings and goings. Although the memory of his childhood nannies had dimmed, these people felt very familiar and safe to him.

'You want to watch yourself, young fella,' he'd often be told, when it became known where he'd set up camp. 'They're *myall*, that lot – wild buggers. Spear ya in your sleep if you're not careful.'

'You need to roll your swag out somewhere else, mate. No good comes of mixing with the blacks. Better you stick with your own kind, if you want to keep working round here.'

He'd heard it all too often. But it was not always smooth going when he did mix with his own kind, he'd found – although exactly who his own kind were was unclear to him. What he did know was that the people deemed society's outcasts seemed to possess a better moral code that many of 'his own kind'. What Bill provided with his rifle was often reciprocated with a lesson in hunting other game, or identifying bush tucker and medicines.

Bill loved his life, crossing the country with Addy and Missus, camping under the Milky Way, watching for shooting stars. Addy thrived in these conditions, building muscle mass and endurance, and Bill got to test her out in a few bush races along the way. He found nothing lazy or uncooperative about her. She responded well to Bill's gentle approach. Unregistered bush events could be wild and woolly affairs, so he was selective about which ones he would enter her in. She didn't win often, but Bill put that down to his lack of experience with the strategy of horseracing rather than his Adelaide girl, who impressed the crowds regardless.

By the early summer of 1921, Bill and his entourage of animals had collected a new member who travelled with them for a while – a mixed dingo pup that Bill called Ding, in keeping with the usual pragmatic way his animals were named. Those months spent crisscrossing the country with his horses and Ding were some of the best times of his life so far. When the pup got tired, Bill would lift him up and cradle him on the front of the saddle. There were days when Bill encountered no one, but that never made him feel lonely. In fact, those were the days he enjoyed most. The only company he ever missed was Catherine's.

'She would have loved you, Ding,' he'd say to the pup, who would cock his head to one side, trying to make sense of the conversation. Bill loved to imagine Catherine there, travelling together with him and Addy, Missus and Ding. But it had been almost three years, and he had to accept that he was never likely to see his friend again. She would have completed her time at Cranbrook and could be anywhere by now – could even be married, he supposed.

When his thoughts headed down this path, it would leave Bill feeling a melancholy that would take some days to lift. At these times it would have been easy to stay away from people altogether, but Bill knew he needed to earn some more money and give his horses a break for a bit; so before it got too hot, he headed to a property near Moree that had put the word out for a farmhand.

Staying anywhere too long always brought with it inevitable risks. Bill was happy at the property in the beginning, being the only farmhand on the station that summer. Not because there wasn't plenty of work for more men, but because the owner, Bert Bloomfield, was known for his stinginess. If he could get by doing things on the cheap, he would.

Bill didn't mind the long days. He had the quarters to himself, which he preferred to the close-lived conditions of the railway gangs he occasionally joined for some quick money. Plus Addy and Missus were kept in feed as part of the deal. But things took a dark turn when Ding didn't come when he called him for supper one night. Bill called for his little mate until it was almost sunset, and then took Addy out along the fence line to look for him. It didn't take long before a familiar silhouette became visible in the dusk, in a horrible, unfamiliar pose – lifeless, draped over a post.

Bill's heartache was every bit as strong as with the other losses in his life. It wasn't unexpected, though, as Ding had been targeted before for his wild dog heritage. Bill cradled Ding one last time on Addy's back, before burying him beneath a river gum on the property. Bloomfield swore he hadn't shot the dog, but said he would have, if he'd thought for a minute he was a dingo. Bill didn't believe him, and old Bert knew it.

Not long after the incident, an old Sydney newspaper was left on the table in the bunkhouse. Its front page shook Bill to the core. 'MAN-WOMAN MURDERESS!' screamed the headline from back in August the previous year. Man-woman. Bill read the article from the yellowed pages, about a woman who dressed as a man and was charged with murdering her 'wife'. Wife. Murder. How could it be? The photographs, and the details of the story, were shocking. Bill had never heard of anything like it. To go about dressed as a man was one thing, but to convince a woman to marry you – that was something else again. And then, to have it end with murder. Bill recalled what Catherine had said all those years ago – that they would be arrested for deviancy.

'Have you ever seen anything like this?' said Bert later that morning while they were having smoko, making a point of showing Bill the front page of the old paper. 'Bloody sheila getting around as a bloke,' he said. 'Some queer business, that.'

Bill just continued sipping on his cuppa, not making eye contact even though he could feel Bert's eyes fixed on him. Bert Bloomfield was a prickly character at the best of times, and was not well regarded around the area, where it was noted that workers seemed to turn over with haste on his property. Bill hadn't intended to stay long, and after Ding's demise he had promised himself this would be his last week.

When he was given his next pay, he noticed it was far less than he had received previously.

'Here you go, *Son*,' said Bert as he handed it over, the stressed word not lost on Bill. 'Consider yourself lucky I'm a generous *man*. That's what we pay the domestics – seems only right for your kind, I reckon.'

'I don't think so, Bloomfield. You pay me what you owe me, or this place will be blacklisted before sundown.'

'Go on with ya. Piss off.'

Bill was not one for conflict of any kind, but he hated more than anything a person as mean-spirited as Bert Bloomfield. He tapped him on the shoulder as Bert was walking away from him and landed a blow on the boss's nose as he turned, causing it to gush with bright-red blood that fell like rain on the baked earth between them. Both men fixed their eyes on the droplets, neither moving until Bill reached over, pulled some notes from Bert's shirt pocket and peeled off what he was owed, throwing the remainder back at the farmer's feet.

'That's for Ding, ya mean bastard.'

Bill didn't expect Bert to be telling anyone about who'd given him his bloody nose, but he knew he needed to get out of the region and start again somewhere else. *Your kind*. Bill showed him what he thought of his *generosity* and of *his kind*, and was gone with his horses the same day.

26

A letter from the Adelaide Steamship Company eventually caught up with Bill, but not the one he longed for. There had been nothing at all from Catherine, but that didn't diminish his yearning to see her again. This letter was an offer of work, on a vessel running around the top of Cape York. After his close call with old Bloomfield, Bill thought it might be good to start up again somewhere well away.

He headed across to Brisbane, where he agisted Adelaide and Missus on a property north of the city, promising them both he would be back as soon as he could make arrangements for them closer to wherever he might be based.

'You two be good, now,' he said to the mares, nuzzling into each one's neck as he spoke to them in turn. 'You've worked hard, my darlin's – time for a well-deserved break. It might be a while before I'm settled, so don't fret. I'll be back for you when I can.'

Bill hated leaving his horses, but he had never been up north before. He wanted to check things out before putting them through a journey that long. The new ship was to run between Townsville and Darwin, so he took the next steamer up to join his new crew. It was the worst time of year to be starting, with the Build-up to the Wet in full swing and cyclones frequent all around the Cape, but Bill didn't mind working on the water again.

The first run to Darwin wasn't too bad. There was not the same camaraderie as there had been on the *Mandura*, however. The crew of the much smaller SS *Brighton* was an unpleasant lot, Bill thought, and it did not take long to notice other differences. For one thing, they all, including the captain, liked their drink. Captain Hannigan on the *Mandura* would tolerate no man who couldn't wait until they docked to have his ale or whisky or whatever else of his choosing. That's how Bill had got the job on the *Winfield* in the first place, and Captain Hannigan's reference to sober habits was as good an endorsement as he might give. The *Brighton* crew was the opposite: suspicious of anyone who wouldn't take a drink.

After several trips to Darwin and back, managing to avoid the nightly binge sessions most of the crew engaged in, Bill found himself trapped one evening while they waited out a cyclone brewing off the coast.

'Go on, Son – take a swig. It'll put hairs on your chest,' said the chief stoker, Frank Stewart, holding an enamel mug under Bill's nose. Backed into a corner, there was nowhere to go. Despite the nauseating smell of ale and sweat combined, Bill took a sip, then involuntarily spat it out down Stewart's front.

'Jesus, Boy – don't waste the bloody stuff!' Stewart said, pulling the mug away before draining it himself in one go.

'He is only a boy, after all,' said Tobias, the ship's second officer. 'Best leave the kid alone, eh Frank.'

'And why is that, now, Tobes old mate? You want to look after the *boy* yourself, now, do you?'

The word 'boy' was said laden with something that made Bill's nerves pay attention. Even though he was now in his early twenties, and hard work had changed his body physically, he still appeared younger and, of course, less masculine – that was undeniable – than his crewmates. The memory of his run-in at the farm caused him to shudder.

With time alone – just him and his horses, making their way slowly to Brisbane – Bill had wondered briefly if it might be wise to return to his feminine self. But who was that, exactly? For some reason that Bill never fully understood, he had long ago stopped having to deal with the challenges of what would certainly have given away his sex. Early on during his time on the steamships, he had been able to discretely dispose of his bloodied rags in the furnace when that time of the month came, but this had become unnecessary in the past few years. First there had been little more than a day or two of spotting, and then nothing. Bill took that as a blessing, and never questioned the change. Even if it signified some health concern, there would be no going to a doctor, that was for certain.

Now, sun-bronzed and muscular as a result of living a working man's life, his walk perfected, comfortable in his trousers and shirts, his fingers stained yellow with tobacco, Bill was unsure he could even find the female self he'd left behind. But he also knew that there were attributes and behaviours that left him vulnerable in the world of men. His voice, in particular, was a potential source of betrayal and another reason to keep to himself.

He took the bottle from Frank's hand, leaving him with the empty mug, and took a couple of large gulps to show them his mettle. It made his head swim almost immediately, but he swiped his mouth with his shirtsleeve and declared, 'I've had better brews,' before pushing past Frank and up onto the deck for some fresh air.

Bill was shaking. He felt exposed and unsafe. He continued to sail with the *Brighton* for most of a year, but there was always a whiff of danger among the men on this ship. He could handle most of their taunts, but there were certain behaviours he found hard to witness. Like the way some of them spoke about women, and pressed Bill to share his exploits. There were no exploits to share, of course, and he could only repeat some of the less offensive things he had heard others say about the women they'd left behind. The tameness of Bill's contributions quickly bored the others, who moved on to someone else's more ribald tales.

With the approach of another Build-up marking almost a year since he had joined the vessel, Bill reminded himself that staying too long in any one place was always a risk, and decided he had been too long with the crew of the *Brighton*. He determined that once they got back to Townsville, he would head south to Brisbane to collect his horses and find himself another job. But that decision would be taken out of his hands when they were just a day out of Cairns on the return journey.

~

The weather hung heavy as they sat off the coast. Everyone moved slowly, except when it came to reaching for the grog. There were no passengers on board the *Brighton*, only freight. Bill wondered if that explained the lowered standards among the crew. Or was it the environment? There was less scrutiny up north, so far from the company's head office. There was also more irritability, as every day inched slowly through scorching heat and humidity to torment with storm clouds that withheld their relief. It was as if the heavens were playing games with the tiny humans below.

Bill tried to keep to himself as much as possible in the close confines of the ship's quarters. They were three days into their return trip from Darwin, and he was thinking more seriously about where to go next. He would first retrieve his horses, Addy and Missus, from Brisbane but then, who knew which direction they might go? All he knew was that the mares had already been left too long, and he'd promised himself that this would be his last trip with this crew.

Off-watch, trying to catch some sleep before the changeover, Bill was alone in the bunk, with his back to the door, when he heard someone enter.

'There's my boy. Shhhh. The lad's sleeping. Don't want to wake the little fella.' It was Tobias's voice.

Bill's body stiffened. He tried to stay still, hoping Tobias would go away. What was he doing down here? Who was he talking to? Next moment Frank's slurred voice joined in.

'Shhhhoosh yourself, ya bloody idiot. You prefer 'em awake anyway, don't ya?'

Bill lay there, unable to move. He had no idea what they might be doing, but it made his skin itch. Should he try to get out of the room? Would they go away if he just lay there? His body began to shake.

'There, there, little Billy boy, you're alright.'

A hand reached for the top of Bill's trousers, trying awkwardly to slide down inside. He slapped at it with force, swinging around to see Tobias sitting on the edge of the bunk and Frank swaying in the background, a strange look on his face.

'What do you think you're doing? Get out of here!' Bill yelled.

'Now, lad, don't pretend like you don't know what's going on. Sweet little arse like yours made for fun, eh boy.'

Both of Tobias's hands were now reaching for the top of Bill's pants. Bill tried to wrestle them away, gripping his trousers with all he had, kicking out with his legs and bracing with his shoulder to push the man away, but Tobias was stronger. Bill continued fighting, even biting Tobias at one point. This was met with a punch to the face, causing Bill's head to snap backwards and hit the bunk board, hard.

'Fucking little bastard. Give us a hand, Frank, you useless turd,' said Tobias as he struggled to flip Bill onto his stomach. Now barely conscious, blood ran down into Bill's mouth, and one eye felt strangely puffy. Frank continued to stand back.

'Nah, you like the backdoor boys. Not me. He's all yours, old mate.'

Tobias rubbed a hand over Bill's bare buttocks and groaned with a distorted pleasure, awaking in Bill a violent memory of Sister Perpetuata and Catherine. Tobias's other hand reached around and down the front of Bill's pants, as he used his upper body to pin his victim to the bunk. Bill twisted and turned and tried to rip the snaking fingers from between his legs, when they suddenly withdrew without further fight. Tobias jumped up off the bed.

'Aw, *Jesus*! It's a fucking *girl*!'

'What?!'

'He's a *she*!' said Tobias, shock and disappointment mingled on his face.

Frank looked from Tobias to the violently shivering figure curled up in the bed. If Bill had any hope that his ordeal was over, it was short-lived.

'Well, let me in there,' said Frank, shoving Tobias out of the way. 'I don't mind a bit of young cunt.'

In one swift movement he turned Bill over and ripped his shirt open. Frank paused briefly, staring at the bindings around Bill's breasts. Perplexed but not put off, Frank was trying to get his own pants down when Bill responded by smashing a palm straight into his nose.

'*Fuck*, you little *bitch*!' Frank howled, pinching at his nose as blood gushed down his shirt and onto the bunk.

'Come on, leave it. Let's get out of here,' said Tobias. 'Bloody sheila on a ship is only going to bring trouble and this one's a fuckin' freak as well.'

Frank ran his sleeve across his face and stood upright, staring at Bill crammed back as far as possible into the corner. He leaned so close into Bill's face that his bristles touched in places. Bill focused on the white flecks flying from the monster's mouth as he spoke.

'*You*, Billy *boy*, better keep your sick mouth shut, or you might not make it back to Townsville.'

Townsville. There was no way Bill was staying on the ship a minute past the next port. He knew he couldn't remain on board.

All that night he stayed awake, staring at the door, until it was time for his watch. His last watch. As soon as they docked in Cairns early the next morning, Bill, his bag over his shoulder, pushed past Tobias and onto the wharf.

'Oi! Where you going, *boy*? Who said you could go ashore?' Tobias yelled after him, but Bill didn't turn back. When he got to the Esplanade he started to run – as far from the water as he could. As far from the ugliness and exposure as he could.

27

When Bill finally stopped running, the vulnerability of having been discovered and the agony of being alone overwhelmed him. There had been other incidents such as these over the years. The fear of them had made it impossible for him to get close to anyone. He had almost allowed himself to forget his other self, having inhabited Bill for several years now. So much so that his body had changed with the physicality and psychology of working in the world of men. He *was* Bill now.

It was still early morning when the adrenaline finally subsided from his bloodstream. He walked through a park populated with massive Moreton Bay figs, decorated with the upside-down bodies of hundreds of flying foxes. The heat was beginning to bite. He sat down on one of the big tree roots. A short distance away, under another tree, was a small group of Aboriginal people – men, women and children. They looked like they had slept in the park. Some were trying to restart a small cooking fire. Bill watched as the group noticed him sitting there. He didn't feel anxious or worried. He had always felt safer among them than he did among whitefellas. He'd worked alongside plenty of Aboriginal blokes on the railways in New South Wales, and had spent weeks at a time around the camps along the riverbank near Moree and Dubbo.

'Hey, brother, you look like you could use a cuppa,' one of the men called. He was rake thin with a mop of sun-bleached, curly hair.

Bill waved away the offer, assuring the man he was fine.

'Suit yourself – plenty here if you change your mind, mate.'

Bill closed his eyes for a bit. When he opened them, two of the children were staring at him. He held his hand up to shield his eyes from the rising sun slipping through the branches and tried to smile at them. The kids ran back to their families. Bill got up and walked over to the group.

'G'day.'

'G'day,' several said back in harmony.

'I was wondering if there's a train back to Townsville?'

'Not yet, brother. It's on its way,' said the man who had offered the cup of tea earlier.

'What time will it be here?' Bill asked.

'About a year or two – track's not finished yet, but it's coming,' said the same fellow, causing everyone to laugh.

'Oh, right then,' said Bill, warm with embarrassment.

'Here, have this and sit down a while. What's your hurry? You need to be somewhere, bud?'

'I need to get back down south – pick up my horses. Or I might need to get a job, then pick up my horses.' Bill was voicing his thoughts aloud more than really speaking to the man.

'A job, eh? Not me,' said the lanky one. 'I'm waiting for my government block for fighting in that Great War. Like that train – be here sometime, eh.'

'Cut it out, Boonie. Can't you see young fulla's had a rough time?' said an older woman. The advice was promptly taken.

'Sure you don't want that brew, brother?' asked the woman.

Bill smiled and nodded, and accepted the tin cup she held out.

'If you don't need to get back right away, you might pick up a bit of work here. You said you got horses – why don't you try over the track? Sometimes they're looking for blokes. If you don't mind shovelling horse shit,' she said, not lifting her eyes as she sipped at her tea.

'I've shovelled plenty before – all my life, really.'

'That long, eh?' she smiled.

'I'll be needing to earn a quid, I suppose, to even get back south,' said Bill, considering for the first time that his hasty departure from the ship meant he would not be paid off. 'Which way is the track?'

The woman nodded her head westward, towards the Ranges.

'Keep going down that road over there, cross over Chinamen's Creek – you can't miss it.'

'Thank you, Missus. I'll give it a go,' Bill said, draining the cup before handing it back.

'Here, have some more,' she said, offering a refill. 'You look like you could use a pick-me-up.'

Bill had no argument with that, and settled into the cradle of the twisting tree roots. The idea of working at the racetrack appealed. He'd often thought about how his young mare, Adelaide, might go as a racer, and her bush experiences showed promise. She had the conformation of a horse built for speed. It was Bill who would need to learn the skills and strategies to ride with the professionals. He vividly recalled an incident from his childhood that had given him his first taste of what it must be like to ride a horse at full gallop.

~

Willie was about seven when she stuck her hand into a thorny bush to retrieve her hat and earned two little bleeding pinpricks for her trouble. She walked over to show her father how brave she was for not crying. On presenting her hand to her father, who had been breaking his newest stallion, he immediately went pale and, without a word between them, wrapped her arm tightly with his neckerchief. He then swung Willie up onto the still-frisky mount, swung himself up behind her and deftly opened the gate before galloping off towards the town road. Willie was shocked by the suddenness of it all but felt the thrill of a thousand-pound beast beneath her – thundering yet graceful, ears back, nostrils flared – and the rhythmic embrace of her father's arms.

'Did ya see it, girl?'

'See what, Dad?'

'What kind that bit ya?'

'Nothing bit me. I cut myself on the rosebush.'

Albert brought the horse to a sudden halt, sending dust and stones flying.

'You didn't see no snake, you sayin'?'

'No. Did you?'

Her father turned the stallion back towards the yards. It was some time before he had her up on a horse again, and she had to content herself with watching from a distance.

~

That feeling, perhaps more than any other from childhood, had remained strong, and now had begun to evolve into the idea of becoming a jockey. As Bill sat sipping on the tea that the strangers had shared with him, the events of the previous night began to rise in his body's cellular memory and he began to shake. The elderly woman, who had chided the lanky one earlier, raised her eyebrows and indicated with a nod of her head for Boonie to sit with the newcomer.

'Hey, you must be too hot in all that clobber, eh?' the man said to Bill. 'You shaking there, young fulla. You right?'

'I'm fine, thanks, mate. Little weary's all.'

'Well, you rest here a bit. No one going to bother you here.'

'Did you really fight in the War?'

'True story, brother. Now they want me to go sit down on the mission and say thank you,' he said.

'My father was in the Light Horse. Did you ever see any of that lot?'

'Light Horse. Big fullas, that lot. Nah, mate. I was 34th Battalion – mostly France and Belgium. Up to our elbows in mud every day.'

Bill felt the small glimmer of hope of some connection to his father fade away. As he sipped on the strong brew, his hands clamped around the enamel cup, Bill began to breathe deeply, relaxing back against the trunk of the fig. When he opened his eyes again, he was alone. The makeshift camp was gone, noiselessly and completely, except for the cup still cradled in his hands. He stood to brush himself down and noticed a mounted constable walking his horse across the grass towards him.

'You see any half-castes camped here this morning?'

'No, can't say I have,' said Bill, tossing the cold remains of his tea onto the ground, before leaning down to stow the cup in his pack.

'They often hang around here. Keep absconding from the mission. Sneaky buggers. You be careful, young fella.'

'I will,' said Bill, reaching out to scratch the horse's lips, which tried to nibble a few fingers as he did. 'I'm not staying here. On my way to the racetrack.'

'You a jockey, Son?'

'Not yet. Done plenty of work with horses, though. Thought I might give it a go.'

'You got the build for it, I reckon. Try old McInnes's stable. He often has new lads, because he doesn't tolerate any shenanigans. That's where I'd start.'

'Appreciate the advice, constable.'

With that, Bill dusted down his trousers, grabbed his kit and tipped his hat to the police officer, wondering how the group had managed to disappear so silently. As he walked away, he took note of the stockwhip roped around the officer's saddle horn. Bill wondered why a constable would need such an item, but he suspected the group would not be unaware of its purpose, given their stealthy departure. Bill hated brutality of any kind. Before he got to the edge of the park, his body finally released the violence it had been subjected to, and he vomited into a bush.

When Bill gathered himself, he wondered why he hadn't thought of it sooner. He already knew how to handle horses, and he was strong enough to manage thoroughbreds. He would be able to get his horses up from down south if he had somewhere to keep them. 'That's it! I'm going to be a jockey. No more ships for me.' In that moment Bill knew what he wanted. Racing required a distinct set of skills, but he knew he would be able to learn them. Everything he'd learned so far, he'd learned from careful observation. He also knew that he could not be caught out again, like he had been on the ship. Living in close quarters with others was no longer an option.

Bill Smith considered the money carefully stashed away in the inside pocket of his vest. Leaving the ship so suddenly meant a big financial blow. He wondered whether he would be able to recoup any wages owed, but the thought of going back to the waterfront made him shudder. If he could pick up work at the track quickly, he might just get by. But he would need something that paid a bit more than a start-up job. Still, he could check things out, at least, and then look for somewhere to stay.

When he reached the vicinity of the racecourse, Bill strolled along the laneway that ran behind the track. There he found individuals and whole families who seemed to have established themselves around the stables, well set up with camp stretchers, kerosene lamps and cooking areas. No one gave the young fella a second glance as he made his way along the lane. They were too engrossed in the busyness of the morning routine – bringing horses in and out of the stalls, washing them down, checking their feet. A few young kids – who should have been at school, Bill thought – were having too much fun running around, throwing hay and horse shit at each other, getting growled at by their mothers and then coming to a sudden halt when one of the men gave the closest boy a boot up the backside.

It was a tableau that he could have watched all day, but he needed to sort out somewhere to stay. As he left the laneway, he found himself in a street with several houses built high on thick stumps. It was a style of building Bill had only seen since travelling in the tropics. He loved the wide verandahs and open breezeways. He kept walking, without any real idea of where he was heading or what to do, until he passed a place that had a sign on the gate: *Room to rent. Single gentleman preferred.*

The room was a sleep-out – an enclosed end of a verandah that he could access via his own stairs without going into the main house. That should suit fine, he thought. Mrs Cleland was recently widowed, and let Bill know very promptly that there would be no visitors entertained in his room and no reason for him to enter the main house, unless invited, but that she would expect a bit of help with the garden in exchange for an evening meal if he so desired.

'That's if you're up for it. My Harold was quite a keen gardener – and a fair bit sturdier-looking than you, young fella. Are you sure you could handle the bougainvillea? It takes a bit of wrangling.'

'No problem, Mrs Cleland. Sounds fine. I don't expect to be here too long. I'm after some work at the track, so if I get something I'll be able to get my own place.'

'The track. The devil's playground, you mean. Hope you're not a gambling man? The late Mr Cleland was a little too fond of a bet. When they built this new racetrack here, he was over there every chance. Beer in one hand and betting ticket in the other, he was happy as a pig in mud. But his heart gave out last year. That's why I need to take in lodgers – but it doesn't mean I'm not particular.'

'Of course. Sorry to hear that. I just like being with the horses.'

'Not a drinker, are you? I wouldn't be tolerating a drinker in the house.'

'I don't drink, Missus. Never cared for it. I even got a reference from the ship's captain that'll tell you.'

Mrs Cleland gave the young man a thorough twice-over, before giving in to his conviction.

'Well then. I'll give you a week, and we'll see how you go.'

~

The room was small, but the bed was the best Bill had slept on for some time. Maybe ever, he thought, lying back and letting cool air flow over him. There was a mosquito net hung from the ceiling, and wooden shutters at one end. It was all he needed for now. His possessions were few. He considered his clothes now hanging on the couple of hooks behind the door and, as he lay there, he began to think about Catherine and the first time she'd seen him dressed as a man.

'So, what then? I'd be your sweetheart, would I? I think you've lost your mind, Willie Smith.'

The idea was ludicrous. Even Bill had thought the disguise would be temporary, but the longer it went on the more natural it became. The transformation suited a life on the move, but now, for the first time in ages, Bill found himself thinking about settling somewhere. The Aboriginal family in the park, the families living behind the racetrack – each had something that Bill's life was missing. They had laughter, and they had each other.

Bill hadn't had someone to laugh with since Catherine. There had been some good times with the crew of the *Mandura*, and a few of the fellows from the Sailors' Rest, and some of the people he'd met working in the outback – but no one had ever come close to filling the gaping hole that Catherine's absence had left in his life. There was little to laugh about, anyway, he thought.

Bill could still feel the shock of being assaulted, and the fear that it could have been worse. Would it have been worse, he wondered? Would dying have been worse than what Tobias had in mind to do? Male or female, either way, Bill felt a wave of nausea rise in his throat. He tried hard to push it down. But there was something more to it than the feeling of danger. Something that followed Bill even into the safer places he occupied.

It occurred to him that this was loneliness. Being alone and feeling lonely were two different things, he realised. Getting close to anyone was always going to be risky. He studied himself in the tiny mirror left on the nightstand next to a washbowl and towel. How lovely would it be to feel someone's touch that was not brutal or threatening? He put his hand to his face, where the memory of Catherine's last touch could not be erased. *'No. No. Can't be. I have to keep myself to myself. That's all there is to it.'*

28

The travel clock was a piece of ingenuity, perfect for someone who didn't have a lot of room for a more ornate or bulky timekeeper. Its alarm was loud enough to shake him from his sleep, but not so loud as to annoy Mrs Cleland in the house. It had belonged to Mr Cleland, but the new lodger seemed to have won the approval of the landlady and she had given it to him to use while he was there. Set for 4am, wound five times and turned away from the bed, because the luminous paint on its hands and numbers was surprisingly bright.

He'd got a job at the new Northern Brewery, but Bill saw it as only temporary. He just wanted to keep it long enough to make the money to get his horses up from Brisbane, cover his rent and hopefully find a job doing trackwork or, if he was lucky, riding as a jockey. But the brewery was to prove a lifeline for the leaner times, and Bill had a job anytime he needed for years to come.

His shift at the brewery didn't start until 7am, giving him a good few hours to spend at the track beforehand. Most mornings he would set off before dawn, slide under the cyclone fence that surrounded the track and wander down to the 6-furlong mark. No one could see him in the still dark. The cool of the night meeting the building heat of the tropical morning created a mix of sea mist and morning fog. Bill observed the horses, the riders and especially the trainers. He listened to their instructions and to the discussions afterwards. He loved this time of day. Cannon Park was one of the bigger racecourses in the north and a busy place, pre-dawn, for trainers and trackwork.

This was his routine for several weeks, until the day big-name jockey Joe Grech fell from his mount in front of Bill. It wasn't a friendly welcome. It put him on the wrong side of Grech from the start, who didn't appreciate the 'girly-lookin' bludger' making him look foolish and trying to ingratiate himself with the trainer, Charlie McInnes. Bill's youthful appearance and less-than-masculine voice earned him the nickname of 'Girly' that day – intended as an insult by Joe Grech but taken on more amicably by the old trainer. Bill 'Girly' Smith didn't know it then, but the birth of that nickname was also the start of his racing career, which would last nearly fifty years.

Charlie McInnes had one of the bigger stables north of Townsville. Although he could attract the elite riders, he was also open to training up his own jockeys, who usually started as stablehands and strappers until Charlie gave them the nod. He was discerning about who he let ride his horses. Every day there would be several young hopefuls, sitting on what looked to Bill like rocking horses for grown-ups – models made for practice, with crops and reins, before you got anywhere near a thoroughbred. Bill didn't mind. He was up for learning all he could about riding to race. It was a few weeks after he'd started as a stablehand that McInnes decided to give Bill some trackwork.

'I can see you got a way with the horses, but can you ride to instructions, Girly?'

'Sure can, Mr McInnes. I can ride exactly how you want me to. I don't even need a whip – I know how to get the best out of any horse here,' said Bill.

'Steady on, now. I don't need you to get the best out my horses, I need to know you can follow instructions. It's my job to bring them along.'

Bill could see the old trainer having second thoughts, and he tried desperately to reel in his excitement.

'Ride to instructions, Boss. Absolutely I can.'

'Grech's pissing off down to Townsville for a bit, so I need someone on Proud Dancer for next month. Reckon you and young Barrett can try a few starts for me? Run them about 3 furlongs, and then go back to the starting line and do it again. See how fast you can get away.'

Bill's body was tense with anticipation, his eyes fixed ahead, waiting for the signal. The first few times, Barrett's horse got away quicker, until Bill started to sense the drop of the rope and feel Dancer's readiness through the bit. It was a feeling like no other, when the mass of muscle and sinew thundered away down the track in one explosive burst from the start, Bill falling in with the rhythm, letting Dancer do what Dancer – and Bill – seemed born to do.

After a few days of trackwork, Charlie thrust his stable's racing gear at Bill.

'This Saturday. Race One on Son of Amar, the gelding, and then you can have Dancer for Race Two. You up for it?'

'Too right I am, Mr McInnes. You won't regret it,' said Bill.

'We'll see come Saturday, eh.'

Bill took the McInnes colours back to Mrs Cleland's that evening and asked her to help him take in the pants a little. As he studied the full effect in the mirror, Bill's excitement spiralled into panic. He would be expected to get changed before the race in the jockeys' room with all the boys. His joy fell away momentarily, until he came up with an idea.

~

As the jockeys were bustling around the jockeys' room getting ready for the first race, Charlie McInnes put his head in, searching for his new rider.

'Where the bloody hell is Smith? Has anyone seen him?'

'Not yet, Mr McInnes.'

'Nah, he's probably in the dunny, shitting himself,' said one of the jockeys, gaining a smattering of laughter from the hoops and a scowl from the old trainer, who walked off muttering about knowing better than to trust a bloody drifter.

Just as McInnes was considering a replacement rider, Bill arrived, looking dapper in his pinstriped trousers, vest and coat, matched with a little green fedora.

'You're late, Smith. I was just about to give the ride to someone else. Hurry up and get yourself changed and get out here so I can give you your instructions.'

'It's alright, Boss. I'm ready to go – be back in a tick.'

Bill walked briskly into the jockeys' room and removed his coat, vest and shirt to reveal McInnes's stable colours underneath. He slipped off his trousers that hid his breeches, folded them neatly on the bench and pulled on his riding boots. None of the other jockeys were taking too much notice of the new rider as they each busied themselves for the first race.

Bill went back outside to find Charlie rolling a cigarette, binoculars tucked under his arm.

'Ready, Boss.'

Charlie looked around at the jockey, fully kitted, eager to go.

'Strewth, that was quick, Girly. If you're half as quick out there today, it'll be a fine thing.'

29

His first official race at Cannon Park was enough for Bill to know that he was meant to ride. He didn't win the first run, but he did come a respectable fourth on Son of Amar, a horse just back from a spell. His next ride, on Proud Dancer, was exactly as he had envisaged it. Dancer was a horse that loved to gallop. She needed little encouragement to get out front and stay there.

If Bill was expecting praise from the trainer for his first-ever win, he would have been disappointed – but it wasn't winning that most attracted Bill. It was the build-up – the pulsing activity as jockeys, strappers and trainers exchanged instructions; the cheers from the crowd when their horses appeared in the saddling enclosure; the owners backslapping and promising a little something extra if their jockey brought it home that day. It was an energy that Bill could feel in his bones. An energy that drove him on the track.

'A jockey who can ride to instructions – about bloody time,' said Charlie on Bill's first win, showing no more emotion than if he had come dead last. It was enough for Bill. He was exactly where he wanted to be. He loved the way Dancer seemed to know that this whole carnival was about them. For some horses, the bigger crowds made them a little anxious, and a good rider knew how to settle the skittish ones; but most thoroughbreds, like Proud Dancer, knew that it was their day – the way she pranced and snorted and flicked her mane, as if to say, 'That's right, look at me.' Bill couldn't help noticing that there were a few jockeys who seemed to share the same vanity.

~

The first time Bill met Nifty Peters he was holding court in the jockeys' room at Cannon Park having returned from a season in Townsville. The other jockeys seemed to be loving Nifty's tall stories and bawdy jokes. Most of them, at least. The men were in various states of dress, coming and going from the showers, some naked, some with towels wrapped around their waists. Nifty was standing starkers in the middle of the room, apparently convinced that his was an impressive member that warranted viewing by all and sundry.

'Put some pants on, for gawd's sake, Nifty,' yelled the chief steward as he entered the room. 'You're not a bloody stallion, you know.'

'A couple of ladies might disagree with you there, Mr Bannon,' said Nifty, giving a wink to the others as he pulled on his silks.

'Well, what have we got here, boys?' said Nifty, noticing the jockey he had only heard about, but not yet met, stowing his gear in the corner of the room.

Bill was dressed in his street clothes, which wasn't unusual in itself. Everyone turned up in their street clothes, but always with their riding gear in a kit bag. But Bill didn't have any colours to hang on the peg. As he took off his shirt, Nifty noticed that Bill was already wearing his colours underneath. It was the same with the bottom half. All he needed to do was to take off his outer clothes and pull on his boots.

'What's this, then?' said Nifty. 'We got a shy little petal here, have we?'

Bill continued with the business of getting ready for his first race of the day.

'Oi. You. New chum,' said Nifty. 'What's the go? Heard about Nifty's knob and feel a bit intimidated, eh?'

The others in the room laughed. Bill didn't look up. One of the other riders stood up and placed himself between Bill and Nifty, holding out his hand.

'Welcome, mate. We haven't met yet, have we? Fred Jackson. Jacko,' he said with a grin.

Bill offered his hand in return and pulled it away after a brief shake.

'Thanks, mate. Bill Smith.'

'*Girly* Smith, you mean,' said Nifty. 'That's what they call you, I heard.' Nifty turned back to his fan club, those jockeys who hung on his every word. He rolled his eyes and made a gesture that had them all in stitches. He crooked his little finger and held it in front of his crotch, which everyone understood meant to imply that the new fellow was shy for a reason.

'Time to move, gentlemen,' said Mr Bannon. There followed a flurry of shirts being buttoned and tucked in, boots stamped into place and helmets, goggles and crops collected. Bill was happy to be the last out into the mounting yard.

'You right there, Son? Don't mind Nifty. He loves an audience,' said Mr Bannon.

'I'm good, thank you, Sir.'

'Strewth. You're not from around here, are you? Manners, boys. Did you hear that?' he said, nodding at the other stewards.

An instant warmth for the chief steward flooded Bill. It was a feeling of safety. As he took his place in the line-up by the 11-furlong mark, Bill silently urged his horse, Grey Moon, to also feel safe and to trust him to look after them both.

'They're all set now, waiting for the starter's gun in the Maiden Guineas here at Cannon Park.'

'Hey, Girly. You'll be squealing for your mummy if you get in my way out there.' Nifty Peters was well known for trying to get under the skin of other riders just before the jump.

'Don't take any notice of that one, Bill. He's all mouth,' said Jacko.

Bill smiled at Jacko, whose eyes suddenly fixed on the starting ropes, causing him to do the same. The clatter of surging mounts, forty hooves on the hard dirt track, was deafening. Despite getting out well on Grey Moon, his first of three rides for McInnes that day, Bill was boxed in for most of the race. By the time he found a gap, Nifty Peters was raising his whip in the air as he sailed past the finishing post.

Back in the saddling yard, the trainer was already negotiating for a change of rider for the next start. It was meant to be Bill's second race on Proud Dancer.

'I'll do better, Mr McInnes. Don't take me off Dancer. I just—'

'I know what you "just", lad,' replied Charlie McInnes. 'You just got boxed in like a fucken fruitcake sent for Christmas. Can't risk it, Girly. You sit this one out. You got lucky here last time. You just need a little more time to learn the game.'

Bill pulled the saddle off Grey Moon and walked briskly to the weighing room, wiping his hand roughly across his face in an effort to remove the tears that he didn't want anyone to see. Nifty was all smugness as he pushed past Bill into the room.

'Looks like old McInnes finally come to his senses. I'll take Dancer for a spin now. Grech knew how to handle her – she'll be doing the quickstep for me when I'm on her.'

Bill stepped onto the scales to have his weight recorded before heading to the change area, where he stood in the middle of the empty room.

'I'll flog your bloody guts if you hurt Dancer,' he said to no one.

But Nifty had followed him back into the changing room.

'What are you on about, Girly?'

Bill didn't respond. He was worried that if he did, he might not be able to pull himself up from wanting to pound on Nifty's head. Nifty grabbed the colours for the McInnes stable and started to put them on, when he noticed a small tear in the back. Superstitions kept close company with a lot of riders, and Nifty Peters had one about his silks.

'Hey, give us your kit, will ya? This one's torn to buggery,' he said to Bill, who was still wearing his own silks but would be sitting out this next race.

'I'm not giving you my shirt.'

Nifty moved right up close to Bill, who stood defiant in return. The irate rider grabbed Bill by the shirtfront and pulled him up so their noses were nearly touching.

'Give us ya bleeding colours, ya bludger.'

Bill was on tiptoes, but not giving in.

'No one wears my kit but me, so bugger off,' he said, a tremor in his voice betraying the strength of his words.

Just as Nifty was pulling back one arm and making a fist, Jacko stepped between them, having entered the change room just in time to hear the threat.

'Take these, Nift. I won't need them till the fifth,' he said, holding up a McInnes stable shirt.

Nifty reluctantly released his grip on Bill's shirtfront, but not without a solid shove that put Bill back on the bench. He grabbed the shirt from Jacko and said, 'Something queer about that bugger,' adding over his shoulder at Bill, 'Don't think there'll always be someone around to save your arse, either.'

Bill did all he could to hide the trembling of his body as Jacko slapped him on the back as he went past to ready himself for the next race, saying, 'Better luck next time, Girly. You won't let that happen again, I bet.'

'Cheers, Jacko – mate.'

Mate. Could Bill really say they were mates? He wanted to be. He just didn't really know how. Besides, being mates would bring with it a whole lot of expectations that Bill wouldn't be able to meet – like joining in drinking sessions, talking about women in the ways men did. The very things he'd had to run from before.

30

Bill's habit of arriving in his street clothes and stripping down to reveal his silks beneath inevitably attracted even wider attention. Most were amused by this peculiarity, but their entertainment was also tinged with curiosity that sometimes turned to obsession. Was he just a shy bloke, acting, as his nickname suggested, a little 'girly'? What didn't he want anyone to see?

As he grew older, he learned to deal with the inquisitiveness more assertively, outwitting all the planners and schemers who hoped to solve the mystery of why Girly Smith behaved as he did. Still, it was exhausting always having to be alert to those who might let their curiosity run riot.

'How would he get on with a sheila if he can't even get his kit off in front of the blokes?' fellow jockey Ray Falco snickered one day as the riders were getting ready for their next race, up at the Tolga track on the Tablelands.

'If that fella's ever been with a woman, I'll walk backwards to Bourke,' said Nifty Peters.

'Reckon he's a virgin, do ya, Nifty – that what you're saying?'

'Course he bloody is! Dainty little petal. Only thing he's ever ridden'd be something with four legs.'

'Well, you'd know, Nifty. If anyone'd know about being a virgin, you would, I reckon,' said Falco.

'That's right,' said Nifty, taking a moment to consider whether he was meant to agree or take offence.

Nifty had a swag of speculations about Bill that he entertained the boys with between races, and not discreetly. Bill heard every word but, as always, kept his mind on what he was there for.

But not everyone thought Nifty was funny. One of the apprentices tried to come to Bill's defence. Ted 'Tadpole' Barrett knew what it was like to be bullied. His own stammer robbed Tadpole of being taken seriously, but it didn't stop him from speaking up

'D-did youse ever think maybe he's got a t-terrible injury that he d-doesn't want no one to see?' Tadpole said, when he thought Bill wasn't listening.

'Has he? Is that why he won't get changed in front of us?' asked Ray Falco. 'Have you seen something?'

'No. I just don't think it's right carrying on about a bloke who's not hurting anyone, that's all.'

Some of the jockeys busied themselves with their race preparations, feeling a little sheepish about their interest, but others were now more intrigued than ever, and waited for Bill to leave the room before putting their heads together in a conspiratorial huddle. Bill sensed something going on and, ever on the alert, stopped just outside the door, pretending to fix his boot.

'Right, we're going to settle this once and for all,' said Nifty. 'We're gonna drill a couple of holes in the lavatory wall before the last race. Girly always uses the same cubicle, so when he goes in there we'll be able to get around the other side and see what all the fuss is about.'

'But he doesn't get changed,' said Ray Falco. 'He just puts his clothes on over his silks.'

'Yeah, but a man's gotta take a leak sometime, doesn't he? And he always goes in that far one, have you noticed?'

'Come to think of it, I've never seen Girly use the urinals,' said Ray. 'Reckon you're onto something there, Nifty.'

The boys were wound up like clock springs in anticipation after Ray went and grabbed a drill from the maintenance shed and, under Nifty's instructions, made a couple of peepholes in the toilet wall in readiness. The remaining races were almost secondary in the minds of a lot of the fellas on the day of Nifty's masterplan. Bill seemed to be the only one with his focus on business. When he found himself in the winner's circle on three races out of an eight-card draw, he was happy, to say the least.

'Good on you, Girly! That'll shut their t-traps up good and proper,' said Tadpole as he unsaddled after coming in a reasonable fourth. Clearly Tadpole was no stranger to being the subject of derision himself, and Bill felt a little sorry for the youngster.

After the last race, the jockeys tried to act normal, but all eyes flickered from Bill to Nifty, Nifty to Bill.

'Ya did good out there today, Girly,' said Nifty.

Nifty had pulled off his colours and his boots and flung a towel over his shoulder as if readying to go into the showers. Bill made no such effort to disrobe, as was his usual routine, and nodded in acknowledgement at Nifty's faint praise. He finally grabbed his street clothes and walked down to the toilets. When he did, Nifty put his shirt back on and headed around to the outside of the cubicle that Bill now occupied. Tadpole was anxious, as he knew what was about to go down.

'Why d-don't you leave the poor bloke alone?' said Tadpole as Nifty pushed past him.

'W-w-w-why don't you fuck off and mind your own business?' said Nifty. 'Or do you want us to find out what you got down there as well?'

Nifty was eager to take up his position at one of the holes, his gormless offsiders busily jostling for who would go first to peer through the other. He swung around angrily and signalled at them with no ambiguity to shut the fuck up, before returning to his position. The implicit hierarchy established, Ray Falco elbowed his way in beside Nifty, and they looked at each other for a moment in anticipation of what they were about to see. Like soldiers going into combat, Nifty gave the nod and they each pressed an eye up against one of the tiny holes.

'Jesus, bloody hell. My eye, my eye!' yelped Nifty immediately.

'Shit almighty, that stings – what the bloody hell?' said Ray.

As the two stepped back, rubbing their eyes furiously, they appeared to be making it worse, spreading the pain from one side of their faces to the other. Nifty tentatively touched his cheek and brought his fingers up to his nose. He could smell the unmistakable shock of horse liniment, which had been smeared around the peepholes.

Even with Nifty and Ray jumping around in a stinging mess, a couple of the others decided to put their eyes up to the holes as well, catching enough of the residue to become similarly uncomfortable, but also catching a glimpse of Bill staring calmly back at them, still wearing his colours.

When Bill walked out of the toilet block and past the little gang, they were still trying to wipe the liniment from their faces.

'See ya next week, fellas. You should get that eye seen to, Nifty. Looks nasty, eh.'

31

Bill's time at Mrs Cleland's had been comfortable and enjoyable. It worked well having his own private access, and the occasional meal with Mrs Cleland was appreciated now and then, but Bill was now keen to get back to Brisbane to retrieve Addy and Missus. Addy had been a racehorse briefly, but her owners had given up on her and sold her to the milk cart driver who, of course, found her unsuited to that line of work. Bill could never bring himself to think poorly of a horse – it had to be the people who were wrong. He had seen Addy's potential as he'd galloped her along Henley Beach back in her namesake city, and in the couple of bush races he had entered her in. He was excited to see more of what she could do.

Bill was about to tell Mrs Cleland of his plans when she got in first to tell him that she would be moving to Innisfail to be with her sister, who had fallen ill and needed full-time care, so Bill would have to find other accommodation as soon as possible. He thanked her for taking him in, for cooking for him and for lending him the travel clock so he could get up early. And he told her that he would miss her. This woman who had been so gruff and suspicious initially had turned out to have a big, generous heart, and Bill realised he had grown quite fond of her.

'Go on with you – don't be getting all sentimental,' she said, eyes glistening.

'Let me get your alarm clock before I forget.'

'You keep that, young fella. Mr Cleland bought that in Townsville, but the ticking always kept me awake. No, you keep it, and that's that,' she said, turning to go.

~

Before heading to Brisbane to retrieve his horses, Bill found a place with stables to rent, on the south side of Cannon Park. Or, rather, he found stables, with a small bunk room attached, but it was all he would need for now. He couldn't wait to bring his horses back and let McInnes have a look at his Adelaide girl.

But on arriving at the property north of Brisbane where he had agisted them, all his excitement was quickly punctured. Bill was not someone who left debts behind. He had paid his agistment fees regularly, and when he was ready to head south to collect his horses, he had sent a telegram advising the landowner of his arrival date. There had been no return communication suggesting that anything was amiss in the arrangement.

'What do you mean, they're gone? I sent you a telegram.'

'Yeah, well, like I said, the yards were sold, so I needed all the horses gone. Not my bloody fault, now, is it? How was I to know you were really coming back for them – they'd been here over a year.'

'Yes, and I was paying you – and you kept taking my payments, eh.'

His two mares had been sent to the slaughterhouse only two days before he arrived. There was no point in arguing. What was done was done.

Bill was shattered with grief and guilt. He hung around Brisbane for several days, going from knackery to knackery in the hope of finding his girls still alive. The landowner had been strangely vague about where they might have been sent. Bill was about to give up when he decided to check one more slaughterhouse near Caboolture, where he found a record of Missus having been accepted for 'dispatch'. She had been 'processed' two days earlier, he was told. There was no record of Adelaide at all.

Bill's heartbreak was palpable. The two mares had been such reliable friends – especially his darling Addy. So steadfast, so affectionate. It took several days before he could muster up the will to get moving again. He had lain in his bed in the boarding house where he'd booked a room – not bothering to eat, not wanting to interact with anyone – until the manager knocked on the door to check whether he was alive or not.

'I'm alive,' said Bill, with a tinge of disappointment in his voice. 'I'll head off in the morning, if that's alright.'

In an effort to pick himself up a bit before heading back to Cairns, Bill decided to attend Brisbane's famous Eagle Farm Racecourse. It was much grander than the courses he was used to, and the facilities would be envied by those up north. He was wandering around the stalls where the strappers and horses waited between races when he caught a glimpse of a big chestnut mare that looked all too familiar. She looked like Addy, but had a blaze on her forehead. Bill thought his grief was getting the better of him. The feet were different, as well – this mare had two front socks. 'You're being a goose,' he said to himself, but still he moved closer to get a look at the mare's brand, which also was just different enough from Addy's to make him question whether this wasn't the saddest ever case of wishful thinking. That was until the owner of the agistment property arrived, form guide in hand, binoculars strung around his thick neck, and – oblivious to Bill's presence – told the strapper to make sure his horse was ready because there was a lot riding on her today.

'You scheming, mongrel bastard!' yelled Bill from behind him.

At first, the would-be racehorse owner tried to protest that Bill had it wrong.

'What are you on about?'

'That's my Adelaide!'

'Your bloody Adelaide went to the knackery, because you didn't come to collect her. This is my horse, Bella Lady.'

'Be figged it is,' said Bill, approaching the mare, who had already started to pull at her halter on hearing a familiar voice. Bill grabbed a nearby water bucket and wiped the mare's face where the star-shaped blaze was, only to see it melt away.

The crowd that had gathered and the wide-eyed young strapper didn't know who to listen to, until Bill threatened to call the constables and the bloke began to lose his false indignation.

'Take her, then. We'll call it even for what you owe me,' he said, to the crowd more than to Bill.

'What *I* owe *you*? You lying, thieving bastard!' shouted Bill, striding purposefully towards the man.

With that, the would-be horse thief turned and legged it before the constabulary arrived.

Bill took his mare, and promised her he would never leave her again. The joy of being reunited with Addy, however, was tempered by the grief of losing Missus in such an awful way. Never again would any animal of Bill Smith's end its life hung from a hook, defleshed and dissected. He hated knackeries, and the cruel bastards who often delighted in their work there. Bill made it his mission to wreak mischief on their operations at any opportunity, and helped many an animal escape from them over the years.

~

Riding for Charlie McInnes, Bill learned all he could from the old trainer. He learned about what kind of feed to give a horse in the lead-up to race days, when to turn a horse out for a spell, what to do about any lameness or sore spots. Bill was a quick study of all things equine. People, however, were another matter. During his first ten years in Cairns he rode mostly for McInnes, who always treated him fairly. So it came as a terrible blow one morning, in March 1940, to learn that the old trainer had passed away in his sleep. All the strappers and riders standing around in the dawn light that morning, waiting for McInnes who had always turned up before them, sensed that something was amiss. It was Bill who offered to go to his house near the track to check on the old man, only to find the doctor consoling Charlie's wife.

As Bill turned to go back and tell the others at the track, Mrs McInnes called him over. 'You'll be needing this,' she said, placing Charlie's trainer's watch in Bill's hands.

'I can't take this, Missus.'

'You can and you will, Girly. Charlie had a soft spot for you, and he reckoned you'd make a good trainer one day. It was the last thing he won, only last year. He won't be needing it anymore.'

~

Bill Smith didn't achieve the accolades of some of the big-name jockeys, but he was reliable and trustworthy and seemed to be able to bring home the hardware on the big occasions. With the crowds chanting 'Go, Girly!' and 'You beauty, Girly!' the nickname wasn't going anywhere, but it came to be said with real affection, as the peculiar rider with a reputation for keeping to himself and his animals became a permanent feature of North Queensland racing for nearly fifty years.

Charlie McInnes had helped Bill to train up Adelaide, and they'd shared some successes at the smaller tracks around the Tablelands. They had got through some hard years together, including the Great Depression, which had affected the whole world. McInnes's stables were just picking up again when another World War loomed. Unlike the first one, which had been fought so far from home, this war was right on their doorstep – but Charlie would not be around to see it.

As the men of the district started joining up, Bill was quietly relieved that he exceeded the age limit by just a year. He had no idea how he might explain not being called up otherwise. But he was also torn, wanting to do his bit for the war effort.

With the American military taking over Cannon Park Racecourse, and large numbers of women and children sent south, Bill was sure that horseracing was likely to end for the duration of the war. He and everyone else, however, were pleasantly surprised to find that the government was determined to keep it going, to help keep up morale and divert attention from the fact that the Japanese had already made it to Papua New Guinea.

~

Bill had now lived through two World Wars, Spanish flu, the Great Depression and almost three decades in the saddle – but he still didn't have any place to call his own. Or any*one* to call his own. His special mare, Adelaide, had lived until the age of about thirty. Bill was having his morning cuppa one day, in the squatter's chair outside the bunk room attached to his rented stables, watching her standing under an old

Moreton Bay fig when she just dropped to the ground. He threw down his cup and ran over to the old horse. He cradled her head in his lap, stroking her face as he watched the life quickly fade out of her.

It broke his heart to see his beautiful mare, his last connection to South Australia, being hauled up by a crane and taken away. He couldn't bear the thought of Addy ending up like Missus, so he raced out to stop the truck before it got to the gate.

'I'll give you twenty quid if you'll help me bury her instead,' he implored the driver.

'Not allowed to do that these days, mate.'

'Who needs to know? We can dig a hole over in that corner,' replied Bill, with such pain in his voice that the driver couldn't refuse.

Bill took some comfort, in his grief, in the fact that Addy had just dropped from old age, and that he hadn't had to use a bullet on her. There was no way he could have looked into her trusting eyes and pulled the trigger on his old friend. Not with Addy. He would eventually have to do it with other animals whose endings would not come so peacefully, but he was grateful that Addy had gone down easy.

~

Girly Smith was still riding in his mid-fifties, but his ability to bounce back from the odd fall or bump had lessened noticeably. He was now feeling every ache, and it was getting harder to argue with trainers that he was still fit enough to hold his own with the younger crop of jockeys in the north. Townsville and Cairns had begun to attract elite riders and horses after the War, with prize money worth the journey for southern racing people.

He was sitting in his squatter's chair one day, looking out towards the sea. The clouds rolling in from the east had a familiar greenish tinge to them. The cyclone off the coast was meant to be weakening, but instead it had turned back towards the city, threatening to make landfall over the weekend. Mangoes littered the ground, helped along by the strengthening winds. The aroma was overwhelming. Bill started to think about how many cyclones he had endured, and pictured some of the places he had been to up on the Tablelands. A good place to retire, he thought.

His little mate, a stray dog that had recently made itself at home in the corner of one of the horse stalls, came to sit beside him.

'You still here, are you?' said Bill. 'I told you before you'd best find some other soft touch.'

The dog just glanced at Bill and flopped down, paws outstretched, as if to say, 'I don't believe you.'

'You look a little like Ding, did I ever tell you that? Only you're a bit of a rustier colour than he was. Rusty. Yes, that's what you are.'

That was enough. The dog now had a name, and Bill had another dog. There'd been a few over the years, each of whom had found Bill, despite his repeated insistence of 'never again' as they had each eventually succumbed to accident, illness or malevolence. They'd each found a way in that people had not. This was a smart little dog, too. Knew enough to keep away from the horses' feet, was good at catching snakes and was a good listener. Rusty watched Bill now as he surveyed the sky and announced, 'Well, we'd best secure everything, eh Rus, or we might just find a croc in the Johnstone River wearing one of our bridles.'

~

As Bill entered his late fifties, he began to think more seriously about a life after riding and the possibility of moving to the Tablelands. He'd already had a longevity as a jockey that few got to enjoy. But before he could retire, he needed a win. Not a believer in keeping money in banks – a hangover from the Depression era – Bill's tin of pound notes was looking nothing short of grim. Driving up the Gillies Range now to a Tablelands meet with his current mare, a gentle giant known as Stella May, the old truck's gears kept slipping. He couldn't afford for the truck to go on him. If there was no place today, there'd be no repair to the truck, and without the truck, there'd be no travelling on the circuit.

Realistically, Bill knew this would be his last ride anyway. A doctor really should've seen him after that fall onto his elbow last year, but he'd never been one for doctors. It had happened during trackwork early in the morning and, with no one around to notice, Bill reckoned paying it no attention himself was the best approach. As it turned out, although his expert home remedies were renowned when it came to horses, fixing his own fractured elbow was a stretch too far. Now the elbow was stiff and as bowed as his legs, and he struggled to pull up a thoroughbred at full gallop.

Riding had been Bill's longest relationship. As he brushed down Stella May, he took his time.

'Well, girl, be good to old Bill today. It'll be our last outing together. Don't you tell anyone, now. Don't want any fuss.'

He flung the saddlecloth across Stella's back and ducked beneath her neck. The track-smart mare turned her head and, grabbing the cloth in her teeth, flung it to the ground. Bill's hands found air instead of the other side of the saddlecloth.

'Gonna be like that is it, Missy?' He stepped back around to pick up the cloth, shook it out and replaced it carefully in position. 'Hope you're going to leave it there this time?' he said, eyeballing Stella. 'We need the purse today, girl. If I'm going to be able to hand the riding over to a younger fella, we at least need to place. So, no nonsense if it's all the same to you, darlin' heart.'

It had taken a lot of years, but Bill 'Girly' Smith had finally won the respect of many of his fellow hoops – not to mention the crowds, who loved the long odds he usually got. He hadn't won an exceptional number of races as a jockey, but he did have a way of pulling off the big events when it really counted. He hoped today would be one of those days.

The race caller ran through the field. Bill took his time in the enclosure. He could feel every painful joint. He tried to bend his bung elbow, but it was now permanently fused in place at an angle of about 110 degrees. If anyone had ever noticed that boomerang-shaped left arm, they'd never said. Bill usually had his crop, his binoculars or the reins tucked in there so it appeared mostly natural, but he knew he was riding with only half power. He took one last look around the grounds before heading out onto the track.

'Hey, Girly, I put twenty quid on you, mate – don't ride like one out there,' yelled someone from the crowd.

Bill had heard it all before. He ran his hand down Stella's neck, stood up in the stirrups and let her take herself out to the starting gates.

'Go, Girly!'

'Onya, Girly!'

'You show 'em, Girly!'

For all the taunts and teasing, there was also a lot of support for the colourful and quirky 'Girly' Smith. He would miss being in the saddle, but at least he now had his trainer's registration, and there would be many years left with his much-loved horses.

'Let's go, Stell.'

It wasn't his best ride. Bill's action was severely compromised by his left elbow, but he managed to place third. The prize money, even for first place, would barely have covered the costs of getting to the track; but Bill Smith did something that day that he had never done, and the shame of it stayed with him for a long time afterwards. He'd placed a large bet two days earlier with one of the unregistered bookies on another horse at longer odds – Flight of Fancy, ridden by a young apprentice. When Flight of Fancy began to push through the pack at the last turn, Bill had eased off the pressure on Stella. Could they have won? He had to convince himself that they couldn't – and he also had to convince the stewards, who wanted a closer look at the race. His reputation had always been for playing a straight bat, and he did not want his last race to be marred with a charge of not riding his mount to capacity.

'Fair dinkum, Mr Ross,' he said, addressing the steward's inquiry. 'She just run out of steam on me on the straight. Her fitness could do with a little more work, is all – and I'll make sure she gets it, now that I'm hanging up my saddle.' Bill eyed the panel to see who'd picked up the cue.

'You retiring, Girly?'

'From riding, I reckon. Gonna give training my full attention. The old body's not what it used to be.'

'Well, that sounds like a fine idea. I think we can put this one to bed, eh gentlemen?'

'Good luck, Girly.'

'All the best, old mate.'

He accepted their well wishes, handshakes and back slaps. Later, he would collect his winnings from the bookie, who was from down south and hadn't recognised the jockey when he'd placed the bet, but would give him a curious study before handing over the money.

Bill knew how close he had come to ruin. He headed back to the jockeys' room, where he made himself a solemn promise to never again compromise himself or one of his horses like that. He pulled his clothes on over his silks for the last time. From now on, he would be WA Smith, Trainer, and his street clothes would do just fine.

Part 4

Far North Queensland, 1978

Put me back the way I was ...

32

Nursing notes: 18/5/78 06:30. Restless o/night. Spiking temps. Increased confusion.

'Don't take me off Dancer, Mr McInnes. I'll do better, I promise.'

Bill was talking in his sleep, his scrapbook opened to a page with a photograph of a horse labelled Proud Dancer. Nurse Maureen Bannon, having just come on shift, observed her patient closely. His body was shaking. He seemed to be talking to people who were not in the room. She felt his forehead. Maureen thought it best to rouse him, as she was concerned about his temperature.

'You alright there, Mr Smith?'

Bill opened his eyes, taking a moment to orient himself.

'Oh, it's you, Missy. I thought I was back at the track for a bit there.'

'You were having a bit of a chat in your sleep. You were talking about a horse, I think – Dancer? Was she a favourite?'

'She was. Although they were all favourites, really, but Dancer was special. She needed gentling, not bullying. We were great mates – bit like

Phar Lap and Tommy Woodcock, you could say.'

Maureen smiled. 'What about the jockeys – were any of them your mates?'

'There were some good fellas, but I kept myself to myself most of the time.'

'Must have been lonely, eh?'

'I had my horses, and a few good dogs over the years. They were all the company I needed.'

'Really? You didn't need any people company?' she asked, shaking the thermometer several times before indicating that she wanted to take his temperature. He opened his mouth and clamped his tongue over the glass tube. His eyes moistened slightly, but he squeezed them shut tight. Then he remembered Maureen's connection to Mick Bannon. Bill studied the young nurse's face, and for the first time saw the family resemblance.

'You look like Mick,' he said.

Maureen removed the thermometer from under his tongue and held it up to gauge the level of the thin line of mercury.

'Do I? I always thought I took more after Mum's side.'

'I can see it now. You could do worse. He was a very good-looking fellow.'

'Is that right?' said Maureen, focusing on the numbers she was now recording on his chart. 'Your temperature's a little high. I might get some paracetamol for you,' she said.

'You do that,' he said, his attention diverted back to the photograph of Proud Dancer.

~

Dancer had come out strong, snorting, ears back and in full flight. It took all of Bill's strength to pull her back and allow the others to go by. Even with room to pass there was still the obligatory abuse and jostling of horses, the slapping of flesh and leather as they manoeuvred into position. At a well-known point in the race, indiscretions increased as a brief blind spot for the race officials made it an opportunity for mayhem. Not for the first time, Bill felt the sting of someone else's crop across his thigh. All was fair game out on the track and, supposedly, it would all be forgiven back in the jockeys' room.

But Bill didn't much like to spend time in the jockeys' room. He didn't like to hear the deals and conspiracies that went on between some of the riders. No one could say horseracing wasn't a gamble. Even the trainers had no idea at times what the jockeys decided between them – let alone the owners and their shareholders. Bill always rode to win, but riding to win was not always appreciated – as Nifty Peters would later discover when he got involved with a nasty gang of race fixers and ended up going over the Barron Falls in a tobacco sack, his body later found down around Freshwater.

The memory made Bill's whole body jump. 'Poor bloody Nifty,' said Bill to himself. No bugger deserved that.

~

Maureen headed back to the nurses' station. She was worried about Mr Smith's deteriorating health, and hoped Petra might be able to offer some reassurance. The more senior nurse had cared for him on the night shift – but she had little with which to console Maureen.

'I know,' Petra said. 'His temp's been spiking all night. I sponged him down, and he's had everything we can give him for now.'

'I don't think we're going to get him home again, are we?' said Maureen.

'Hard to say, Maurs. He's a tough little bugger, though. And he's fond of you. That book you did for him perked him up no end.'

'I hope so. It upsets him as well, though, sometimes. Some of the memories – not all good ones, it seems.'

'At least he's talking to you. I think he just needs to know that someone is interested. He really appreciates it. Now, I'm off to get horizontal. Four night shifts in a row – I'm knackered.'

Maureen sat on the CWA chair, spinning slowly around and around, thinking about Mr Smith's life and the fact that there was no one in it now except for the staff of Leichhardt Memorial Hospital. She thought about her grandfather, who had known Bill Smith and yet not really known Bill Smith. The sense that time was running out hit Maureen, and she knew it applied to more than just Mr Smith. All those wasted days of not talking to or seeing her grandfather. She had already lost Nan Bannon, and what was worse was that it had happened when Maureen was meant to be looking after her. Mick had relied on Maureen to be with his wife, to keep an eye on her after that turn she'd had earlier.

It was as if time itself suddenly waved its hand in Maureen's face and demanded an end to the merry-go-round games on chairs. She would visit her grandfather on her next day off like she had promised him, and she would make things right again. There was no undoing the past – only acknowledging it and grabbing hold of the present. She headed back to Mr Smith's room to see if he was in the mood for another story. Since she'd given him the scrapbook and visited his home, he seemed to have a greater desire to share as much of his life story as he could, and Maureen was happy to hear it.

~

'How many horses did you have all up?'

'Let me think now. My last mare died in '72 – that was Stella. There was Star, or Starlight Miss – she won the Bracelet. And Nor East. And I had Adventure Boy – he was a bit long in the tooth, but we still did alright. Long before them all was Addy and Missus – oh, poor Missus.'

Each name brought a smile to Bill's face, until he got to Missus, the old packhorse he had first purchased when he was in Port Adelaide.

'What's wrong? Why poor Missus?'

'That was a terrible business – terrible. You don't want to know. Let's just say she died, and it was my fault.'

'You don't have to talk about it if you don't want to.'

'She ended up in the knackery, poor old girl. Some thieving bastard sold her off before I could get back to pick her up. I swore then that would never happen to another horse of mine, ever. I didn't like it happening to any horse, really, but that's how it is and for some, there's no other option, but too many good horses ended up at the slaughterhouse just because their owners couldn't see their potential, or because they'd given all they could.'

'That's awful. I didn't mean to get you upset.'

'It's not you, Missy. Don't worry. I was known for helping a few escape from the knackeries now and then. I wasn't too popular – but I didn't care,' said Bill with a grin. 'Did I tell you about the colt that I broke out of the slaughter yards, down in Cairns? What a business. I'd do it all again, too, if I had my chance.'

'Really? You let one out?'

'Not just one, but that was one I got caught in the act with. Lucky I didn't get my block knocked off.'

'Tell me, if you're up to it.'

Bill lay back in his bed, thinking about the first little colt he had set free after the trauma of losing Missus. It had become almost a holy war for him, any time he saw an animal who he thought deserved a second chance – which was all of them in his heart, but only a select few when common sense kicked in. He closed his eyes and pictured that day. Not only pictured it – he could smell the horses, all crowded together, could feel their agitation and fear at their hopeless predicament.

~

When the truck pulled into the saleyards in Cairns, Bill was already there, searching for who he might save. As he stood leaning on the gate, one foot up on the rail, eyeing the scrawny, tormented-looking animals whose owners had given up on them, Bill wished he could take them all. But he knew he couldn't. With images of his own mare Missus vivid in his mind, he knew what needed to be done. As the driver was unlocking the back of his truck, Bill swung open the saleyard gate and silently urged the startled horses to run.

As the dust began to settle, the furious driver spotted the stranger hanging off the now-open gate. He marched over to Bill, grabbed him by the shirtfront and threw him to the ground, then placed a boot square on his chest and screamed down at him: 'What the fuck do you think you're doing, you bloody idiot?' Spit flew from his foaming mouth.

'Geez, I'm sorry mate,' stammered Bill, trying to push back a bit against the pressure of the boot. 'I just leaned on the gate, and it popped open.' He tried to look as startled as the driver did enraged.

'Popped open! I oughtta pop open your numb bloody skull!' roared the driver, leaning down and lifting Bill off the ground by his shirt.

At that moment, a little blue cattle dog ran out of the bushes and grabbed onto the back of the driver's trouser leg, forcing him to let go of his hold on Bill.

'Get on back, Bluey – go on,' Bill said to his saviour, who did exactly that, returning to the bushes where he had been waiting. Bill didn't mind taking a belting for his part, but he wasn't about to let anyone lay into his little mate. Ever since he'd followed Bill home from the river one day, hungry, footsore and without any sign of belonging to anyone, Bluey had never strayed far from his friend.

'Piss off, before I call the coppers,' said the driver. 'And don't let me see you round here again.'

It took a good hour or so for the irate man to round all the escapees into his truck – well, most of them. One roan colt stood at a distance, partly hidden by the surrounding scrub, watching as the others were herded into the pens. Bill had only moved as far away as out of the driver's line of sight. As he was watching and waiting on his haunches with Bluey by his side, he noticed the solitary horse peering out from the scrub behind the yards. As the others were counted back in, the manifest checked and rechecked, Bill saw the driver's face ripen like a tomato.

'There must be one still bloody out there,' he muttered to himself. 'Well, I haven't got time to frig around – good bloody luck to him.'

When the truck was gone, Bill moved around to the stand of melaleuca where the roan had hidden himself. Bill stood still, rolled a cigarette and waited.

'Smart fella we got here, Bluey,' he said. 'Yep, real smart fella. Just like you eh, boy. Why don't you go introduce yourself?' he said, nodding towards the curious but wary horse.

Bluey subordinated himself before the young horse, cautiously moving closer until he was in a vulnerable position where a hoof could at any moment be brought down on his head. Then he stayed quite still. The colt put his nose towards the dog, who returned the gesture, before slowly retreating to stand back beside Bill. Bill gave a soft whistle and began walking slowly away with Bluey by his side. Every few yards he would stop, as would Bluey, and sneak a look over his shoulder. The colt had moved as well, but also stopped, keeping the same distance.

'How did a fine-looking young 'un like you end up heading for the knackery?' he asked the animal as the trio walked on, but the colt offered no answer. The rejected never really know the reason, Bill surmised. The three continued in this start-stop procession down along the river for several miles. As they reached home, Bluey ran ahead and opened the gate to the back stables with the rope that lay on the ground for this purpose. Bill invited the colt to follow, leaving the gate open so that there was no doubt in the young horse's mind that he was free to leave if he chose to. With the water buckets filled and the feed bins topped with a dribble of molasses, the horse settled in for the night, and was still waiting there the next morning.

Over the years, Bill had saved several from the knackery like this. Some, like the colt he'd named Lucky Fella, had gone on to earn just enough from the small country races to pay their own way, but nothing more. What he really needed was one of those wonder horses that the punters loved so much; a rags-to-riches fairytale horse that would help make sure everyone was kept in feed. But life was far from a fairytale, as Bill Smith knew well, especially towards the end of his jockeying days.

33

Nursing notes: 22/5/78 22:00. Resp 38; T 38.2. Decreasing periods of lucidity nocte.

Bill must have gone through the scrapbook at least a dozen times since Maureen had presented it to him. He was at his best in the mornings. He revisited the past in episodes that the book seemed to trigger, as he ran his fingers over faded photographs, yellowed newspaper clippings and copies of old race books that Maureen had somehow managed to find. Franny had helped as well, but the information was sparse overall. Bill didn't mind. The memories were still all there – the scrapbook just helped to bring up a few that needed a dust-off.

~

After the Second World War, Bill was getting on in age, and many of the trainers back then were after younger riders for their mounts. There were still plenty of good years ahead in the saddle for Bill, but he knew that if he wanted longevity in the game, he needed to take greater control over his options.

While on a trip to Brisbane, Bill stepped up to the desk and handed over his application to register as a jockey and a trainer. He had absorbed all he could from Charlie McInnes in those early days, adding to his already substantial knowledge of how to get the best out of horses. He could read every minute change in behaviour, gait, mood – whether in a thoroughbred or common working stock. Breeding didn't matter to Bill. Every horse was a thoroughbred, he thought, and worthy of a thoroughbred's treatment.

The clerk tugged at his tie with irritation, and gave a few up-and-down glances at the stranger who seemed overdressed for both occasion and climate.

'You're a bit long in the tooth for riding, aren't you, Mr ... William Albert Smith?' he enquired, reading from the form before looking up to gauge Bill's reaction. Bill almost smiled. It used to be that he was always trying to convince people he was older than he appeared. The sands had shifted, and he wondered what was now written on his face. He spoke so softly that the clerk had to lean across his desk to hear.

'It's called experience.'

'You been riding amateur for some time. What's taken so long to go for professional status?'

'Just wasn't so important back then. Game's changed a fair bit since the War, eh.'

The clerk remained curious, checking and rechecking the form. He stood up and walked over to a filing cabinet, which almost toppled when its overburdened top drawer was pulled out.

'Smith. Bill Smith. I feel like I've heard of a jockey Smith – only it was Birdy or ... Girly? Something like that. From up your way.'

'That's me. "Girly" Smith. On account of my soft voice or something.'

'I can see that,' said the clerk.

Bill didn't respond; just kept focused on the papers that would give him the freedom to be his own boss.

The clerk returned to his desk and gave the papers a series of pounding stamps on each page. A signature here, initials there. Then it must have been time for a lunch break. The clerk stood up, shook Bill's hand, and placed a 'Back in thirty minutes' sign on his desk.

'Well, there you go. Good luck, Mr William Albert Smith, Registered Jockey and Trainer. Not too many holding both licences.'

Bill stepped outside and stood on the busy Brisbane footpath, studying his registration papers. Registered jockey and trainer. He had never felt happier. There was a gelding waiting at the city's Easter sales that Bill knew had something in common with him. Like Bill, the horse harboured a secret. His owner had put him up for sale because out of nine starts he had not even come close to a place. He was slow off the line, and the owner's conglomerate of hopeful investors had grown impatient. Get rid of him, was the order. Bill would be ready when they did. Now double registered, he would have full control. The bay gelding didn't know it, but his life was about to change for the better.

Adventure Boy was the first of the horses that Bill officially both trained and rode for himself. He hadn't yet received his registration as a trainer when Addy was running, so she was always listed as having been trained by McInnes. Picked up at a bargain price in Brisbane, Adventure Boy lived up to his name as the pair made their way gradually back up north, covering the smaller racetracks along the route where they made enough in prize money to pay for their feed for the month they were on the road. Bill couldn't wait to get the Boy home and show the locals what he could do. No more waiting for a ride or being shafted at the last minute when one of the southern boys turned up looking for a mount.

Adventure Boy's first run on the Tablelands was a memorable one. The excitement of the crowd and the megaphonic crackling of announcements from the newly installed PA system echoed across the grounds. The horses paraded in the saddling enclosure, their temperaments sized up by the punters scrambling to place their last-minute bets.

'They're all out in the mounting yard now, with ten minutes to the start of the third race here at Mareeba, the Open Handicap Race, where all are invited to run. We've got a good field here today. They won't want a delay. You can see a few signs of nerves among the youngsters, they're showing some lather, so they'll try to get them out quickly.'

Bill wanted to make sure he was first out onto the track with the three-year-old gelding. Adventure Boy loved to run, so the plan was to go out first, and hope that no one took too long to go into the gates, as some had a habit of doing. Bill had spent a lot of time working with the new barrier-style starts, but the Boy didn't care for them. When he was put in early there would always be a poor jump from the barrier. If they could get in last and get out quickly, Bill was quietly confident in his mount.

The track was damp. As they cantered out onto the course, mud splattered Bill's face before he'd got far. More reason for his Boy to get out front. His mount was already snorting, ears back, having drawn an advantageous position on the inside.

'Adventure Boy is hanging back at the gate. He's in no rush to go in. Looking good for a mount they'd all but given up on down south. Sporting new colours for his first time from the Smith stable – green, white and violet checkerboard. The others are circling. Mighty Joe, in the blue and white squares, is next to go in. The Ferryman, with red hoops and white on a green field, is in a bit of a mood – it's his first start back after a spell, although he should be worth a gander in this lot.'

The starter took his position.

'Man down! Man down!' came a shout from the middle. The strapper was still in the fifth gate, where a big three-year-old colt was threatening to dislodge his rider. The young lad ran to the back of the barrier and grabbed hold of the colt's tail to stop him rearing up. He gave the nod, and the starter surveyed the line one more time. Bill tried to steady his horse. Thankfully, it wasn't a long delay.

With a sound like gunfire, the barriers snapped open. Adventure Boy did what Bill had hoped he would when he sniffed the air of the hopefuls beside him – he sprinted to the front effortlessly, leading by a length at the first turn. Bill was standing fully in the stirrups, using only hands and heels, the whip tucked in tight against his body. Adventure Boy did not appreciate nor need the whip. As they reached the 5-furlong mark, the Boy was just beginning to relax when Bill found they were three-deep on the fence, with one of the interstate jockeys trying to squeeze through.

'Move over, Girly,' yelled southern hoop Larry Hynes, as his horse bumped Adventure Boy into the rail.

Bill hated his horse copping a hammering from this bloke's careless riding.

'*You* move over,' Bill shouted back over the thundering of hooves and bumping of bodies. 'You're gonna cause an accident, you bloody fool!'

'Squeeze him in, boys,' Larry Hynes yelled, unmoved by Bill's cautions. There was too much riding on this one – including a large chunk of Hynes's own money.

Bill had to get Adventure Boy out of the pack. He steered him so close to the rail that he could feel his boots scraping it and, for the first time, brought out the whip to give him a hurry-up. With that, the Boy surged forward into clear air and into the home straight.

Bill felt sick about taking the whip to his horse. The colt had felt it before with his previous owner, and it wasn't how Bill wanted to handle him. The jockey-turned-trainer was angry with himself for taking the pressure off too soon and letting the others box them in. There was no one else responsible. When he crossed the finish line a good length in front of the dirty challenger, Bill could not feel the joy of the win. As he jumped down from Adventure Boy in the winner's circle, his first concern was to check for any bumps or bruises his mount had sustained. He inspected the Boy's rump and ran his hands down each leg, all the while apologising to his horse.

'I'm sorry, fella – sorry I had to give you a tap. Had to get you out of there. I'm sorry.'

Larry Hynes, who had come into the circle beside him, was unrepentant.

'You old bludger,' he said to Bill, as he pulled his saddle off. 'You cost me. You should have moved over.'

'*I* should have moved over? You boxed us in against the rails! We're lucky we didn't go arse-up!'

Rod Morgan, who had come in third behind Hynes, was not happy with Hynes either. 'You could've caused a bloody pile-up riding like that. Don't worry about him, Girly. Good run, eh.'

~

Bill was muttering loudly enough for Maureen to hear when she came in to check on him again.

'What's got you riled up now, Mr Smith? I might have to take that book off you, if it's getting you too worked up,' Maureen said, as she wrapped the blood-pressure cuff around his arm and began inflating it.

'Who's got your goat now?'

'That bloody southern jockey, Hynes. Fool of a man,' Bill said, tapping the photograph of their race. 'He gave jockeys a bad name. He was careless – got himself in trouble – and he was rough on his mounts.'

'What happened to him?'

'Sad thing – he caused a pile-up in one of the big Townsville races, and several horses had to be put down and a jockey ended up with a broken neck, poor bugger. Hynes copped one of the longest suspensions ever given. Never came back from the ban – not in Queensland, anyway. Don't know what happened to him, but it was a good thing they got rid of him.'

'Gawd, that's terrible. If this book is bringing back too many upsets for you, we should probably put it away for a bit, eh?'

'Over my dead body, Missy. It's the sweetest thing anyone's ever done for me. Anyway, life is full of light and shade. Can't have one without the other.'

'How about we compromise and take a break for now, at least?'

'Aren't you the persuasive one.'

Maureen took the book and put it on the side table.

'Maureen,' he said softly, 'call me Bill, eh.'

'Okay ... Bill.'

Even with the scrapbook closed, Bill's memories didn't stop returning.

34

Nursing notes: 23/5/78 11:00. Pale, increasing dyspnoea, diminished appetite, withdrawn at times.

Maureen had been wanting to ask Bill about Catherine since they'd visited the house, but she was afraid of upsetting her patient, who seemed to be getting frailer by the day. While Bill was more than willing to talk about his beloved horses, certain memorable races and even some of his fellow jockeys, whenever it came to any personal connection he either stopped the conversation altogether or artfully redirected it.

'You'll be rubbing a hole in that photograph if you're not careful,' she said to him one day. 'What's so special about that one?'

'Eh? Oh, nothing really.'

'Really? You seem to look at that page a lot.'

'That was when they changed the bloody currency over. What a business that was.'

'To decimal currency?'

'That's right. I still change it all to pounds and shillings in my head.'

'I remember the song,' said Maureen, singing: '"*In come the dollars and in come the cents, out go the pounds and the shillings and the pence, something, something, on the fourteenth of February 1966.*" I was only in prep, but I remember trying to sing that song.'

'Yeah, well. It certainly made it a challenge there for a bit.'

He continued staring at the photo, his mind elsewhere.

'Bill?'

'That was the day I saw Catherine. Just one time, in Townsville. What were the odds on that, eh? Just after they changed the money over. In February 1966.'

'She's the lady in the clipping from the newspaper? The one we brought back from your place?'

'Yes, that's her.'

'You said you were in a home with her?'

'We were in a girl's home together. Best of friends. We were both orphans – well, my father went off to war and never came back for me, so I supposed I was an orphan by then. She didn't have any family. She looked after me there. They were hard days in that place – terrible. But Catherine made it more bearable. We got up to some mischief, too,' he smiled at the memory, until his face fell into a more melancholy expression.

'Did you keep in touch? Maybe we can get her to come and see you?'

Bill was staring off into space. There it was. The shutdown. As a patient call bell went off in the next room, Maureen had to leave Bill to his memories once more.

~

'Ten quid on Go Lightly in the third.'

'Ten quid or ten dollars do you mean, mate?'

'Eh? Dollars then.'

'Ten dollars Go Lightly at twenty to one to win, Race Three. There you go, mate,' said the bookmaker, handing Bill a ticket covered in an indecipherable scrawl.

'Ten *dollars*. God almighty. How's a bloke supposed to keep up with all these bloody changes?' Bill muttered as he walked away.

He went back to the saddling enclosure, ticket tucked safely away, as they brought in his young mare, Go Lightly. The jockey, Mick Richards, was a good year out of his apprenticeship but still nervous with each ride, as was his mount.

'Now, listen up, Son,' Bill instructed him. 'She can be skittish if she feels crowded, so keep out wide for the first couple of furlongs. Keep her wide to the turn, and then give her the hurry-up. But not too much. No need to flog. She'll go if you give her room.'

Bill couldn't help thinking, with all the changes taking place, that he was getting too old for this game. The currency was one concern, but the idea that racing might one day also be talked of in metric rather than imperial was too much to contemplate. Even the climb up the stairs to the members' stand was taking its toll on his sixty-four-year-old knees.

Bill flopped onto a seat halfway up. He tried to find his rider through the binoculars as all the jockeys cantered out to the starting line. Satisfied that Mick wasn't letting Go Lightly expend too much energy before the race started, he turned his field glasses back across the crowd. A woman caught Bill's attention. She was laughing, from the way she threw her head back. He had seen that laugh before, many years ago. He tried to adjust his binoculars to get a better view and, when he did, he felt his body almost slide to the ground. He had to plant his feet and push himself back up onto his seat. He looked around to see if anyone had noticed his near-fall.

Catherine. Bill was sure it was Catherine. He kept his binoculars fixed on her, even as the starter took his position.

'Hey, Girly, your mare's testing the young fella. Hope he knows to keep her wide.' Bill felt a gentle elbow in his side, and turned to see one of the other trainers, Henry Irving, with his enormous extra-strength binoculars focused on the starting gate.

'He knows, alright.'

'And they're racing in the third here at Townsville's Cluden Park. Mighty River's made a strong start. What's My Name moved over quickly to the inside rail, nudging Go Lightly on the way, who might have clipped a shin there. Go Lightly is falling back on the outside ...'

Bill was watching the race, but his mind was racing in an entirely different way. Could it really be her? Would she recognise me? he wondered. He desperately wanted to turn his glasses back to the crowd and to the woman who had to be Catherine, but he kept them trained on the equine pack moving as one along the far side of the field. When Go Lightly crossed a close third, Bill's attention turned immediately to the throng of people in front of the grandstand, searching desperately for Catherine.

'Well done, Girly. That little mare's going to do well this season.'

'Eh? Oh, yes. She could have done better if Mick took her wide sooner, like I told him. Have to see how that shin pulls up.'

'If anyone can fix a split shin, it's you, eh Girly,' said Henry, giving Bill an overly exuberant slap on the back. Bill had to steady himself before tackling the stairs down to the winners' enclosure. All the while his eyes feverishly scanned the crowd for Catherine. Even when he was with his mare and jockey, his head swivelled, trying to find her, oblivious to the apologetic Mick.

'Really sorry, Boss. I was trying to get her out of the way. Do you think she'll be okay? I didn't want to push her too much in case it opened up. I thought that's what you'd want me to do. Was I right, Boss?'

Bill hadn't even sighted the cut on Go Lightly's shin, nor his jockey.

'Boss? Was I right?'

Bill finally looked at the mare's leg. It was split a good few inches.

'Oh, I'm sorry, little girl,' he said to the mare. 'That's a nasty one. It's alright, Son, we'll get it sorted. That's why I wanted you to go wide. Now you know.'

The old trainer knew Mick was waiting for a serve from him, but Bill left him hanging. The jockey headed off to weigh-in and Bill asked the strapper to walk Go Lightly back, and to hose her down gently until he had a better study of the injury. Bill stood for a time, convinced that he must have been mistaken about the woman in the crowd, before turning to leave the enclosure. As he did, he came face to face with someone whose features he knew so well.

'Catherine?'

'Yes? Have we met?'

Bill had pictured this moment a thousand times since the last touch of Catherine's lips on his cheek almost fifty years ago. The realisation that he was not similarly fixed in Catherine's mind stung, and he had to fight the urge to run.

'It's me. Willie,' he said in a faint voice.

Catherine stared back, unblinking. The hair showing beneath her hat was grey, but the eyes were the same hazel that Bill had kept in his mind and heart's memory from all those years ago. Before she could respond, a well-attired gentleman grabbed her by the elbow, fanning a bunch of the new brightly coloured decimal notes.

'Look, darling. Forty quid. Nice going, eh? No, sorry, that's forty dollars. Aren't they pretty notes?'

Neither Bill nor Catherine had broken the gaze that gripped them.

The gentleman smiled at Catherine and then looked to Bill quizzically, before extending his hand.

'Girly Smith, isn't it? Clive Stimpson,' he said, pumping Bill's hand. 'Nice little mare you have there. Would have had a bigger lead if she hadn't copped that scrape early on. Do you two know each other?'

'No, no, not at all,' Catherine said. 'Mr Smith thought I was someone he used to know, but it's not me. I mean, I'm not her ... I mean ...'

'Oh, well, this gorgeous woman here is my wife of thirty years, would you believe?' Clive said to Bill.

Bill sensed the anxiety rising in Catherine and was relieved that she hadn't said anything. What could she have said? Yes, we were at the girl's home together?

He turned to the man and said, 'Well, it's lovely to meet you – both. I'd best see to the young one. That shin's going to need work. Enjoy the rest of your day.' He tipped his hat to the woman he'd waited so long to see again, and from whom he now had to walk away once more.

When Bill got back to the stall, Go Lightly was pawing at the ground in obvious distress. She was still sweaty from the run, the strapper having tried to cool her down gently as best he could.

'I was getting worried, Boss. Will I hose her down properly now, or what?'

'Sorry, my darling girl,' Bill said, running his hand along the young mare's neck and down the injured foreleg. 'Shouldn't have kept you waiting, sweet lass. Hose her down, and go gentle around the cut. I don't want to open it up, but you'll need to clean it out best you can,' he said to the strapper, patting Go Lightly's rump as she was led out of the stall.

Bill leaned back on the rail and rolled a cigarette. He had always hoped to see his friend again, and yet he had not really thought about how she might react. Why would she expect that her old friend from the girls' home was now Bill Smith – a man, and an elderly one at that, called 'Girly' by all and sundry as if they were all in on the ruse? She must think I'm some kind of freak, he thought to himself. A bloody weirdo. Bill slumped down on a milk crate in the corner of the stall, where the strapper would often sit between races. He watched his mare swirling around in response to the water spray, mesmerised by the reddish tinge to the wash-off running down her leg. He wished it was his own blood draining out of his wretched body, as it had been all those years ago when he'd tried to disappear from the world.

'Gentle, Son. She'll be stinging,' he said to the strapper.

Lost in a cyclone of memories and emotions, Bill didn't notice the shadow of someone now standing at the far end of the stall.

'Willie?'

Bill took a moment to consider whether the voice was a figment of his imagination, a wish on the wind.

'Willie. I'm so sorry. It was a shock … seeing you … like this,' she said.

Aware of the strapper and of the other trainers and stablehands nearby, Bill jumped up and placed a hand on Catherine's arm, directing her back towards the public area.

'Let's move out of the way here, Missus,' he said, walking Catherine out of earshot and away from prying eyes. As they stood beneath one of the African mahogany trees dotted around the course, Bill felt his hands shaking so much that he had to jam them in his pockets.

'I was caught off guard, Willie,' said Catherine quietly to him. 'Never in a million years did I think that if I ever saw you again, you'd still be dressed like a man. I mean, I thought you just dressed that way to get out of Cranbrook – didn't you? But now you're Bill "Girly" Smith. You're practically famous up here.'

'It's still me. They're just clothes, you know.'

‘Are they? What does it mean, Willie? Have you always gone about as a man, since ... way back then?’

Bill looked down, shifting his weight from one foot to the other. All he wanted was to see his friend Catherine again. The only person he had ever thought of as a friend. The only person he had ever loved, other than his father.

‘Seemed easier this way,’ he said.

‘Easier? I can’t imagine it has been,’ she said, touching Bill’s arm tenderly. Years fell away as they stood reunited in that moment.

‘I have to go, Willie – or, should I say, Bill. But I’m so glad to have seen you again. Really, I am. Here’s my address,’ she said, pressing a note into his hand. ‘Write to me, if you like?’

‘I did write you – did you know that? I wrote a bit in the beginning. But I never heard back.’

‘Really? I didn’t know. I wanted to hear from you. I missed you so much.’

Bill stared at the folded paper.

‘I would love to hear from you, Willie, really I would.’

With that, Catherine tentatively placed a kiss on Bill’s cheek, as she had so long ago, but there was an awkwardness in it. She turned and left Bill standing alone beside the contorted roots of the tree.

‘Woohoo, Girly! Got yourself a little lady bird, have you?’ called one of the jockeys as he passed by. No one had seen Bill Smith with a single friend or relative in all the years he had been part of the racing scene. To see him talking so intimately with a woman was sure to raise a few eyebrows.

‘Fuck off,’ said Bill, heading back to the stalls and to his horse needing his attention.

35

Nursing notes: 27/5/78 06:30. Increasing restlessness, pt trying to get out of bed o/night ... Sedation ordered.

'My clothes. Where are my clothes? I want them now.'

A clearly distressed Bill Smith had woken up yelling and rattling at the bedrails, trying to get up. He hadn't been this unsettled in some time. Maureen was by his side as soon as she heard his voice.

'Bill, what's wrong? You're in the hospital, remember?'

'Of course I remember. I want my clothes. I need my clothes. There's something I have to find, in a pocket.'

'I checked all your pockets and put your belongings in the cupboard when you first came in. Tell me what it is, and I'll get it for you.'

'No, no – you won't have found it. Get me my vest. I need to know it's there.'

Maureen retrieved the vest, which had been laundered along with the rest of Bill's vomit-stained clothing when he was first admitted.

'You washed it.'

'Of course. Everything was pretty smelly after your fall. What's wrong? What's got you so upset?'

'Doesn't matter,' said Bill, tears coursing down his hollowed cheeks. He was certain that what he was after would be nothing but pulp by now. He turned his face into the pillow.

Maureen tried to recall the items she had taken from Bill's pockets. Handkerchief, crumbled biscuit. The watch? Apart from those items, there had only been a few dollar notes and a folded piece of paper. She hadn't opened the paper at the time, because it had seemed so fragile and she hadn't seen it as her business, so she'd enclosed it with the money in a small plastic bag. She left Bill now and returned a few minutes later with his belongings.

'Is this what you were looking for? The money's all there. And your watch – and this note.'

Bill pulled his body up with a surprising energy and stared at the nurse holding the small plastic bag. He took it from her and began tossing the contents onto his bed cover. He disregarded the money and the watch and stared at the yellowed paper. He picked it up with both hands and cradled it close to his lips.

'Is that what you were worried about?'

Bill didn't respond. He kept his eyes shut and lay back.

'Can I put all these other things away now?'

But Bill was elsewhere, somewhere that Maureen didn't want to intrude. She went to check on her other patients, leaving him to his thoughts. It had become her routine, whenever Bill seemed upset, not to try to jolly him out of it but to let him be with his memories. He would share when he wanted to, but there were some aspects of his life that remained his alone.

~

The Wet had set in. Every afternoon the clouds would storm across the horizon from the north-east and let go of their load until the ground was a series of rivulets running from the shed down past the working yard and into the gully. Bill had moved several times over the years. When he saw Catherine at the races in Townsville he was renting a place close to the Ranges in Cairns. Mount Bartle Frere was in cloud a lot of the time, but he loved the drama of the clouds as they rolled in, engulfing the winding road up to the Tablelands. There was nothing to do as the rain fell in swathes but settle back in his comfy squatter's chair and read another Zane Grey western.

Seeing Catherine had opened old feelings that Bill had long pushed aside. He put down the magazine and reached into his vest pocket. The neatly folded paper she had placed in his hand before they'd parted ways had not been opened. He held it to his nose, certain it held a faint hint of Catherine's perfume. His fingers trembled as he carefully unfolded the note.

My dearest W.

I have missed you terribly. Write to me if you would.
Friends forever, remember?
Mrs Catherine Stimpson
147 Squire Street
Woolloomooloo, Sydney
Love, C.

Bill slumped back into the chair, the note pressed to his chest.

Catherine had missed Willie. What did that mean? She'd missed *Willie,* but Willie had been gone since the day she'd left Cranbrook and had become someone else. Catherine did not know this other person. She knew her friend, Willie – a teenage girl. What could he say to Catherine that would make sense of the direction his life had taken? *I've missed you, too, my darling Catie.* But would she want Bill Smith to write to her?

Still, he read and reread the note, and held it gently to his lips. The feelings were unfamiliar and confusing. The rain on the corrugated iron hammered like anvil blows, and Bill's temples pounded in unison. He glanced down at his dog, who was considering Bill with a tilt of his head.

'What do you reckon, Rusty boy – would she want to hear from *Mr* Smith?'

Rusty let out a long breath and flopped his head back down on his paws, just the way old Bluey-dog would do.

'No, you're right. Best leave well enough alone, eh boy? Past is past.'

He carefully refolded the paper, tucked it back into his vest pocket and picked up the western.

~

Back at the nurses' station, Maureen's shoulders slumped with frustration.

'He's so alone. I just wish we could find someone he'd want to see.'

'He's made it pretty clear that he doesn't want people knowing,' said Franny.

'Yes, but what about this Catherine? She already knows. Can't we at least try to contact her? We've got an address.'

After their shift, the pair went down to the common lounge and Maureen dialled directory assistance.

'Hello, yes, Sydney residential, please – 147 Squire Street,

Woolloomooloo. Stimpson, Catherine. You've got a Clive Stimpson? That could be it. Yes, thank you. Yes, I've got a pen ...'

'You've got it?'

'I think so. Clive might be her husband. Do you think we should call?'

Now that they had a phone number, the full ramifications of their potential interference began to emerge. What if the husband answered? What if Catherine wanted nothing to do with Bill Smith? What if they told Bill and he got angry with them? What if – what if – what if Matron found out?

Maureen put the number in her pocket and decided it could wait another day. She was looking forward to her next shift, when she'd get the chance to discuss it with Bill.

36

Nursing notes: 1/6/78 14:30. Pressure sore showing signs of necrosis, no granulation, non-stick dressing in situ; 2 hrly positioning.

After Maureen and Fran's visit to his house, Bill had been generally more settled and less anxious, despite the growing realisation that his health was deteriorating. The pressure sore refused to heal, his lungs were stubbornly congested and his bouts of confusion were becoming more frequent. In one of his more lucid moments, Bill asked for Matron. He wanted to discuss his affairs, and Matron Kelly made no effort to offer the patient false hope. It was sensible, she told him. She wished more people could be so prepared.

As Bill opened his eyes on what he realised was another day in Leichhardt Memorial Hospital, he looked across to the photographs on the side table to see that they were still there. Sunlight streamed into the room, lighting up a cobweb that Matron must have missed. How could that be? They're tenacious little buggers, spiders, he thought, reminded of his own battle with the creatures in his blacksmith shed at home. Probably got the run of the place now, he mused. He lay there thinking about the shed down the back. He could smell the coal from the furnace, hear the air wheezing from the bellows, taste the sweat that would run down his face and into the corners of his mouth. He pictured the day he'd first met the little ginger-haired boy in the photograph, and wondered what had become of him.

~

Another cobweb frizzled as the flames from the furnace licked the low-hanging beam. They never seem to learn, Bill thought to himself. You'd think they'd pick a better location than above the bloody fire. He pumped the bellows several times, reigniting the coals, and plunged the hammered steel into the orange glow. Sweat ran down his back and into the top of his work pants.

Confident that he was alone, he took off his damp shirt and laid it over the bench. Enjoying the freedom of bare skin, he gave the bellows a few more pumps before removing the now molten metal and carefully transferring it to the anvil. Glowing metal fragments splintered the darkness of the shed. Bill was captivated by shaping and reshaping a dull piece of metal into a beautifully crafted shoe. When he was satisfied with its form he dropped it into the water bucket, watching the steam billow out as the heat of the metal dissipated and the orange glow drained away. Lost in the rhythmic working of the steel, he didn't notice the young boy standing under the shade of the mango tree.

'Madam will be stepping out in style with these little dainty numbers,' Bill said to no one.

'Sure will. Ladies always love new shoes.'

Bill swung around towards the direction of the voice and then quickly back again. Realising he was not alone, he hunched to the ground, fumbled for his shirt and pulled it over his head.

'What the bloody hell do you think you're doing, sneaking up on a man like that?'

'Sorry, Mr Smith – I didn't mean to startle you.'

Bill smoothed down his rumpled shirt and inspected himself before turning to face the boy.

'Well, you did. Coming up behind like that.'

'I came to see if I could give you a hand. I'm strong, and you've hurt your back, eh? I can help if you'll let me.'

'What? Hurt my back?' Bill realised the boy must have thought the tight bindings were a dressing of some kind, and felt some small relief. 'You don't enter private property without permission. You're lucky Rusty didn't rip your leg off.'

Rusty, who remained an uninterested bystander, glanced up briefly at the sound of his name and then went back to trying to remove a bindi from his paw.

'I – I'm sorry, Mr Smith.'

The boy reached down to scratch Rusty's ear, who returned the favour with a lick of the hand. Bill studied the young fellow, who clearly had Rusty's approval, and recalled a time when he had also asked for a chance from someone.

'Why aren't you in school, boy?'

'School holidays.'

'Haven't you got any friends to play with?'

'Not really. I want to be a jockey. I hope I can leave school in a few years and be an apprentice. I want to be like you, Mr Smith.'

Bill felt an awkward sensation in his chest.

'There's plenty of jockeys you could ask. Why me?'

'I see how you are with horses. When you go by to the river, always talking to them, treating them so kind. You got a special way with them, Mum reckons.'

Bill's face flushed crimson.

'Don't try to gild the lily, boy. You think I'm a soft touch, you'd be wrong.'

'No, I don't think that at all. Everyone knows you're a tough old coot,' the boy said with a grin.

'Do they, now? Well, they'd be right,' said Bill with something the young lad thought could be mistaken for a smile.

'Guess I better go then, before this dog licks me to death?' said the boy with a wider grin that exposed a gap between his two front teeth.

Something about the boy caused the usually reclusive Bill Smith to soften his grumpy demeanour just a little.

'Well, a horse can't wear just one shoe now, can it? Grab that piece over there, since you're here,' he said, indicating a blank steel bar on the bench. 'Got a name, or I keep calling you boy?'

'George. Like the famous jockey, George Moore. But I'm George Fisher.'

'High ambitions, then. Should be easy to remember.'

With that, Bill gave a few bursts of the bellows, breathing life back into the coals once more.

~

Young George Fisher continued to visit the blacksmith shed most afternoons even after the holidays were over. Raking up, refilling the water bucket, even brushing down some of the cobwebs that Bill refused to acknowledge until they sizzled and melted above the forge. Bill made a pretence of tolerating the boy, but the truth was he'd begun to look forward to his little shadow appearing after school. It had been a long time since he'd allowed a human to get so close. He'd had a few young lads help out as strappers over the years, but they rarely wanted to hang around after the jobs were done like this one did. Bill didn't want to admit it, but young George brought a bit of enjoyment to his days – hanging off Bill's every word, trying to take in as much as he could about blacksmithing and horses, the way a young Willie once had with her father.

'Oh, it's you again,' he'd say each day. 'Haven't you got a home to go to?'

'Sure I have, but Mum said it's okay to come over and give you a hand.'

'Did she, now? And why would she think I needed one? More likely trying to get you out from under her feet, I'd say.'

'Maybe, but I don't care. I'd rather be here.'

'Don't know why. Nothing special about here.'

'This place is the best. Like a museum.'

Bill had never thought of his surroundings as being interesting to anyone but himself. He kept things simple. Spent most of his time down at the stables – even sleeping there on occasion when one of his equine family was off their feed or injured. Not that Bill Smith's horses carried many injuries. His house was a place to read the newspaper in his favourite chair, and to display the photographs and memorabilia of his racing and other careers long past. Even cooking was often done on a little stove in the shed, where a tin of baked beans and toast made on a wire rack would be enough for Bill – especially in the days when he'd needed to keep his weight down. The old homemade sweatbox had long been taken over by the spiders, who were welcome to it. He didn't miss that aspect of his riding days.

'Mum reckons you should come to dinner,' young George said one day, after he had been coming to visit for some weeks.

Bill didn't look up from his hammering.

'That's nice of your mother, but tell her I have to keep my weight down – got to stick to a strict diet.'

'But you don't ride anymore. I thought you were only training these days.'

'Think you know all my business, do you, young fella?'

'No. Anyway, that's alright – you can just eat what you want.'

'I don't keep regular hours, Son. Tell Mum thanks very much.'

'We can eat whenever—'

'Jesus, boy, take a bloody hint. I don't want to go to your place for dinner. Don't make me have to say it again.'

Bill gave up on the shoe he'd been fashioning and flung it into the bucket of scrap metal. He looked over at the boy, who was staring into the bucket at the misshapen lump, biting his lip in what seemed like an effort not to cry. Bill Smith was in unfamiliar territory. He hadn't mixed much with children. Most kids in the neighbourhood loved to torment and poke fun at the funny old bloke in his vests and coat jackets no matter the weather. He turned to grab a new piece to work.

'I don't mix much, Son. That's all. Keep myself to myself. Always have. I don't think anyone's ever invited me to dinner before.'

'It's just me and Mum,' said the boy, quietly now. 'And Dad, if he comes home.'

'Does he work late?'

'Only at the pub lifting brown ales, is what Mum reckons. She doesn't wait for him. If he's late then he can ruddy well have it cold, she says.'

'Like that, is it?'

The two stood in silence, watching the glow of the furnace work its alchemy on the lump of steel. In that moment Bill remembered standing beside his father, watching his every move, not wanting to get in the way but wanting to soak up everything his father had to share.

'What about Friday? Check with your mum if that suits.'

'You bet, Mr Smith. It'll be right. Mum won't mind which day.'

Little George never wanted to go home, and always waited until the tone in his mother's voice got that edge of final straw about it, shouting across two backyards to Mr Smith's.

'Why do you always make her call you so many times?' Bill asked him. 'If you were my kid, I'd boot your backside.'

George surveyed Mr Smith sceptically.

'Fair crack of the whip, Mr Smith. I can't imagine you hurting a fly.'

'Well get going then, before I change my mind about Friday.'

With that, George spun on his heels, gave Rusty's ears a parting ruffle and shot off over the side fence towards home.

'I'm only doing this for you, Rusty boy. You seem fond of the little fella. We'll go just this one time, then, eh.'

37

Young George had managed to work his way in through the defences of a lifetime. The following Friday, after he'd fed the horses and put them in their stalls for the night, Bill had a quick shower and got ready for dinner with the young fella and his mum. As was his custom, Bill Smith wore his trademark vest and jacket, and donned his battered felt fedora. One long survey of the mirror and he was ready. Stepping out of his front door, he stopped in the front of his house where some agapanthuses were growing and snipped off a handful with his pocketknife. As he walked up the road, he was careful to avoid stepping on the cane toads that liked to gather under the streetlights.

'Ugly bastards,' he muttered, having to hop to avoid squishing one beneath his shoes. 'Not your fault, though, is it,' he conceded.

Bill stopped at his neighbour's front door and checked his outfit once more, before knocking.

'He's here! Mr Smith's here, Mum!'

Young George flung open the door and urged his guest to come in.

'Something smells good,' said Bill as he stepped inside.

'Mum's done a chook – you don't mind chook, do you?'

'Glad you could come,' said George's mother as she entered the hallway, before he could reply. 'This one never stops talking about you.'

Bill felt a flush come over his face, as he awkwardly pushed the flowers at Mrs Fisher.

'Aggies! Lovely. I often envy your beautiful garden. Come on in. Can I take your hat and coat for you?'

'Just my hat, thank you. I feel the chill at night,' he said, pulling his coat tight around him.

'Really? George, hang up Mr Smith's hat for him and show him into the dining room.'

'Where's the dining room, Mum?'

'George, don't be silly,' said an embarrassed Mrs Fisher, whose dining room was no more than the kitchen, where they all sat around a yellow laminex table.

The two adults sat across from each other, Bill somewhat stiffly, while the boy beamed with delight that his friend had come for dinner. Although it took a while, and a tall glass of ginger beer, Bill found he enjoyed the company as much as the perfectly cooked roast dinner. He couldn't remember the last time he had done so.

'Beats baked beans and toast, eh,' he said as he watched young George wipe his mouth on his sleeve. Mrs Fisher frowned and pushed a serviette across the table, to which the boy remained oblivious.

'Must be hard cooking for one. Have you ever been married?' she asked him.

'Married? Oh, no. No. Happy bachelor, me.'

'Oh, well that's good. Another ginger beer?'

'Thank you.'

'A man who doesn't drink alcohol. That's refreshing,' she said.

Bill Smith shuffled in his seat, and began absently pulling at a thread on the tablecloth. He was about to make his excuses for an early night when Alan Fisher stumbled through the door.

'Well, well. What have we got here, eh?'

'Dad! Mr Smith came for dinner. You should've been here. He was telling us all about racing and—'

Alan dragged a dining chair across the floor and steadied himself on its back as he swayed like an over-ripe mango in a breeze.

'That right?' he said, slurring his words. 'Well, isn't that just ... dandy. "Girly" bloody Smith, eh?'

'Alan, for gawd's sake, sit down. You're making a goat of yourself,' said June Fisher with the weariness of someone too accustomed to her husband doing exactly that.

'Sorry, sorry, Girly – little dainty Girly.'

Bill extended a hand to Alan Fisher, which hung awkwardly without any returned effort.

'You interested in horseracing yourself?' asked Bill, trying to break the moment, but there was no answer.

June's husband sat himself at the head of the table and picked from the chicken carcass, dipping pieces in the remaining gravy that June had poured into a gravy boat for their special visitor. The silence became heavy in the room. Bill made a move to stand, holding his plate.

'Can I help with the dishes, Mrs Fisher?'

'Huh,' sneered Alan Fisher. 'Get the man an apron, love.'

June shot her husband a look that even in his alcohol-fuelled state was not difficult to understand.

'Don't be silly, but thank you for offering,' she said to Bill, taking the plate from his hands. 'If only everyone was as well-mannered as you.'

'Well, thank you very much, Mrs Fisher, George, Mr Fisher. It was a lovely evening, but I'd best be getting home. Early start and all.'

'No, no, no, don't go. Sit down, sit down, Girly. Don't fly away on my account,' said Alan, sending gravy spattering across the clean white tablecloth as he motioned with his greasy hands for Bill to stay. 'My boy spends a lot of time at your place, doesn't he, Girly? A lot of time.'

Bill remained standing. He noticed that the boy was now sitting with his hands tucked tightly beneath his knees, staring at the table.

'Yes, he's a good little helper. You've raised him well.'

'Helper? What's he help you with? That's what I want to know. What does a little boy help a little horse's hoof with?'

'Alan!'

Bill turned to Mrs Fisher.

'It's alright. I know he doesn't mean it.'

'What's he mean, Mum?' asked George, whose eyes were glistening with tears.

'Never you mind. Your father's talking rubbish with the drink.'

'Am I? Have a gander at him – Mr Bill "Girly" Smith. Not exactly the manly type, would you say? People reckon he's a little bit of a queer bird. Man's got a right to ask what his sort's doing hanging around with little boys who aren't his own, doesn't he?'

'Stop that!' his wife snapped. 'Shut your stupid drunken mouth, you old fool.'

Alan Fisher snickered and shoved a handful of stuffing into his mouth, flecks of which stuck to his lips.

'It's alright, Mrs Fisher,' said Bill. 'I'll see myself out.' He grabbed his hat from the hook near the door and stepped out into a night filled with the chorus of cane toads that echoed the ugliness he'd just experienced.

'Mr Smith,' a small voice called behind him. 'Dad had a little too much to drink. I can still come over, can't I? He doesn't mean anything.

He won't even remember tomorrow.'

'That's alright, boy,' Bill said, without looking back, adding quietly to himself as he stepped down off the step, 'I will.'

~

A few days after the dinner, it came as a surprise to Bill when Alan Fisher turned up at his door. He stood on the lower step, his hat in his hand.

'Mr Smith – uh, Bill,' he called through the screen door. 'Would you mind if I come in?'

Bill got up from his seat on the enclosed verandah, where he'd been stitching a leather halter, still with his cutting tool in his hand. He did not know why, but his grip on it was tight.

'What do you want, Mr Fisher?'

'Alan, eh, mate? I wanted to say I'm sorry about Friday night. I was a drunken galah. Nothing coming out of me mouth was worth a pinch.'

Bill remained in the doorway, prompting Alan to take a step back onto the ground.

'I, uh, I always say rubbish when I've had a skinful. Anyway, I wanted to say sorry. I hope you won't hold it against me boy. He loves coming over. I'd appreciate it if you could see a way to still let that happen.'

'Your missus sent you over, did she?' said Bill.

'Well, sort of. But believe me, after you left – the way my boy looked at me, I knew I'd gone too far. I wanted to come myself, to say sorry, mate. It's that bloody rotgut they sell out the back of the pub. I've got to learn to stick to the amber ale. Sorry, Bill, eh?' he said, extending his hand up.

Bill stepped down to meet him and gripped his hand a little more firmly than he might usually.

'Better come in for a proper drink, then. I got a Four-ex open I might need help to finish.'

'I thought you weren't a drinking man?'

'I'm not, as a rule. Some days just call for it.'

Alan Fisher had never been inside his neighbour's house, and Bill was surprised at himself for the invitation. He could have left the man standing out the front, having accepted his apology, but after Catherine's note, he found himself craving company. He pushed a pile of newspapers off the cane chair and offered Alan a seat. Bill went into the kitchen, rinsed an extra glass that he'd never had cause to use before, and poured his and Alan's drinks before settling back in his chair.

'Cheers,' said Alan, who had been studying his surrounds. 'Got a tidy place here for a bachelor,' he added.

Bill felt his jaw tighten, and wondered if this might have been a mistake.

'I was well trained.'

'Oh yeah? Your mum always on you, was she?'

'My mum passed when I was little. No, on the steamships. You had to keep everything squared away. Good lesson for the rest of my life, I reckon.'

'You worked on the steamers? Bloody hard work, that.'

Bill nodded and sipped his beer, hoping there wouldn't be too much of an interrogation to come.

'That boy of yours is a good kid,' he said, changing the subject. 'You and Mrs Fisher have raised him right. Good manners, willing to work.'

'I reckon his mother can have all the credit for that. As you can see, I get meself into a fix now and then. I'm lucky they put up with me.'

The two neighbours spent a good hour or so talking – mostly about the racing game in the north, who was crooked, who was straight and how Bill picked a good horse. Alan was not a big gambler, but he enjoyed going to the races for a drink or two. He would often tell people that Girly Smith was his neighbour, even though this was the first time they had sat down together, other than the fiasco that occurred a few nights prior.

'You got anything in next week at Tolga?' he asked Bill now as he stood readying to leave.

'Yes, if the truck gets me there. Going to give the mare a run.'

'We might all see you there, then – make a day of it. Sure young George would like to see his hero in action.'

The pair exchanged nods, as Alan donned his hat and left. Bill watched him walking up the road and wondered why he had invited him in. He could not remember having had anyone come for a drink before. Bill had enjoyed the afternoon chat over a beer, but he certainly didn't expect it to become a regular event.

'No, best keep myself to myself, I think – better that way, eh, boy?' he said, scruffing Rusty's ear as he sat back down at the bench to finish mending the halter. As usual, Rusty offered neither agreement nor disagreement.

~

Young George was not so easily put off. He still came over the fence most afternoons after school, asking Bill to show him how to make horseshoes and brands. They even went to the races together when they were on at Tolga – with Alan Fisher, who made a real effort to give up the grog for a time, offering to drive them all in his new Holden station wagon; and June who fixed a picnic basket. It felt almost like friendship, albeit a guarded one on Bill's part. In fact, he would realise only years later, looking back at the photograph of the Fisher family from his hospital bed in Leichhardt Memorial, it was the longest relationship he had known since leaving Cranbrook decades prior.

Although he didn't know it at the time, things would change one day at the Tolga Races when Bill found himself the subject of attention from a gang of high school kids.

'Hey, Mister, aren't you Girly Smith?' yelled one long-haired hooligan.

'Girly Smith – ha – Girly!'

'Hey, Girly, show us your tits!'

With that, the group dissolved into laughter.

Young George Fisher was a witness to the encounter. He observed Bill Smith saying nothing in his own defence – not offering any sort of fight back against the taunting teenagers. It was the first time George had really contemplated Bill's quirkiness, his difference from men like his father. He thought he saw tears when their eyes met as the old man disappeared into the members' area.

George felt sick for not standing up for his friend, but he also felt that he shouldn't draw attention to their friendship, lest he become the target of the older boys' torment.

All Bill knew was that George's visits became less frequent after that day. It was something he tried to put down to the boy growing older and chasing different interests – but he couldn't help feeling that things had changed between him and his young mate that day when they saw each other in that vulnerable moment at the track. Bill would feel a twinge every now and then, noticing how empty the blacksmith shed had become in George's absence. He tried not to begrudge it.

'Boys grow up, don't they, eh Rusty? Boys grow up.'

38

Nursing notes: 5/6/78 21:00. Restless o/night. Semiconscious throughout shift. Refusing food/fluids. IV fluids commenced 16:00, removed at pt request 20:30. U/O low. BNO × 2 days.

Arriving for her first night shift after a few days off, Maureen entered the nurses' station for her handover from Franny, who was coming off evening shift. Matron sat silent and still in the swivel chair, waiting for one of the other night-shift nurses, Joy Farthing, to stop scratching at the heavy-denier stockings that were an absurd feature of the uniform in their tropical location. Maureen shuffled in beside Franny, giving her a nudge and trying to whisper of the side of her mouth, 'Why's *she* here?'

It was unusual for Matron to be present at the start of the night shift. Franny stared straight ahead, but reached across to give Maureen's hand a quick squeeze. Maureen gave her a quizzical look, and then met Matron's gaze. It was softer than usual. That in itself was unsettling. Something in Maureen longed for the stony-faced, fear-evoking Matron Kelly.

'If Nurse Farthing has dealt with her itch, we'll begin patient handover. Nurse Patterson?'

Usually the evening staff rattled off the care provided over the past eight hours with an air of gratitude for having reached the end of their shift. Franny was less enthusiastic to give her update. With eyes fixed on her handover notes, it seemed she wasn't so much reading them as using them to avoid meeting anyone's gaze.

> Bed eight: 42-year-old male, three days post-surgery, uneventful shift, cannula in situ left arm, flushed and patent. Bed nine: 54-year-old male, ready for discharge on review in a.m. Bed 11: 76-year-old, acute lower lobe pneumonia, temp low, 35.6; pulse weak, thready, 54; respirations slow. Skin integrity poor; knees, feet, hands mottled ... Patient NFR.

NFR? Maureen tried to catch Franny's attention, but Franny kept her eyes fixed on the paper in her hands. When had Bill become 'not for resuscitation'? Maureen wondered. She had only had a few days off and couldn't believe what she was hearing. He couldn't be dying! They still hadn't had a chance to tell him they'd found a contact number for Catherine. She looked to Matron, who stood up and addressed the team.

'It seems Mr Smith has entered his final hours. Nurse Bannon, I'd like you to be with him tonight – which means the rest of you taking on Nurse Bannon's other patients. Importantly, we have done our best to maintain Mr Smith's privacy and dignity throughout his time here, and I expect that commitment to continue after his passing.' She turned to each staff member for their confirmation. 'I don't want him to be left alone at any time. I know some of you have not yet had to deal with a passing. All I can say is that it is never easy, but if we can give comfort in that time, we have done our jobs.'

Fran took Maureen's hand again, as if to remind her that she was not alone and to give her strength for what was to come. Bill had become a friend. Despite all the advice they'd been given not to get too close to patients, to maintain their 'professional objectivity', Maureen wasn't ready to let go. When everyone else had left to attend to their duties, Matron called her and Fran over.

'Nurse Patterson, would you mind staying with Mr Smith for a few minutes longer while I talk with Nurse Bannon?'

'Not at all, Matron. I'm happy to stay longer if I may. I'm not asking for overtime – I'd just like to be here for Maurs ... for Nurse Bannon, *and* for Mr Smith.'

'Very generous of you.'

With that, Matron Kelly nodded her head in the direction of Bill's room, sending Fran on her way.

'Nurse Bannon,' she said to Maureen, 'I've watched how you've cared for Mr Smith over these weeks. How do you think you will be if he does pass tonight?'

'I don't know, Matron,' said Maureen honestly. 'I've only ever seen my grandmother after she died. I won't lie – I didn't deal with it well. It's why – it's why I've always been a little reluctant to look after old people.'

'Yes, I know. I remember you mentioned that when you first started. Are you going to be able to do this for your patient?'

'I hope so, Matron. I knew Mr Smith was unlikely to recover. But I was shocked to hear that he's NFR already. He's always been such a fighter.'

'He slipped into unconsciousness this evening. You should know he made the decision a few days ago. He had one of his better evenings, and he wanted to make arrangements while he was still able. One thing he specifically hoped for was that you might be with him at the end.'

'He said that?'

'He did. There's something quite special about being with someone in their final hours. Let him know you're there. Talk to him. We don't really know how much a person hears or understands at the end, but I believe they do know we're there and it's a comfort. You can always call me at any time.'

'Thank you, Matron.'

'Nurse, you should feel proud of what you have done for Mr Smith. You and Nurse Patterson and the other girls. Very proud.'

'Thank you, Matron.'

Maureen wanted to leave before big, insistent tears spilled over. She had never before felt anything but anxious whenever Matron spoke to her or looked in her direction. She wasn't sure that this even was Matron Kelly – not the Matron she had known until now – but then, she knew she wasn't the same Maureen Bannon who had tried to offload the 'grumpy old bugger' she had now come to care for. No one was exactly who they had been before their lives had intersected so many weeks ago.

She pulled a chair up alongside Bill's bed. She thought about her last shift, when she'd asked him if he had ever been in love. He had just turned his head to look again at the photographs on the bedside table, and then closed his eyes.

'Better mind my own beeswax, eh?' she'd said to him. 'See you in a few days then, Bill.'

'If Saint Peter doesn't open the Pearly Gates before then.'

'Hey, you tell Saint Peter to hold his horses. You're not even in the mounting yard yet,' Maureen had said, not convincing anyone, least of all herself. Still, it had come as a shock tonight when she'd arrived on shift to find that Mr Smith was not going to rally like he always had previously. Had he been saying goodbye that night, and Maureen just hadn't heard it?

Fran had kept the room lit, but not too bright. Bill was already in the breathing pattern of someone close to death – a shallow intake of breath, followed by an unnerving pause before the next rattly exchange. Maureen reached over and took his hand in hers.

Bill 'Girly' Smith's appearance now reflected the nickname given to him all those years ago, Maureen thought. A tiny, frail, elderly woman, mouth opening now and then, like a baby bird seeking its mother.

'You can go now, Bill,' she said softly. 'Last race run. It's okay to leave.'

Maureen realised in that moment that she had begun to think of Bill as female. Perhaps it was the frailty of the person in front of her that reminded Maureen of her own grandmother, or perhaps it was that Bill no longer needed to hang on to that lifelong secret in the face of death.

Fran walked quietly into the room and handed Maureen the scrapbook.

'This was a lovely thing you did for Bill, Maurs. Why don't you go through it one more time?'

Maureen laid the book on the bed, never letting go of Bill's hand, and read slowly from the first page.

'*Bill Smith, Champion Jockey and Trainer, 1922 to 1968.*'

As the years tumbled off the pages – the people, the places, the horses – Maureen was convinced that Bill was hearing it all. She was certain that at some names, especially of horses, there was a flicker of movement around the eyes. She went through every newspaper cutting, every photograph caption, every race record until she reached the end of the book, then she closed her own eyes for a moment. Fran moved around the bed, checking and rechecking vital signs, before putting a hand on Maureen's shoulder and whispering gently: 'Bill's gone, Maurs.'

'What? No. She – *he* can't be.'

Maureen studied Bill's face and realised that, for the first time in weeks, it was relaxed, as if he was finally sleeping comfortably. No pain, no ragged breathing.

'Oh. He is gone,' she said, placing a hand gently on the now-stilled chest. 'Rest in peace, dear Bill.'

As she and Fran sat there for a time in silence, a thought came to Maureen about how they would need to prepare the body. She grabbed Fran's wrist and looked directly into her friend's glistening eyes.

'Remember what Bill said to us, Franny? Remember when he said, "Put me back the way I was"? That he'd come in here as Mr Smith, and that's how he wanted to be at the end? We need to do that for him now. We need to keep our promise.'

'I know,' said Fran. 'He kept his secret for more years than you or I have been alive. I reckon it's the least we can do to let him take that secret with him.'

'We've got his clothes here, all clean and laundered. Will we put them back on him?'

'I reckon. I'll get everything ready. You wait here with Bill.'

Maureen sat there, thinking back to the feisty little old man she'd first met, fighting her off with surprising strength, the obscenity-filled sprays coming from such a tiny old figure, the slow thawing of hostilities as trust developed – and so much more than trust. She would miss her friend Bill.

~

The nurses knew what had to be done. Matron and Dr Cunningham had already given discreet instructions to all staff involved that Bill Smith's secret would go with him when he died. Matron made sure the funeral home staff were also informed, so there would be no surprises in preparing *Mr* Smith when the time came. They were only too willing to respect the patient's wishes.

Bill Smith was not someone to leave matters disorganised, even when lying in a hospital bed, knowing it was unlikely he would ever return home. On one of his better days, he had asked Matron Kelly if she would help him to organise his affairs. He had not thought about his will in a long time – believing he had little of value to pass on, and no one to give it to if he did. But as he'd shared some of his memories and thumbed through the scrapbook that Maureen had made for him, he had come to view his life differently.

'I'd like to see some of my memorabilia go to either the Jockey Club or the museum, Matron. Do you think they'd be interested?'

'I'm sure they would. That's a lovely idea.'

'And I'd like to give a little something to everyone who's looked after me here – especially those two young ratbags, Bannon and her mate.'

Matron Kelly's eyebrow lifted slightly in acknowledgement of the descriptor.

'That's very generous, Mr Smith, but I'm afraid staff are not allowed to accept gifts from patients – other than perhaps a box of chocolates for the ward.'

'Bugger that, Matron. Those girls have done more for me than anyone in my life, and I won't be taking no for an answer. Now, if you wouldn't mind helping me with arrangements, this is what I want to happen.'

Fran was to receive the squatter's chair from the verandah. Bill had remembered how much she'd gone on about it after their visit to his house. Maureen was to have the trainer's watch. It came as a further surprise to learn that the undertaker had already met Mr Smith some years earlier, when he'd picked out and paid for a spot at the far end of the Leichhardt Cemetery overlooking the valley and his home. Mr Smith would go into an unmarked grave and, just as he had come to expect and want, there would be no fuss.

39

The two nurses gently bathed Bill's diminished body, noting that there were more scars than stories he had shared – more secrets, no doubt, than they had learned about. Maureen sponged the prominent scar on his left breast with such tenderness that Fran started to cry.

'It must have been so bloody hard all his life.'

'Don't cry – you'll set me off, and that'll be the end.'

Franny cradled Bill while Maureen put on his singlet. They helped each other with the clean, pressed blue shirt, vest and trousers that had seen better days. Franny combed Bill's hair back into the masculine style it had been in when he'd arrived.

'He looks so tiny, doesn't he?' Maureen pressed her hands to her temples, as if it was too much to accept that Bill Smith was really gone. She turned to Fran with some confusion in her eyes. 'Bill Smith. Is that the name we should keep using, now that he's— *she's* passed?'

'That's who came in here, and that's who he wanted us to send off,' said Fran. 'Although it did seem a great relief to him in those last few weeks, to be able to give up the disguise for a bit.'

'Was it a disguise, though? It was more than that in the end, don't you think? If he wanted to be female, he could have stopped when he finished riding, a long time ago.'

'Who knows? Maybe.'

When they'd finished dressing Bill, Fran smoothed down his vest and straightened the buttons. Maureen suddenly remembered something, and pulled open the bedside table drawer, rummaging around with some urgency until she felt the crinkle of paper tucked away at the back. She pulled it out and carefully unfolded the fragile, yellowed square.

'It's from Catherine.'

'Let me see,' said Fran, craning over Maureen's shoulder to read it in the darkened room. 'She did want to stay in touch,' she said softly, reading the note Bill had been so anxious to retrieve. 'We've got her phone number. I wonder if she's still alive. Do you think we should try and contact her – let her know what's happened?'

'I don't know. But I know this needs to go back in his pocket and go with him. Let's ask Matron.'

The two lingered at Bill's bedside for a moment longer, before Fran gave Maureen a nudge with her shoulder as another patient's call bell interrupted their reflections on their friend, Mr Smith.

~

When they got back to the nurses' quarters in the early morning, the two nurses lay down together on the bed in Fran's room, as they had so many times before. Maureen thought sometimes that she should be paying rent, she was so often in with Fran rather than in her own room. It was her lifeboat.

'I wish he had gotten to see Catherine.'

'That would have been something, eh.'

'Why, Franny, why? Why did Bill cut himself off like that? People would have understood, wouldn't they?'

'Would they? Remember how Kevin reacted? And that crusty old doctor from Cairns? I don't know. I do know that you shouldn't leave things unsaid, unresolved, and think you'll always have time to make things right later.'

'We still talking about Bill? Not very subtle, Patterson.'

'You don't respond to subtle. You need a sledgehammer.'

'I'm glad we were both there for Bill,' Maureen said, trying to get off the bypass that Fran had led them down.

'Me too.'

Maureen knew Fran was right. She had not told Fran about her phone call to her grandfather, because she was still unsure about how things would go when she saw him again.

'Well, you can finally get off my back, because I will be seeing Pop Bannon this weekend. I called him a few days ago, and he wants to see me.'

'That's wonderful, Maursie! I'm proud of you – and I reckon Bill would be, too.'

~

Maureen and Fran stood in silence as the coffin was lowered into the ground. They were the only mourners there. The minister's detached, robotic words grated on Maureen. She glanced down and noticed that the man responsible for sending Bill off to God was wearing a pair of old Dunlop sandshoes beneath his cassock. She gave Fran a nudge and nodded towards the footwear. The minister was droning on about 'our sister Wilhelmina' now being free to enter the gates of heaven 'as God made her', leaving behind the 'deceit and deviance' that had led her to disguise herself as a man. While Matron had ensured that all the relevant hospital staff and funeral home people knew and respected Bill's wishes, Pastor Wooton was apparently less concerned with privacy and more with what he believed would be a truthful entry to heaven.

The gravediggers were subtly swatting flies and trying to keep a respectful demeanour, but clearly wishing the minister would get on with it, as the tropical heat fuelled up with a seeming disregard for the start of winter.

Fran could feel Maureen's growing anger with the minister and tried to reach out a settling hand. But it was too late – Maureen was already in fight mode.

'Hoi, Father,' Maureen interrupted.

The droning paused. 'I'm a minister, child, so it's Pastor, not Father, but yes? Did you wish to say a few words about our sister Wilhelmina?'

'Minister, Pope or Pasta Marinara,' replied Maureen, 'it's *Bill*, not Wilhelmina, who we're farewelling today. And Bill Smith was no deviant, so say your amens and let's get on with it.'

Fran was trying hard to stifle her laughter, which was made worse by seeing the expression on Pastor Wooton's face, but Maureen wasn't laughing.

'If one began life as Wilhelmina,' said the thin-lipped minister, 'then one ought to be buried as Wilhelmina. But I can tell that you are grieving for your friend, dear, so I forgive you. We commend the departed to thy hands, Lord. A-MEN.'

And with that emphatic conclusion, he turned and headed off in haste, not bothering to wait until he was back inside the chapel before beginning to remove his cassock and reveal the casualwear beneath.

'Got a tennis game to get to, have ya?' Maureen called after him, but

Pastor Wooton was not about to dignify that remark with a response.

'Come on, Maurs – he didn't mean any harm.'

Maureen wasn't so sure.

The first gravedigger moved forward to begin shovelling the rich, black Tablelands soil over the coffin, eyeing the two young women respectfully to confirm that they were ready to say goodbye. Fran nodded, and the other fellow stepped forward to help finish the job. With an arm around Maureen's shoulders, Fran gently guided her friend away from the graveside.

'Well, he *wasn't* a deviant,' Maureen said. 'And he wasn't Wilhelmina.'

'No, that's right, Maurs. He was *Mr* Smith to you – you cheeky little twerp.'

Maureen laughed. Franny always knew how to lighten even the darkest day.

'Rest in peace, *Mr* Smith,' she said aloud.

40

Even though the phone call had gone better than she'd hoped, it took no less courage for Maureen to walk through the door of Mick Bannon's aged care unit, two days after Bill's funeral.

'Hello, stranger,' she said to the figure sitting in a comfortable-looking armchair.

She was shocked by her grandfather's frailty, and almost took a step back. Mick's eyes were watery, greyish-yellow – nothing like the sparkling hazel she remembered. Maureen could see the cataracts that had clouded them over. He was still sprightly enough on his feet, though. He got up from the chair and opened his arms wide.

Maureen had steeled herself for a stark reception. She knew she deserved it. A younger Maureen Bannon had been selfish, self-absorbed and irresponsible. Could her grandfather already see that this was not the same girl that he'd said would never be welcome in his house again?

Maureen knew he had found it hard to forgive her. She had promised to stay with her grandmother while Mick was away in Cairns. Maureen had begged Pop Bannon to trust her – all would be fine. He'd been understandably reluctant to leave his wife alone since she'd taken that turn that she'd told him was nothing to worry about. But he was reassured by his granddaughter that he could relax. She would take care of everything. She was almost sixteen, after all. So he'd kissed his wife and then-favourite grandchild goodbye, promising to bring back some coral trout if he got the chance.

Mick wouldn't even have been down the Range by the time Maureen broke her promise. Staying over at Nan and Pop's was always a great opportunity for a taste of freedom, and Nan was a bit of a pushover with Maureen.

'You don't mind if I meet my friends at the pool, do you, Nan?'

'Not at all, love. Off you go. Enjoy yourself.'

'And tonight, a few of the kids are going to the drive-in. You don't mind if I go too, do you?'

'Of course not, pet. I'll be fine here.'

Mick could not recover from the fact that his wife had died alone, in their house – from a stroke that might not have been fatal had someone been with her as he had been promised. And yet, here he was, his arms wrapped tightly around his granddaughter. Maureen dissolved into tears.

'I'm so sorry, Pop. You don't know how sorry. I was selfish. I could have saved her.'

Mick stepped back from the embrace, and bent his large frame down to meet his granddaughter's eyes.

'That's all I wanted to hear, my girl. I know there's no guarantee that we'd still have her, but she wouldn't have died alone. I entrusted her to you, and you let me down. You let Nan down.'

'I know. I know. I can't ever forgive myself, but I couldn't bear it if you never forgive me.'

'I forgave you a long time ago, my girl. I was just waiting for you to realise.'

'Love you, Pop.'

'Love you too, darling girl.'

All the pain, the hurtful words and distance dissolved away over the course of the afternoon they now spent together. They cleaned up all the johnnycakes over several cups of tea. Mick showed off his prize orchids, Maureen admired his ferns and together they looked through old photo albums and agreed that Grace Bannon would be happy to know that they were together again.

Maureen was getting up to leave when she tentatively put one more question to her grandfather.

'Hey, Pop, do you remember a jockey from around here, Bill Smith? Some people called him Girly.'

'Girly? Yes, I remember Girly well. Why, love?'

'I guess it's okay to tell you now. He was in hospital, but he passed away a few days ago.'

'Fair dinkum. Poor Girly. I wish I'd known – I'd have gone over to visit.'

'Yeah, we aren't allowed to say who's in hospital. And Bill was pretty private.'

'Not surprised. He'd never get changed in front of anyone, no matter what. Funny bugger.'

'He was very fond of you, did you know? He talked about you a lot.'

'Is that so? Some of the boys used to torment him, make fun of him. I wasn't having any of that business. Bill Smith, eh,' he said, shaking his head in a way that jogged a memory. 'You know, there was some of us who suspected Bill might have been a woman.'

'A woman?'

'Yeah. He had a funny little voice, and just something about him – the way he was so shy. Anyway, he could handle a horse, that's for sure, God bless him.'

Maureen reached up to kiss her grandfather goodbye, and promised to visit again before too long.

Epilogue

Sydney, 1979
To the lady rider ...

'Hurry up, Franny. We're going to miss the train,' said Maureen.

'We're not going to miss the train, Maurs – stop worrying.'

But Maureen was running along the Cairns platform, searching for their second-class sleeper car. The *Sunlander* must have been nearly a kilometre long, its carriages snaking around the corner beyond the station proper. The train had already shunted forward to allow passengers in the rear cars to embark, and now it was the turn of those lucky enough to be in the sleeping section.

'I can't believe it. We're finally going to Sydney – and we're going to meet Catherine!' said Maureen, her voice an octave higher than usual.

'I know.'

Maureen thought her heart was going to explode when she opened the compartment door that would be their private space for the next two-and-a-half days. Eighteen hundred kilometres of steel ribbon running down the coast between Cairns and Brisbane, overnight at the People's

Palace and then another full day on to Sydney.

'We've got our own washbasin!' she squealed as she investigated every lever, button and switch. And we're nice and close to the dining car.'

'Bags bottom bunk,' said Fran, before Maureen had time to claim it.

'That's okay. I wanted to sleep up top anyway.'

With that, the train jolted several times before the final whistle sounded their departure.

~

With his final instructions, Bill had included a special request. He'd left money for the two nurses to travel to Sydney to deliver the Marsfield Bracelet to Mrs Catherine Stimpson of 147 Squire Street, Woolloomooloo, if she was still known at that address. They had already obtained her phone number before Bill had died. When they made the call they were able to explain everything, and Catherine was only too willing to agree to their visit.

Catherine Stimpson accepted the gift with gratitude and great affection. She invited the two nurses into her home for afternoon tea, and they spent several hours sharing experiences of their mutual friend.

'I knew we were going to be the best of friends the first day Willie arrived at the home,' Catherine told them. 'She was ... scared, hurting ... but brave at the same time. She didn't understand why her father had abandoned her, and she never really accepted being there. She could cope with a lot of things, but she could not cope with cruelty. And there was plenty of that at Cranbrook. She was too gentle for that place.'

'Well, that didn't change. Bill hated anyone who was cruel, especially to animals,' said Maureen.

'It's funny hearing you talk about "her" and "she"', said Fran. 'We met

"Mr Smith", and even at the end, that's who Bill wanted to be.'

Catherine turned the bracelet over in her hand, then placed it on her wrist. 'She will always just be Willie to me,' she said.

They were about to leave when Catherine suggested that perhaps, in memory of Willie, she could take them to Royal Randwick Racecourse on Saturday. They willingly agreed.

Maureen had never seen a crowd the size of Randwick before, or heard a noise like the sound of thousands of racegoers urging on their horses and jostling each other to get their bets on with the bookies. Cairns was the biggest race meeting Maureen had ever attended in her life. The roses lining the fence billowed perfume, and she could hardly take her eyes off the clerk of the course in his bright-red jacket, his magnificent dappled grey mare with plaited tail and chequerboard pattern across her rump. All of Maureen's senses were engaged as they made their way through the crowd to watch the jockeys and their mounts enter the saddling enclosure.

Catherine filled their glasses with champagne and gave a toast to their mutual friend and each shared their personal recollections until the announcer's call caught their attention. The three women stood, ears craning to hear the crackle of the public address system over the crowd.

'*And now we head to Southport on the Gold Coast for what has to be a bit of history in the making, as Miss Pam O'Neill becomes the first registered Australian female jockey to have a start. First of three races here today for the lady rider. And it's all steady for the start of Race Three. Lights flashing – and they're off ...*'

'To the lady rider,' said Catherine with a wink, as three glasses clinked together.

Author's note

Mr Smith to You is a work of fiction inspired by the real life of an Australian steamship worker, bushman, brewery worker, jockey, trainer and more, who lived for most of the 20th century. A remarkable life by any measure, made even more remarkable by the fact that Bill Smith was identified as female at birth. Living in an era when there was no language to adequately and safely describe or understand an individual who appeared not to fit the binary gender constructs of their biological sex, Bill Smith's real life was shrouded in mystery and contradictions.

Was Bill Smith a woman disguised as a man, living 'under false pretences', as some have suggested? Or was Smith 'a feminist hero', presenting as a man to break through the societal restrictions of his birth sex, as others have asserted? Or perhaps Smith was someone simply living their own truth as they perceived it? Even those few who had some first-hand knowledge of Bill Smith don't seem to know the answer, which is why I chose to imagine a character and their circumstances rather than try to present any assertion of facts.

People like Bill Smith were not unknown in the era in which Smith lived, nor in times before or since, but they were perhaps unknown on a deeper level. In the same era that Bill was described in Sydney's *Truth* newspaper (18 August 1929) as 'masquerading as a man', there were others who were also the subject of public discourse. These individuals generally fell into two categories, according to academic Ruth Ford: they were characterised either as heroic battlers or as deceitful deviants. Those whose stories revealed no hint of an intimate relationship were regarded simply as trying to survive in a man's world that disadvantaged women. Those known or suspected to have been engaging in any kind of sexual relationship, however, were viewed less sympathetically. The concept of transgenderism seemed to have no space in the discourse about or the responses to those assigned female at birth but who later presented to the world as male.

My own interest in Bill Smith started with a conversation with my uncle, who was a horse trainer in North Queensland. He has been quoted as a source in several articles about 'Australia's first registered female jockey' having known Bill through the industry. This post-mortem descriptor, however, did not sit comfortably with me, given that Bill did not identify, nor was perceived at the time, as female. Bill lived, worked and gender-identified to the world as male, until his hospitalisation late in life revealed his biological sex to be female.

Further investigations into the character who arrived at race meetings with his riding gear already on under his clothes revealed only scant information, and some of it contradictory. Still, I was intrigued by Bill's story of having been able to survive in a world of men, and what that must have been like – especially in the period in which Bill lived. Did Bill have any intimate relationships, or did he have to isolate himself for fear of rejection, or worse?

In writing this book, I discovered numerous other stories of people assigned female at birth who, for whatever reason, later presented as male.

Some stories were of people who had made pragmatic decisions to help them survive or achieve a specific goal denied to women at the time. Others had less obvious reasons, and then others were people who might identify as transgender today. Throughout this book, I have used the pronouns appropriate to the era and to the gender that Bill was inhabiting at various stages of life.

I chose to fictionalise the character of Wilhelmina/Bill Smith because I did not feel there was enough certainty about this individual to write anything but fiction. Others may be in a better position – such as the nurse with whom Bill shared some details of his life and who kept his secret as asked, only recently revealing certain aspects in the 2020 publication by Laurence Murphy, *Under False Pretences*. Also, as I encountered more characters and more contradictory information, it felt less constraining to use fiction to tell what could have been not only Bill's story but that of others with similar experiences. The fictional Bill Smith is therefore a composite figure, and only some elements of this story are verifiable – such as the incident of the steward stepping in to prevent an assault by other jockeys.

What is believed known about the Bill Smith who inspired this work is as follows.

According to Laurence Murphy, Bill Smith was born Wilhelmina in the US in 1886. She came to Melbourne with her family as a child. Her mother died when she was young, and her father was described as having been brutal to the child. Wilhelmina started dressing in boys' clothes to get work from a young age. She died in 1975, aged eighty-eight having confided some of her story to a Nurse McConnell, quoted in Murphy's 2020 publication. These insights focused mainly on Bill's life prior to becoming a jockey.

Other sources suggest that Wilhelmina was born in Western Australia, while others say she was born in Sydney. I changed Wilhelmina's age, dates of birth and death and backstory, as other details attributed to Bill Smith indicate that he didn't start his career as a jockey until he was in his early forties, so would have been still riding when he was in his mid-sixties. This may have been true, but as Bill was purported to have such a strong passion for horses, I chose to introduce my character to the profession much earlier.

Bill Smith was a registered jockey and horse trainer, although there is some suggestion that Bill's records were mixed with those of another jockey who died in a race fall, attributing some achievements erroneously. The aforementioned sensational 1929 story from the *Truth* newspaper described a court case involving a 'William Smith' of New South Wales as a complainant seeking payment for wages withheld by an employer due to the belief that Bill was a woman and therefore not entitled to a man's wage. In the surrounding publicity, Bill was described as 'Australia's most romantic figure' – a true Aussie battler. The irony was, of course, that Bill seemed in fact to have avoided any hint of romance, for fear of rejection and derision.

The findings of that case were that Bill was 'biologically female' but had lived and worked so long as a male and been able to do the work of a male so should be paid accordingly. Bill was described in the case as being 'in the early days of her make-believe', just trying to scratch out a living. He was, therefore, 'not like the shameless fraud, Captain Barker', an English individual identified female at birth who presented as a male and had convinced a woman to marry them; or, later, the Australian case of Harry Crawford, described as a 'man-woman', who married two women and was charged with the murder of one of them.

There was also the reported case of Bill Bailey, another or possibly the same individual who, in the early 1920s, sailed on coastal steamers until being hospitalised in Adelaide with rheumatic fever. Public sympathy was with this Bill, who by all accounts was a hard worker and well liked, and only exposed by illness after having lived as a man for twenty years.

Dates cross over, locations and events are blurred at times, but for me, what was important was that Bill Smith was obviously not the only individual to live outside the narrow confines of biology. Whether they identified as transgender or not is not for me to say. I was more interested in the lengths to which individuals might go in order to avoid rejection, violence, poverty, disadvantage; to make others feel comfortable and not disturbed by difference; to stay small and unseen.

But at what cost? With the best of intentions, Bill Smith may effectively have been erased by being claimed posthumously as Australia's first registered female jockey or even as the first transgender jockey. Bill Smith was not known to ask for or claim either accolade. But whatever Bill's truth, not seeing or recognising their existence in the world ensures that erasure.

Fictionalising Bill's story has, I hope, given a nod to all those who, for whatever reasons and whatever their personal situation, refused to be constrained by the sex they were assigned at birth. It is also my hope that this is a story about more than an individual – that it offers a glimpse into a period of Australian history marked by great social change and upheaval, and conveys the importance of simply having witnesses to a life lived.

Acknowledgements

I never really appreciated the irony of having a single author name on the cover of a novel until completing this, my first. I'd read acknowledgement sections of other novels and sometimes wondered how they could possibly be so long. Now I'm struggling to keep it brief. I sincerely hope I haven't overlooked anyone.

Here goes: In 2019 I attended a retreat in Scotland with acclaimed nature and fiction writer Inga Simpson that would prove life changing. I can almost see Inga's note in the margin calling me out on this cliché. It's a truth though. Before the end of that trip, I had been gifted a year of mentoring with Inga by someone who had joined our group briefly.

Laurie Truce was a stranger to me before the retreat, but we made an instant connection through sharing our writing. Unfortunately, he had to leave early, and I thought that was probably the end of our brief connection. However, before he left, Laurie had arranged a year of mentoring with Inga Simpson for me, someone he hardly knew, for no other reason than: 'He liked your writing.' It was a gift I couldn't refuse and one that prompted me to stop treating my relationship with writing casually and give it the commitment Laurie's generosity deserved.

Inga proved incredibly generous with her time and expertise, making 12 months stretch miraculously to the end of a completed novel. No matter how many times I declared my manuscript done, completed, finished, she would roll her eyes (I imagined) and send it back for 'just one more go over'. I cannot thank Inga and Laurie enough for dragging me out of my own way to make this book happen.

Before Inga and Laurie, I was fortunate enough to have met and been mentored by international bestselling author Joanne Fedler. I met her in a similarly – what are some synonyms for life changing? Metamorphic, transformative, life altering? – *transformative* retreat, walking and writing in Tuscany in 2011. Jo has said to me that she can't take credit for this novel, but that is far from true. I was to do many more workshops and mentoring sessions with Joanne and she is directly responsible for bringing this book to the attention of just the right people. Joanne believed in me long before I ever did, and that belief and support have brought this book into the world. She is the doula of aspiring writers and has helped dozens of writers, especially women, to find their voices and achieve their writing goals. Thank you for everything, dear Jo!

So, I'm more than a page down and I haven't even mentioned the many friends and chosen family who were my 'very-drafty, draft' readers, critical friends and providers of fabulous feedback. I truly appreciate every single one of you who has taken the time and been gracious enough to read the many iterations of this story and help shape it into what it is now. It's been a long ride, but a fun one for me. Thank you all (in alphabetical order as I couldn't possibly do it any other way): Lisa Benson, Xanti Bootcov, Carolyn Cartwright, Penny Drysdale, Gill Evans, Lani Foulger, Kylie Gwynne, Vicki James, Linda Jervis, Gai Keniry, Steve Keniry, Glenda (Muriel) Lucas, Nerida Nettlebeck, Yvonne Owens, Chris Prestwidge, Janet Rattigan, Doreen Taylor, Fiona Taylor, Annie Zon. And I will never forget Clare, '*in my corner*' helping me get here.

To the team at Affirm Press: Kelly Doust – thank you for taking a chance on me and embracing this story in the way you have; Elizabeth Robinson-Griffith – thank you for fielding every question and anxiety with patience and grace. Thank you also to Leila Jabbour, Arlie Alizzi and Brooke Lyons.

Finally, my greatest gratitude goes to my chosen family – darlin' heart Nungarrayi and Vick – the latter without whom this book would have been finished years ago! And I wouldn't have it any other way.

Book Club Questions

1. We first meet Bill Smith towards the end of his life, still carrying a secret that he tried hard to keep, but ultimately could not. What impact did this secret have on Bill throughout his life, and when it was eventually shared?
2. The character of Bill Smith has been fictionalised in this work, out of respect for the fact that the real Bill's motivations, perceptions, experiences and decisions could only be known to them. What do the motivations, perceptions, experiences and decisions presented in this story reveal about the fictionalised Bill Smith?
3. The individual who inspired this story has more recently been memorialised as either a 'feminist hero', for being Australia's first registered 'female' jockey, or a 'trans pioneer'. How do these characterisations sit with the fictional Bill Smith?
4. What did the two main protagonists, Bill and Maureen, gain from their relationship with each other?
5. How does the historical context influence this story?
6. How do the outback, tropics and other settings influence Bill's ability to 'fit in' with others?

7. Bill seemed to avoid any kind of intimate relationship throughout his adult life. How would this story differ if Bill had been in an adult relationship?
8. Bill lived at a time when there was no vocabulary to help understand and articulate issues of gender identity. What did this mean for Bill and others who, for whatever reason, sought to live differently to the sex they were assigned at birth?
9. What internalised messages did a young Wilhelmina receive from their father, Catherine, and others they encountered during their early life?
10. There were instances of kindness and acceptance throughout Bill's life, so why was it hard for Bill to trust other people?
11. How did you interpret the ending of this story?